Queer AND LOATHING on the YELLOW BRICK ROAD

Published by
Dog Horn Publishing
45 Monk Ings, Birstall, Batley WF17 9HU
United Kingdom
doghornpublishing.com

Editing by
Victoria Hooper

Typesetting by
Adam Lowe

Cover by
Matt Truiano

Distribution: Central Books
99 Wallis Road, London, E9 5LN, United Kingdom
orders@centralbooks.com
Phone:+44 (0) 845 458 9911
Fax: +44 (0) 845 458 9912

Overseas (Non-UK) Distribution:
Contact the publisher

by
Deb Hoag

Dedication here

Chapter One
Dorothy: The Meeting

I don't know much, but I know this: magic is all around us, every day. It's in the air we breath, the water we drink. Sometimes it's wonderful, and sometimes it's absolutely horrid. Magical things are happening to all of us, all the time, without rhyme or reason, without a care in the world about who deserves it or who doesn't.

Magical things have happened to me. My name is Dorothy, and this is my story.

I met Frannie in the spring of 1890, the night I got thrown into the hoosegow for getting overly friendly with a couple of guys at the local saloon. I stomped into the cell and threw myself dramatically on the bunk, except it wasn't the bunk I landed on—it was another woman. I hadn't seen her there in the dim light leaking in from the booking room.

She made an '*oofing*' noise and I jumped off the bed faster than I had jumped on, and the guard laughed. A small horde of adolescent jitterbugs that were prancing around on the ceiling giggled shrilly, but my mundane companions didn't notice.

"Well, *excuse* me," the woman said with a sniff, sitting up and putting a hand to a hairdo that had seen better days.

"Sorry, sister," I replied, scooting over to the wall, where I slid down into a sitting position.

The jitterbugs went back to their endless, intricate mating dance, having approximately the same attention span as the gnats they so closely resembled.

The tiny flashing disco light was annoying, but I did my best to ignore it. I'd learned early that people who see things no one else does get a one-way ticket to the nearest loony bin. Even jail was better than that, which reminded me of exactly where I was. Jail. *Fuck!*

I thunked the back of my head against the concrete. It hurt like hell, so I did it a couple more times. Stupid, stupid, stupid getting caught like that! A few more dollars and I would have been on my way back to Kansas, chasing cyclones till I could find one that would take me back to Oz.

"Hey, honey, it can't be that bad," said the woman, eying me with alarm.

I stopped banging my head and sighed. "I was this close to going home, and I got picked up by some needle-dick copper for soliciting. Now I'm stuck here until I can see the judge, pay a fine, maybe a bribe, and then earn the money I'd saved all over again. And I'm on a deadline. I need to get back to Kansas before cyclone season hits."

She laughed. "If you can make enough money out of these hayseeds to bribe a judge, you're even better than you look. Most of these hicks would rather boink a sheep than pay money for a tumble with an actual woman."

I sighed again. Completely true. I should have known two guys with cash money in a frontier town like Aberdeen, South Dakota were too much of a good thing.

"Look," I said, "I didn't mean to sit on you. I really didn't know you were there. I'm Dorothy. I just blew into town a couple of weeks ago. Who are you?"

She shook her head sadly. "I'm Frannie, from right here. For the last few years, at least. I hale from back east, originally."

"God, you actually live in this podunk town? You poor thing."

We sat in companionable silence. Eventually, my thoughts brought me back around to what I'd been doing that landed me in jail, and from that to what my cellie had been doing that landed *her* in jail.

"So, what exactly got *you* thrown in here?"

Her face grew sulky. "I committed a lewd act in public."

"Wow. What constitutes a lewd act around here?"

She shrugged and looked annoyed. "Looking cross-eyed on a Tuesday, if the constable is in a bad mood. It wasn't really even in public. We were in a perfectly respectable alley. It just happened that the alley was behind the police chief's house, and his wife picked that very moment to look out the bedroom window."

"Gee, that sucks."

"Yes, and so did I. That's why I got arrested."

I laughed out loud. Frannie started laughing too. Just like that, I knew we were going to be good friends.

When we stopped laughing, Frannie stretched on the narrow cot and stood up. "I've got an extra blanket," she said. "It gets quite cold in here at night. You want it?"

"Sure," I said, and she walked over to drape it around my shoulders.

When she stood up, the jitterbugs' disco ball illuminated her face and figure. She had a square, short jaw, and lush, full lips. Her nose was a little large for her small face, but it lent humor to an otherwise serious visage and her eyes were beautiful and large, thickly lashed. In the dim light she was altogether pretty, and she had a grace of movement that gave her lithe frame an inviting wiggle when she moved, top-heavy the way men liked. The farmers probably ate her up. She looked closer to thirty than twenty, but I prefer older women, myself. She wore boots she must have sent all the way to New York for, and had the goodies wrapped up in a scarlet silk dress that suggested all kinds of mischief.

If I wasn't heartbroken over Glinda, that wicked bitch, I might have eaten her right up myself.

I must have been staring, because she blushed, and reached up a hand to check her hair again. Her hands were large but well-shaped, with long, sensitive fingers. When she tucked the blanket around me, I smiled up at her, and noticed an unfortunate Adam's apple, nearly as large as a ma--

Was that a wisp of mustache on her upper lip?

"Are you ... ah, you wouldn't happen to be ... I know this sounds crazy, but are you a man?" I blurted out, watching as her painted cheek turned even rosier than it already was.

Frannie raised one of those large hands to tidy hair I realized now was a wig, askew on her head. I reached up and gave it a tug to set it

9

straight.

She slid down to the floor and leaned against the wall a scant distance from me.

"You've found me out. Our guard doesn't know that I sat next to him on a pew just last Sunday in a suit coat and tie. Are you going to tell him?"

"Your secret is safe with me. It's no skin off my nose."

Frannie blinked. "Really? That's a refreshing attitude. You didn't grow up around here, did you?"

"Well, I'm from Kansas, originally, but ...."

"I've been to Kansas. I didn't realize they grew 'em so liberal there."

"Oh, Kansas isn't really my home."

"Then why do you want to get back there?"

"It's a long story."

She laughed. "Sister, time is one thing we both have plenty of, given the present circumstances."

I had to agree.

I didn't suppose for a second that she would believe a word I said, but I didn't think she'd call the local loony bin about me, either.

I nestled in more comfortably to begin my tale.

"It all started in New Orleans . . . "

Chapter Two
Dorothy's Story: the Louisiana years

My mother was a small-town girl. She ran off from her parents' Kansas farm with my father, a gambler passing through on his way from California, and she never looked back. "I had to get out of there before I turned as gray as everything else in Kansas, Dorothy," she used to say. "You wouldn't want to have some old, gray nanny goat for a mother, would you?" Then she'd laugh and sing a song, or recite some silly poem and twine ribbons in my hair, and we'd be off for another adventure. She never showed an ounce of regret for what she'd left behind.

My memories are of a pretty, laughing woman who never said 'no' to a good time. I think she was determined, in the second half of her life, to make up for everything she'd missed out on in the first half. My father was a rambler by nature, and while he did his best by my mother and I, he had itching feet and a suitcase that he never fully unpacked. Eventually, we heard that he met his death at the wrong end of a vengeful mark's pistol, and my mother wept at his loss. But her grief didn't stop her perpetual party for long, and her tears soon dried up.

If she continued to grieve for my father in the years that followed, she kept up a good front, because I never knew her as anything but happy, with a song and a smile for every situation. As a matter of fact, after my father died, that's how she supported us, playing piano or guitar, singing and dancing in the clubs and saloons attached to Walnut Hall, one of New Orleans' most opulent bordellos. I was usually with her, tucked quietly away in a corner watching my beautiful mother charm the crowds that came to drink and have a good time.

As she got older, my mom developed a fondness for patent pills and liquor that hastened her death, I'm sure. Mercifully, she had a quick end, and by the time the doctor we'd called for arrived, she'd already passed on. The elderly medic just shook his head. "That's what comes from too much pills and liquor," he observed, and I knew he was right, but still, she was the happiest corpse I'd ever seen.

When my mother died, Lilly Spanks, the madam at Walnut Hall, offered me a job singing in the saloon that was attached to the bordello, just like my mother had done, and I was seriously considering taking her up on her offer. There were worse ways to make a living, and I liked the Walnut Hall, with its swank furnishings, lively girls, closets full of pretty clothes, and rowdy clientele. Lilly herself was a goddess in perpetual white, with a pile of carefully coiffed auburn hair nearly a foot high on her head, and bracelets jingling all the way up her chubby forearms.

Have you ever been to a New Orleans funeral? There's dancing, singing, loud music and a procession from the funeral home to the grave site that's more like a parade than a death march. New Orleans funerals are so much fun you almost forget that someone died. Lilly paid for the whole thing, and there was a huge feast planned back at the bordello after the graveside ceremony concluded.

When the funeral was over, the rest of the girls were departing on a wave of expensive perfume, and Lilly was paying off the musicians, when I was approached by a rail-thin stranger in a dusty, ancient suit. As soon as I saw him, I got an uneasy feeling.

"Dorothy? Dorothy Gale?" said the man, and I got the impression he half-hoped I would deny it.

Instead, I gave him a curtsey and nodded. "I am. And who are you? I thought I knew all of my mother's friends, but you are unfamiliar to me, sir."

He sighed. "I'm not surprised. I'm your Uncle Henry, Dorothy— your mother Mary's older brother. I've come to take you back to Kansas with me."

I nearly laughed in his face. "There's some mistake. I have never asked to be taken to Kansas. I have a job here, and am perfectly capable of taking care of myself. Thank you very much for your kind offer ... *Uncle*, but I am not in need of your protection or your home."

He frowned at me in the absent way people do when confronted by someone speaking a tongue entirely foreign to them.

"Dorothy, don't be silly. Of course you're going to come home with me. You're a child, and an orphan. I've already gotten a paper from the court that says you belong with us now. You need to be taken care of. I'm the only kin you have left. Auntie Em has already had a bed put into the house just for you. And a little dresser for your clothes."

I tapped a foot. What was this hick's problem? Didn't he hear what I was saying? I had no intention of going back to Kansas with him, and if he thought some stupid paper from a judge was going to change that, he was *crazy*.

There was a noise behind me, and I heard Lilly's voice. "Is there a problem here, sir?"

Uncle Henry slowly peeled his frowning gray glance away from me to look at Lilly.

"The girl's my niece, and I'm taking her back to Kansas to live on the farm with me and my wife. I've got the court paper that says so."

Lilly glanced at me, then back at Uncle Henry. "We were just getting ready to go back and have supper together, Mr..."

"Gale," said Uncle Henry.

"Mr. Gale. Why don't you join us? It will take a little while to get Dorothy's things together anyways, and you might as well do it sitting down with a plate of good New Orleans food in your hand as standing up in the sun and heat." She gave him a pretty smile.

"Well, I don't know... was Dorothy staying with you?"

"She was," said Lilly, linking her arm through Uncle Henry's and leading him toward the cemetery gates. "Dorothy and Maria both."

"Maria? You mean Mary—my sister Mary," said Uncle Henry.

Lilly nodded. "She liked to be called Maria, after she arrived in New Orleans. She thought it sounded more exotic. I was her best friend here, and when she took ill, Dorothy and I nursed her together. Please come back with us? We'll have a nice meal, and you can relax and wash some of that travel dust out of your throat, and

Dorothy can get her things together." As they walked, Lilly looked over her shoulder and gave me a wink. "We'll get it all sorted out back at my place."

Which is how Henry Gale, the original gray man, ended up at Walnut Hall, the finest little whorehouse in New Orleans.

From the outside, in the drenching heat of a New Orleans summer day, Walnut Hall looks quite impressive, with lush lawns and sprawling trees to shade the three-story brick mansion with its snowy trim work and wrought-iron fixtures. It's in the middle of the notorious red-light district, but in the afternoon, even the streetwalkers are fagged by the mid-day heat and tucked away somewhere waiting for it to cool off enough to ply their trade.

In the front parlor, even, the facade of respectability is carefully maintained, with ornate furniture and heavy drapes to keep the sun at bay. There is elegant flocked wallpaper and velvet-covered furniture that sits on thick ornamental rugs. Which is exactly where Lilly installed Uncle Henry when we arrived. Catalina pulled off his jacket while Lilly fussed around and sent Paula for a nice cool drink of lemonade, "and some of that cherry cordial we put by, if you please. Oh, and chip off lots of ice for Mr. Gale's lemonade!"

Once Uncle Henry was seated, Lilly insisted on making a plate for him herself, piling it high with fried chicken and sliced ham, cold salads and thick slices of bread with butter, all fresh made by the cook that morning. I noticed she skipped the jambalaya and *file* gumbo and all the other spicy New Orleans specialties. As she passed me with his heaping plate, she muttered to me out of the corner of her mouth, "Keep an eye out for that court paper, kid. Check that jacket we just shucked him out of."

I went to do her bidding as she took a seat next to Uncle Henry and began chattering brightly while he sipped lemonade and balanced his plate on his knee.

Dinah must have been in on the plan, because she kept that cordial glass topped up, and while I didn't find the documents giving custody of me to the Gales in Uncle Henry's jacket pocket, I had faith that with enough cordial and sweet-talk, the girls at Walnut

Hall could talk him out of whatever other clothes we needed to go through as well.

I drifted closer to hear what Lilly and my uncle were talking about.

"You sure have a lot of young ladies here, Miz Lilly. They can't all be your daughters. You run a school here or something?"

Amazingly, Lilly kept a straight face. "Oh, yes, Mr. Gale. A school for young ladies. We would so like to persuade you to let Dorothy stay here with us, in this familiar setting in her time of grief and loss. Moving her now would be so... difficult for her, don't you think, away from everything she knows and cares about?"

It might have been the effects of the cordial, but Uncle Henry actually looked as if he were considering it.

Just then Felicity came running in, stopping when she got to Lilly. "Miz Lilly, there's a . . . handyman . . . at the door—what did you want us to do about that?"

Lilly frowned at Felicity, then glanced meaningfully at Uncle Henry. "Please tell him we've company in today, and we'll have to ask him to come back tomorrow."

Uncle Henry shook his head. "Don't stop the work on my account, Miz Lilly. You go right on about your business. I insist."

Felicity gave Lilly a pleading look. "He's my best . . . handyman. I hate to turn him away once he's got here. And Mr. Gale wants us to go on about our business, the sweetie-pie. Please, Miz Lilly?"

Lilly frowned some more, but with Uncle Henry's eyes on her, she finally gave a reluctant nod. "Alright. Take the . . . *handyman* around the back, Felicity, and explain to him he'll need to keep the noise down—we're in mourning."

"What kind of work you having done here, Miz Lilly?" asked my uncle in an interested tone.

"Just a little . . . woodwork. You know these old southern mansions. Always something to do."

Felicity snickered, and Lilly shooed her out of the room.

"I'd be glad to take a look at it for you, if you like," said Uncle Henry. "No offense, but those handymen will take advantage of a

lady without blinkin' an eye, if they think they can get away with it."
He made a move to shift his plate over the little pie crust table next
to his chair, and stood up.

"Oh, oh, no, Mr. Gale," said Lilly, pushing him back down into
the chair. Uncle Henry looked at her with surprise. Lilly's small, but
she's strong. "I mean, that is ... you're our guest, and you just lost
your sister. I wouldn't dream of having you do any such thing as
work here today."

"And the handyman is *very* handy," purred Dinah.

Uncle Henry gave her an odd look, at the same time as I saw a
scantily clad Felicity bounding down the hallway, closely pursued
by her 'handyman'—a middle-aged banker who was a regular
customer, and who was clutching most of Felicity's cast-off clothing
in his hands.

I moved quickly to shut the door to the hallway, and Lilly topped
off Uncle Henry's cordial. "Oh, my, it's awful warm in here, still,
isn't it now? Mr. Gale, why don't you take off that vest and loosen
up your tie? We're not on ceremony here—Dorothy is just like one
of my own girls, and that makes us practically relatives, don't you
think?"

Uncle Henry obligingly shrugged off his gray vest, and Lilly
said, "Dorothy, why don't you just go hang that up with your uncle's
jacket, now, like a good girl?" I moved to do as she bid, and quickly
went through the pockets on my way, as Lilly continued. "Now, Mr.
Gale, what a fine shirt that is! I would just love to get one made like
that for one of my nephews. Does that have pockets in it?"

Half an hour later, Uncle Henry was slumped back in his chair,
a pile of chicken bones on the plate at his side and most of a bottle
of cherry cordial inside him. We still hadn't found the damn court
papers, but it looked as if he might start nodding off any second, and
there wasn't a girl in the joint who couldn't roll a sleeping mark in
one note.

Without warning, a heavy pounding started overhead.

"Huh? What's that?" snorted Uncle Henry, sitting up straighter.

"It's ... ah ... it's that darn handyman, Uncle. I'll go tell him to quiet down," I said, knowing it was Felicity and her banker.

"There's no cause for him to be bangin' around like that," said Uncle Henry indignantly. "He'll bring this whole place down around your head, Miz Lilly! I'm gonna go give him a talking to!"

"No!" we both yelled in unison, sparking a look of alarm on poor old Uncle Henry's face.

"I mean, no, Mr. Gale. You will not go supervise that careless handyman. You sit right here with your niece. Dinah, you go tell them to cut the noise, right now!" said Lilly.

From upstairs, I could hear Felicity start to moan with great enthusiasm.

"What the bejezus is that?" said my uncle, looking at the ceiling as if he could stare through it.

"Why ... it's pipes, Uncle Henry," I said earnestly. "You know how these old houses are. Plumbing's awful."

"Wouldn't know about that, Dorothy, as we don't have indoor plumbin' back on the farm."

Lilly and I exchanged horrified looks, and Felicity moaned again.

"That is not pipes," said Uncle Henry firmly. "What is the matter with you women? Somebody's in pain up there. I can hear it plain as day. I'm going to take a look."

And before we could stop him, he had bolted out the door and headed for the stairs.

Lilly threw herself in front of him. "Don't you go up there, Henry Gale, I won't have it! There's nothing going on up there but some good old-fashioned woodworking. It's just Felicity polishing up the knobs, that's all. She likes to sing while she works, and she's the worst singer you've ever heard. Isn't she, Dorothy?"

I squinted at the ceiling, where Felicity was fast approaching a crescendo. The pounding was furious.

With one hand, Uncle Henry moved Lilly out of his way and headed up the stairs.

Helpless, we followed him to the second floor. I was right behind him when he flung open the door to Felicity's room. She was holding a riding crop and sprawled naked across the banker, who had been tied hand and foot to the bedposts. Red welts decorated his thighs, and a satisfied look decorated his face. When the door flew open, Felicity looked up, sweaty and replete and gave Uncle Henry the prettiest, friendliest smile you can imagine. "Why, hello, Uncle Henry. I've tuckered this one out. Would you like to add a little Felicity to *your* day, too?"

Uncle Henry turned bright red and started sputtering. I was in a buggy headed for Kansas before you could say "dust bowl."

Chapter Three
Dorothy: In the Still of the Night

Even the jitterbugs were winding down, and I could hear the guard snoring loudly from his chair in the adjoining room. "I need a drink of water," I said. "My throat's getting dry from all this talking."

Frannie stretched. "Me too. And I'm getting a little stiff from sitting here."

I stood up and walked over to the pitcher to get some tepid water. It tasted like minerals and the tin cup I drank it out of.

"It must have been awful—having your mother die, and then having your uncle show up and take you away from everything and everyone you knew and loved."

I nodded agreement. "It was horrible. Don't get me wrong—Uncle Henry and Auntie Em weren't bad people or anything. But going from a brothel in New Orleans to a farm in Kansas was like going to another planet as far as I was concerned. New Orleans is vibrant, lush, bursting with color and noise and people and music."

"And Kansas?"

"Kansas is completely devoid of anything that makes life worth living. Even color. The farmhouse was gray weathered wood, the fields were gray, the dirt was gray, the sky was gray, even Uncle Henry and Auntie Em were gray. Nobody laughed, nobody sang, nobody danced or cracked jokes. I remember one day when one of the hired hands that worked on the farm was showing off, walking on top of the plank fence that kept the hogs in. He lost his balance and fell right into the pigs' mud hole. You should have seen those hogs jumping and grunting! I couldn't help myself—I started laughing so hard I thought I'd bust. Auntie Em shrieked and fainted. She thought some wild animal had gotten loose in the house. It was horrible. Can you imagine someone not recognizing the sound of laughter when they heard it?

Uncle Henry worked all day, from daybreak to sunset out in the fields, and Auntie Em did the same thing inside the house, canning, cleaning, cooking, washing. You name it, they did it. By hand. Over and over and over. Without ever turning a profit, or having a damn thing to show for it, except more wrinkles. Oh, and more dust."

"Why didn't they just pack it in and go somewhere else?"

"I have no idea. Some horribly misguided Norwegian protestant Bible-belt work ethic, I think."

We were both silent for a moment, contemplating the horror that results when Christian morals and rural American work ethics collide in a stolid Norwegian brain.

"I'm tired of talking," I said. "Why don't you tell me a little bit about you? How'd a sophisticated urbanite like you end up in the ass-end of nowhere?"

Frannie leaned back against the wall and patted the floor next to her. I came and sat down and she put her arm around me. I snuggled against that lovely expanse of bosom. Her breasts might have been fake, but they sure were soft.

She cleared her throat and began. "I spent my childhood in upstate New York..."

Chapter Four
Frannie: The Tin Man

I was born to a wealthy family in a small town. As you can imagine, we were the biggest frogs in our little pond, and from my earliest memories, the demands on me were excessive: to be a manly little man, to stand up straight, to take my punishments without flinching, to rule my toy box with an iron fist. All of it I rejected, of course, as any sensible and intelligent child would. I cried when I got switched, let my toys fall where they may, and slouched when I should have been standing at attention.

My father regarded me as an utter failure; my mother as her sensitive little angel. Between the two of them, I became the prize ceremonial object in their marital tug of war, the eternal contest between the 19th Century ramrod Republican captain of industry and the soft-hearted, passive-aggressive flower of genteel society. From the moment they met, they were as doomed to conflict as they had been to marry in the first place. I merely gave them new and fertile fields over which to wage their battles.

What they were both equally incapable of perceiving was that, right from the first, I was my own person, not theirs. They schemed and (in the case of my mother) bribed and manipulated; they plotted and (in the case of my father) threatened and punished. But I pursued my own path, regardless, playing each of them as best I could to my own ends. By the time I was out of the nursery, I myself was quite adept at both manipulation and bullying, if I do say so myself.

As a very small child, I had a tendency toward febrile seizures—those sudden, cataclysmic, drooling, foaming personal earthquakes where the temperature spikes up for the least provocation and the victim is left writhing and pissing themselves until the episode passes—guaranteed to strike horror into any tender-hearted mother. By the time I was old enough to leave the nursery I rarely had them any longer, but I had so perfected their likeness that even my father was fooled. It was one of the best weapons in my defensive arsenal.

As most youths do, I blamed much of my confusion about my own identity and about life in general on my parents; as I grew older, however, I came to realize that the confusion I felt was much more fundamental than that of a sensitive, intelligent child caught up in parental conflict.

Inside, I was quite positive I was a girl, but the external evidence, and the testimony of everyone around me, assured me that I was a boy.

In my extreme youth, it was assumed that I simply didn't understand what I was saying, when I kept insisting that I was a girl, not a boy. I'd get patted on the head and ignored, or someone would explain kindly that I was mistaken, as if I were too stupid to see the evidence in hand.

As I grew older, my assertions caused first consternation, and then whippings from my father, until I learned to hold my tongue. Occasionally, a maid would catch me trying on something of my mother's and look at me askance, but I had learned to be as sneaky and as ruthless as the adults around me, and there were few in the household who dared to cross me that were not blood relatives.

I first heard of Greek love when a cousin, Tobias, told me a snickering story about an uncle who lived on the continent and was shunned by the rest of the family. He pranced around in woman's clothing and accepted the physical love of other men with wanton abandon. With a shock, but also with an exhilarating sense of rightness, I realized that the love of one man for another was the ultimate, logical conclusion of my strange belief that I was indeed a woman in spirit if not in body—for if I were indeed a woman, would not the most natural thing in the world be to love a man as did all of the other women in the world?

I wished I could meet this uncle, talk with him, question him about this queer affliction we apparently shared, but he was thousands of miles and an ocean away. After having spent the first decade of my life completely isolated and alone with this feeling of differentness, surrounded by rough masculine figures such as my father for my role models, and total twits for maidenly companionship, I longed for a strong, powerful woman or a delicate, feminine man who could demonstrate for me a middle path to walk in which I could own both the powerful intellect and feminine grace which I felt pulsing inside of myself.

Alas! No such role model appeared, and I was forced to spend my tender years in a societal oubliette of shame and deception.

When I was about twelve, our Irish groom, a handsome young man named Nick, returned from the war. He had lost both an arm and a leg in battle, but managed to convince my father that his lack of limbs would be an advantage in the competitive world of Syracuse horse-racing, where every ounce a jockey weighed could help determine the outcome of a race.

My father had the finest prostheses possible made for him, fashioned out of a lightweight but durable tin, and with his racing colors on, Nick was still a fine figure of a man. His prosthetic hand was fashioned so that the reins could be looped tightly through the tin fingers. With gloves on, and a little misdirection, no one but us and the tinsmith realized the hand wasn't real. My father was careful that Nick was only seen by those outside our own stable fully mounted, and few were aware of the extent of his injury, thinking his two stiffened limbs were merely damaged, not replaced entirely.

His missing limbs only added to his fascination as far as I was concerned, and I spent endless hours in the stable admiring his handsome visage and listening to his tales of glory on the battlefield. I found myself, against my conscious will, quite smitten. He was a friendly fellow, handsome and manly, dominating the other stable hands in a way that made me long to be under his hand myself. In spite of his commanding presence, he was barely taller than I was, but his forceful personality made him seem twice that size. Despite his rough masculinity, however, there was a grace about him—an indefinable sensitivity—which lurked beneath the surface and which made me wonder if at last I had found someone in the world besides myself and my absentee uncle who was attracted to other men.

Occasionally we would take a ride together out to one of the farther pastures, to check on the horses. On one such ride, I was embarrassed and aroused to observe a stallion attempting to mount a yearling. Nick watched with open interest and some amusement as the younger horse attempted to shift and deflect the stallion.

"'Tis not that unusual in nature to find one fine beast attempting to mount another," said Nick, watching me out of the corner of his eye.

I wasn't sure if he had realized that the horse the stallion was attempting to mount was another male, and felt obliged to point this out.

"Most think that what he's doing is unnatural in the extreme," I said. "He's trying to mount another male, not a female."

"Do you think I don't see his fine young member there between his legs?" laughed Nick. "What kind of horseman do you think me to be? And it would be hard to miss, considering the way it's raising its handsome head, now, don't you think?"

I looked again, and sure enough, the younger horse's prick was becoming erect as the stallion continued trying to mount him.

"Now, I ask you, could it be so unnatural an act when nature itself thus supports it?"

I nodded, not sure what to say.

"And if a man himself had such urges, surely he could not be blamed for following them, if even the mighty stallion in the field occasionally indulges himself in such harmless pleasures?"

Now my eyes flew to Nick's, as the impact of what he was saying struck home.

He smiled, a smile I felt all the way down to the toes of my fashionable leather boots, but before I could think of an adequate reply, one of the grooms thundered up and commanded me back to the house for luncheon.

Irritated and unsettled, but obedient nonetheless, I turned my horse and headed back to the house. Fear of my father's wrath overcame even my extreme interest in Nick and his opinions about one male mounting another. But I determined we would continue the conversation at the next opportunity.

I developed a fervent new interest in riding, which surprised and delighted my father and quite puzzled my mother, who preferred a sedate carriage ride herself. I spent hours there every day, grooming the horses, polishing the fine leather saddles until they gleamed, feeling an unaccountable excitement whenever I came across Nick carrying a riding crop and tapping it smartly against one of our magnificent horses' flanks. My father was preparing Nick to take up the mantle of first jockey in our stables, however, and the demands on his time were many. I was unable to find time alone with him, and remained frustrated (literally and figuratively) in my attempts to continue our talk.

The first several races of the new season went well, and despite the lack of two limbs, Nick's proficiency as a jockey was apparently untrammeled.

At least, as long as the sun was shining.

It was an overcast Sunday morning when the fateful race took place. The spring sky was thickly coated with heavy gray clouds as the horses and jockeys took their places at the starting gate. When the starting bell rang, Nick looked a winner indeed in his silver and white racing threads, reins tightly looped through the curved fingers of his prosthetic hand, flesh leg and tin alike tucked snugly against Juniper Moon's chestnut flanks, booted feet thrust through the stirrups drawn up high under the skirt of the fancy leather saddle.

Despite the threat of rain, the stands were jammed with fashionable spectators, and I remember cheering lustily for my hero, Nick, who was already in the lead on the first turn.

There was a peal of thunder, and the heavens let loose a rain so dense it seemed as if buckets of water were being poured directly onto our heads.

A shriek cut through the watered air.

I followed the pointing arm of a nearby matron to see Nick nearly unseated, bouncing painfully as Juniper Moon made the next turn. It was then that the true difficulty of jockeying with only one arm and one leg became apparent—as the polished leather saddle became slick with rain, Nick was unable to retain his balance on the slippery seat. I watched in horror as Nick fell from the saddle and rolled on the muddy ground, narrowly avoiding being trampled by the thundering hooves of the other horses as they raced by.

A chorus of new screams, these infused with a rising horror, assailed my ears. Right in front of me, a fat woman fainted, her large hat striking my cheek as she fell. Several of her compatriots immediately followed suit. I battled feathers out of the way to see what I thought would be Nick's trampled corpse and saw instead that the people surrounding me were gaping at Juniper Moon, who had come to a stop, chest heaving, a tin arm dangling from his reins and a tin leg trailing from the right stirrup.

For those who didn't know Nick was a double amputee, it must have appeared that the fall had yanked Nick's flesh right from his body.

I bolted over the side of the stands to reach Nick's side, and pounded him on the back as he coughed out mud and track dust. The left side of his face was scraped and raw, and he gave me a rueful look out of those handsome dark eyes.

"Well, boyo, looks like I've botched this race up good and proper.

Before I could reply, my father had reached us, face a coppery red even in the chilling rain. He hauled Nick up onto his one good leg and shook him like a terrier shakes a rat, screaming about how Nick had failed him. It took two track officials to force him to relinquish his grip on the defenseless jockey, who was half his size. Father was still threatening to use Nick's own crop against him as they dragged him back to the owner's box for several potent tots of whiskey.

By then, the artificial nature of Nick's severed limbs had been ascertained, and a semblance of order restored to the shocked crowd.

While there was no rule, per say, against racing while wearing an artificial limb, the pains that father had gone to prevent Nick's handicap from being public knowledge weighed heavily against him in public sentiment, and it was assured that Nick would no longer be racing on behalf of my father's stables.

That evening, I heard from the upstairs maid that on the morrow, Nick was being given severance wages sufficient to buy him a one-way train ticket to family on the other side of the Niagara. I made my way with all haste to the stables to say my goodbyes.

Imagine my surprise when I found my hero slumped amongst a loose pile of hay, whiskey bottle clutched in his one remaining hand, obviously three sheets to the wind.

"Nick?" I said, somewhat shocked. I associated the drinking of whiskey with my father and his cronies, and didn't know what to make of Nick's obvious intoxication.

"Hello, there, boyo. Come to report back to your father how low I've sunk?"

"Nick!" I protested. "I like my father no better than you do. If I could stop him from discharging you, I would do so, gladly. But he listens to me no more than he does to the hounds and the geese."

He sighed and nodded. "True words, lad. Forgive my bitterness. It's the first time I've ever been sacked, and I'm not myself this night. Give me a hand up, so I may make myself presentable?"

I approached and slung his good arm around my shoulder, and heaved. We almost made it, but at the last minute, Nick's leg gave out from under him and we both tipped back into the hay.

Nick blinked in surprise, and then gestured with the whiskey bottle, which had miraculously remained upright throughout our fall. "If a few sips of the Irish makes me lose my balance, maybe a few sips more will see me right again. What say you to that?"

"I . . . I don't know. I've never heard that before."

"Well, one way to find out. Will you join me, and have a drink to toast me on my way?"

Put like that, how could I refuse? I took the whiskey bottle and tipped some of the fiery liquid down my innocent throat. It burned on the way down, and detonated in my stomach like a Chinese firework, sending heat and sparks directly into my brain.

From my spot under Nick's arm, my back cushioned by the sweet-smelling hay, I gave my drinking partner my most charming smile.

Nick's eyes met mine, and those beautifully sculpted lips curved up. Did his hand tighten slightly on my shoulder? Suddenly, the world was alive with possibilities.

We passed the bottle back and forth, and I persuaded him to show me his truncated left arm. I did not bother to turn away my avid gaze as he doffed his shirt. I looked my fill at the smooth white skin of his chest, the rippling muscle that chased itself across his fine form, before turning my gaze to the stump that ended a few inches below his shoulder. The skin was smooth and stretched tautly down until the area which had been ripped asunder, first by shrapnel from a cannon, and then by a surgeon's blade. From there, the flesh irrupted red and gnarled, a miniature topography of tortured mountain and sulfurous valley.

One of the horses whickered sleepily, then lifted his head over the side of his stall for a closer look at our activity. Hesitant but compelled, I reached up a hand and ran my forefinger over the rough scarring, then placed my palm firmly against the torn flesh and rocked it there as I looked into Nick's eyes. He put down the whiskey bottle and reached out with his good hand to stroke his fingers through my hair.

"And here I am the stallion, and you the yearling, now, unless I'm mistaken," he said, in a soft voice. "Think you're ready for your first ride?"

My throat went dry, but I nodded.

"Well, then," he whispered, and slid his hand down to cup my cheek.

Once freed of my constraints, my hunger, and my curiosity, knew no bounds. I slicked palms wet with sweat over Nick's body, hands trembling in my desire to divest him of his remaining clothes so we could slither together skin-to-skin, whiskey soaked heat-to-heat. I was kneeling in front of him when the door to the stable burst open and my father burst in with two of the servants, bellowing for me.

"Your mother wants you, you elusive cur! How dare you slip from your bed, you reprehensible excuse for a--"

As my father caught sight of us, Nick's rapidly wilting member between my eager lips, there was dead silence in the stable for a full five seconds. Even the horses seemed to hold their breaths as they waited for the storm to break.

I never saw Nick again, and barely got to say goodbye to my mother. Welts still fresh and bleeding, I was shipped to military school the very next day.

Chapter Five
Dorothy: Sprung!

During Frannie's recitation, the sun had finally poked its tousled head above the horizon. Our guard brought us breakfast and news together.

"The judge is coming in special just to deal with you two. He'll be here in about an hour, and he's not very happy about it," the man informed us while we ate. "Better get your story together and make it a good one."

Frannie and I exchanged looks. "Frannie, do you have any cash on you?"

She reached under her dress and pulled a small coin purse out from under a limp garter. "I think I've probably got about twenty dollars, minus a few bits."

"That's a lot of lewd acts. I know, because I've got about the same."

Frannie smiled but shook her head. "Don't I wish! I work for a living. What's the going rate?"

I told her and she whistled. "That *is* a lot of lewd acts. You must have wanted to get home awfully bad."

"I do. There's no place like home."

The door to the booking room banged open. The copper stuck his big, ugly mug in. "Judge is here, and so is your lawyer. Shake your skirts, ladies. Court in five minutes."

"Lawyer?" I mouthed to Frannie. She looked just as puzzled as I was, and we hurried to follow the copper out of the holding area.

The courtroom was a small one, adjacent to the jail. There were a handful of people in it when we arrived. A bailiff who stood ready to swear us in, a corpulent man in a dusty suit and tie who sat at a long plank table facing the judge's bench, and a woman sitting on a bench at the very back of the room who might have been the ugliest female

I had ever seen in my entire life. She had a large, square face with a lantern jaw and a long, hooked nose that would have been singularly unfortunate even on a man.

When Frannie saw the woman seated in the back of the room, she winced a little, and I assumed that this was one of the relatives she had mentioned. We took our places at the table where the fat man was sitting, and he leaned over me to shake hands with Frannie.

"Good morning, Miss Akers. I'm your attorney, John Tok. I was hired by that lady over there to represent you in this matter. So, let's oblige the lady and get you out of here, shall we?"

"And my friend," said Frannie in a low, firm voice.

"I beg your pardon?" said the lawyer, obviously flummoxed.

Frannie looked back at the woman by the door. "And my friend," she repeated, in the same unshakable tone.

"I'll have to check with my employer," said the lawyer, who waddled back to the ugly woman. They had a brief conference and the woman nodded her head, but I could tell she wasn't happy.

The lawyer returned to our side just as the bailiff stood and clicked his heels together. A prune-faced, gray-haired man swirled into the room in a flurry of black robes.

"All rise for the Honorable Judge Hognettle of the Aberdeen County Court," said the bailiff.

The sour-puss took a look at Frannie and me on the bench, and his face, if possible, puckered even more.

"You may be seated," said the bailiff.

"I hear tell," began the judge, "that I have *hoors* in my courtroom. I don't like hoors, and my missus likes 'em even less. You hoors want to explain to me what you're doing in my town, dragging me into court at seven o'clock in the Goddamn morning?"

"Your Honor," said our attorney, rising to his feet.

"Tic-Tok, that you?" asked his honor, squinting, as if he had not noticed the big, fat lawyer sitting next to us before that very moment.

"Yes, your honor," he replied.

"You representin' these hoors, Tic-Tok?"

31

The fat man sighed. "Yes, Your Honor. In a manner of speaking. I'm actually working for this lady right here, who has asked me to take on their case." As he spoke, he pointed at the ugly woman in the back of the courtroom.

"And who exactly are you, madam? These friends of yours?" demanded the judge, turning his rheumy eyes to her.

"Your Honor," she began, rising and stepping forward. Her figure was no more feminine than her face, and her clothes, dark and plain as mud, didn't help.

"Wait a minute," said the judge. "I know you. You're the daughter of *that*... woman. That sign-carrying, protesting, *suffragette* woman. Is your mother involved in this somehow? Is this one of those protest things? Are you going to try to pull some *shee*-nanigans in my courtroom?"

"No, no, and no," replied the woman calmly.

The judge was showing real alarm. "You want to take responsibility for these hoors? Rehabilitate 'em or something, I suppose?"

She nodded. "Yes, your Honor."

He whacked his gavel on the table in front of him. "Case dismissed, as long as I don't see no picket signs. We clear on that?"

"As crystal, Judge," chimed in the lawyer, who seemed rather baffled at the turn of events.

The judge turned and huffed indignantly at the bailiff. "Well, this was a waste of a good Saturday morning. Someone should have let me know this case involved suffragettes and protesters before I got dragged out of bed this morning!"

From the look in his eye, it was clear that the *somebody* in question was the bailiff, who visibly quailed.

"Come along, before he changes his mind, what little there is of it," hissed the woman, grabbing Frannie's arm and dragging her out the door. On the steps of the courtroom we halted, while the woman fished in her purse.

"You understand, madam, that regardless of the circumstances under which the judge decides to dismiss the charges, my fee remains constant. Think of me as a giant watch, wound and ready to spring to the defense. If my defense is not needed, still, compensation for my winding and my readiness--"

"Yes, yes, Tic-Tok. I'm not arguing your fee, I'm just ... ah, here it is! Now go away and spout off to someone else and leave us alone." The fat man waddled away without another word.

"Well, we just paid for his breakfast," said the woman with some heat. "And I suppose you have a perfectly good explanation for this, and for her," she continued, with a jerk of that heavy chin in my direction.

"Of course I do. Don't be silly," said Frannie. "Maud, I'd like you to meet Dorothy Gale from Kansas. Dorothy, this is my wife, Maud."

Well, you could have knocked me over with a feather, I can tell you that. Maud blushed and hushed Frannie, dragging her down the courtroom steps and over to a waiting carriage. I followed and hopped in next to Frannie as Maud took the driver's seat and giddyapped the horses. With a shudder and the slap of leather on horseflesh, we left the courtroom—and the jail - behind us.

There was a neat stack of clothing piled on the bench beside us, and as soon as we were out of sight of the town, Frannie changed from her rustling red silk dress to the modest habiliment of a frontier businessman. The final touch was a large, bristling mustachio that he attached with the aid of a tube of spirit gum. When he was done, wig, dress and Frannie's high-heeled boots were tucked into a bag and stowed beneath the seat.

The man before me turned and gave me a sheepish smile. "I'm afraid we haven't been properly introduced. "I'm Frank Baum, operator of Baum's Bizarre and editor-in-chief of the *Aberdeen Saturday Pioneer*. Pleased to meet you." He held out a hand, and numbly, I shook it. The transformation was amazing.

"Huh. Well, pleased to meet you, Mr. Frank Baum."

We arrived at the Baum's house after a short drive. "Where are the boys?" asked Frank as Maud unhooked the horses and turned them into the big pasture to the left of the drive.

"My mother took them fishing," said Maud calmly.

Then she swung a meaty fist at her husband, connecting with enough force to knock him cold. She could have knocked a tree down with that blow, if there had been any around.

She surveyed her handiwork, then, as calm as a cucumber, gave me a friendly smile. "I bet you'd like to wash up and get into some clean clothes. Come along then. Frank will be in in a minute." She motioned for me to follow her as if planting a haymaker on her husband were the most natural thing in the world.

Glancing nervously over my shoulder at the prostrate Frank, I hurried after her. Maud was one housewife I was determined not to cross.

After refreshing myself, I returned to the kitchen. Frank had come into the house, and was sitting at the kitchen table, watching Maud cook.

Maud turned from the stove, a kettle in one hand, a cup in the other. "Here you go, Dorothy. I've got some flapjacks coming up in just a minute. You like bacon, I hope." With that, she poured out the coffee and Frank handed me a sugar bowl and a little pitcher of cream in the shape of a cow.

By the time I got my coffee fixed Maud plunked three plates filled with toasted bread, flapjacks drowned in molasses and thick rashers of bacon on the table and sat down to join us. Whatever had passed between them seemed to have cleared the air, and they were the model of the loving couple over breakfast.

I finished before my two companions, having a smaller appetite, and was enjoying a second cup of coffee when the front door crashed open with enough whooping and screaming to suggest we were being invaded by Indians. Not entirely incredible, considering the nearby battle at Wounded Knee Creek was just a few years in the past.

Frank and Maud, however, remained calmly in their seats, and Maud gave an expectant smile. Three rambunctious young boys burst into the kitchen, one of them sopping wet, followed by a petite middle-aged woman with graying hair and fierce eyes.

"Well, the youngest one fell in the creek—again! But all in all, we not only survived but managed to have quite a good time and ate up every bite of that huge lunch you packed for us, Maudie. Now, what's this I hear about your marching a bunch of women down Main Street carrying signs and yelling about lynching the judge over a dozen prostitutes? I never heard such a bunch of chat--"

The older woman stopped in her tracks as she spotted me. I got a slow, thoughtful once over, then her gaze went to Frank, who was blushing profusely. To my surprise, she burst into laughter. "Oh, my Gawd, that was Frankie, wasn't it? And I suppose you must have been involved in this miscreant's adventures somehow, young lady, weren't you?"

This last was directed at me, and I nodded, not sure what to say.

Fortunately, Maud stepped in. "If I was going to lead a lynch mob down Main Street after that disgusting old man who calls himself a judge, you wouldn't be hearing him talk about it afterwards."

"True enough," said the older woman. Then she gave me a pointed look. "Now, are you going to introduce yourself and tell me what you're doing at my daughter's kitchen table, or am I going to have to wrestle it out of you?"

Considering that the older woman, despite her petite frame, bore a striking resemblance to Maud, that was a rather alarming proposition, so I introduced myself right away.

"And I'm Matilda Gage, nationally renowned suffragette," she said, shaking my hand firmly.

I'd never met a suffragette in person before, let alone a nationally renowned one, so I looked at her with interest, but she just looked like a more petite, more feminine version of Maud to me, which was probably saying enough, all things considered.

"She and I were swapping stories while we were sitting in jail. Dorothy's got quite a tale to tell," said Frank.

"Well, I love a good story, myself," exclaimed Matilda. "Let me get the boys upstairs and settled in for naps, and I'll be down to listen. Make it a good one, girl, and don't leave out the juicy parts."

"You really want to hear my sob story?" I asked. "I'm willing, but you'll just think it's a bunch of crazy talk, anyway, more likely than not."

"Oh," said Maud, "We listen to Frank's crazy stories all the time, don't we, Mother? We love them. The crazier the better."

"Absolutely," agreed Matilda. "Maud, come help me get these hooligans set to rights."

"Yes, mother," said Maud obediently, following her out of the room, children in tow.

"Your wife is quite ... unusual," I observed.

"She's a hermaphrodite," he said, in an almost whisper. "She's got woman parts and man parts. The man parts are rather small, but they all work."

"They must," I said, thinking about the kids.

He smirked. I didn't blame him.

It raised some pretty interesting questions. "So, does she pee sitting down or standing up?"

"Well, it's interesting. See--"

Then another thought occurred to me. "She didn't get *herself* knocked up, did she?"

"No, no, no," Frank said, looking both shocked and intrigued. "We never even thought of it. Besides, I don't think it would bend that way."

"How do you ... you know. Do *it*. Is it hard?"

"Well, of course it is, Dorothy. How do you think we'd have managed otherwise?" We both snickered.

Maud bustled back in and started the kettle for more coffee, followed by her mother.

Matilda took the seat next to me at the table. She leaned forward and gave me a challenging look. "I bet you think my daughter and my son-in-law are a pair of funny duddies, don't you, girl?"

I wasn't sure exactly what a 'funny duddy' was, but I had the general idea that it was an insult of some kind. "Oh, no ma'am. I like Maud and Frannie—I mean, Frank, very much. I think they're both great guys. Gals. Whatever. Male, female or fire truck dog, they're my friends, and that's that." I lowered my voice. "But I do think the mustache is a little much, don't you?"

She snorted out a laugh. "I've told Frank that, but he says it helps him get in character."

I nodded. "I guess that makes as much sense as anything. I have a friend who goes back and forth, and sometimes she has a horrible time keeping straight who and what she is at any particular time. She gets very confused."

The old lady looked interested. "Do tell? I suppose in your line of work, you meet all kinds."

"Oh, I've met all sorts of folks. Why, where I come from—"

Maud took her seat, bringing with her a tray bearing fresh coffee, along with fresh plates and a thick slab of chocolate cake. I sat back in my chair, mug of fragrant coffee between my hands.

"Now, let's see. Where was I? Oh, yes. I had decided I needed to leave that awful farm no matter what . . ."

Chapter Six
Dorothy: Escape from Kansas

From my very first day in Kansas, I knew it wasn't my kind of place. For one thing, Auntie Em was crazy as a loon. Oh, sure, she did all the day-to-day stuff just fine. But there was something just not right about her. For one thing, she didn't really smile; she had this kind of daft grimace that seemed to serve the same purpose, though, and she'd lay one on me, then skitter off most of the time, as if I had something she was afraid to catch. It made me jittery, watching her bare her teeth and then run like seven devils were after her, every time we passed each other in the hallway.

She was more comfortable when Uncle Henry was around, and would have earnest, meaningless conversations with him at night when it got too dark to work anymore.

"I put the kettle in the coconut bottle today, Henry," she'd say, face all serious.

He'd pat her hand and answer, "That's nice, Em."

"The grow wart is placidly mowing."

"I figured that would happen, sooner or later," he'd respond as he washed the dirt off his hands and face.

"Petulant cacophony in the fire starter," she'd finish on a triumphant note.

"Exactly," he'd say. "Is dinner ready?"

And we'd sit down to eat, like everything was just fine and dandy.

On top of everything else, they had rules for everything. How I wore my hair (two demure pigtails, secured with blue ribbon). What kind of clothes I wore (a never-ending series of blue gingham dresses, made from leftover curtain fabric, which Auntie Em had gotten at a bargain at the local dry goods store). My shoes were a plain and serviceable brown leather, with soles like wooden planks. I wore plain white ankle socks to keep those damn shoes from giving me blisters. Or splinters. Whatever. Even my underwear was under

Auntie Em's control, plain white cotton panties and thin white tee shirts that did nothing for the boobs I was beginning to grow.

I pinned my hopes on school being better than home, but that didn't work out so well, either. On the very first day, some pimply oaf tried to grab my boobs. "Nice melons you got there, babe," he said, putting out his hands.

I socked him in the head with the bucket full of lunch Auntie Em had packed for me that morning.

"Hey, ow! What was that for?" he said from the ground, rubbing his head.

"In the first place, why do all you hick farmers compare everything to produce? Do you have any idea how insulting that is? And in the second place, you can't just walk up and grab a lady's tits." Miss Lilly and Felicity had taught me well. "That'll cost you at least a nickle." After that, things were going pretty well, and I was well on the way to earning my first two bits of travel money, when sharp, strong fingers grabbed me by the ear and pulled me away from my customers. "Hey, hey, HEY!" I yelled, struggling against the grip of death. "Let go of me already!"

"Slut," hissed a voice by my damaged ear. "We don't have that kind of behavior here in the Norfstodan Dyrendaldorum School for Primary Education!" The stranger shook me like a dog, and I could feel my earlobe stretching. "You'll stop that if I have to beat it out of you."

The satisfaction in the voice convinced me that a beating from that source was the last thing any sane person wanted, and I held up my hands in submission.

"Hey, okay, no beatings necessary. I'm sorry! Look, put me down, I'll apologize. Whatever you want. But no beatings, okay?" There was a disappointed sniff, but I was lowered back to the ground, much to my relief. I turned around to get a look at my torturer. It was a thin, dried-up broad with a whomping nose and an evil eye, clad entirely in black. I wasn't sure, but it looked like she was sprouting the beginnings of quite a hunch on her back.

"Who are you?"

She snorted. "I'm the principal here. Almira Bendickson. And no need to introduce yourself; I already know who you are, Dorothy Gale. Why, when I tell your Auntie Em what I caught you doing here today, she'll...."

The bitch actually licked her lips.

I gave her a steely look. "She'll what? Tell me to put the baby back in the cannonball?"

The evil eye fixed on me. "You have a smart mouth on you, for an orphan."

I almost told her what I thought she had on her, but good sense stopped me. She waited for a full minute, but I didn't say anything, and finally she turned on her heel, summoning me with a clawlike hand to follow her, and led me away to class.

Wonderful. First day at school and I'd already pissed off the wicked witch.

From there, it was all downhill.

Even Kansas itself seemed out to get me. I hated the storms. They started out as great gusts of nasty, dirty wind. The dust hits you like sandpaper, a vile, scratching thing, and hot enough to make you sweat, turning the grit into mud on your skin—mud that soaks into every crease, making it look like an angry child took a felt tip pen and drew all over you.

The grit gets in your ears and up your nose and in your eyes, causing dirty tears. It gets into your lungs, and can rack your body with coughing fits that make it feel as if you have consumption. People have died from it, breathing in the dust and blowing dirt of Kansas. They hack up chunks of bloody lung as their bodies try to force out the clinging dust that's forced its way into them.

It gets into your food, and into your water, and into your fricking underpants and socks and bed and sheets and howls in your ears until you think you're going crazy; it carries a stink like the stink of a centuries old mummy, dry death and the faint scent of rot, and it taints everything it touches, and it touches everything.

You'd think the rain would make it better, but somehow it doesn't, as the rain itself falls through the sullen, filthy air and becomes mud before it even hits the ground, making that evil smell bloom when it should be washing everything clear and clean.

The slashing rain is a lie and a cheat. It fills all the cracks and crevasses, and turns dry pasture into ripping currents and tiny creeks into torrential rivers. Because the land is so dry between rains, there's nothing on the prairie to hold back the water. The clay-like ground cracks and dries into thick plates, so the water can't seep and soak into it. Instead, the runoff roars across the fields and looks to drown and destroy anything in its path, like a living thing—a living thing with a malicious consciousness and a willful hatred of us puny humans.

When I finally got up the gumption - and traveling money - to leave Auntie Em and Uncle Henry, it turned out to be the worst day for storms in the history of Kansas. It was dark and rainy, and Uncle Henry was muttering under his breath about twisters and the root cellar, but now that I was ready to go, a patch of nasty weather wasn't going to stop me.

If I sat in that damn gray farmhouse through one more storm, listening to the wind howl and shriek, hearing the rain battering like blows from a fist on the roof and walls and windows, I thought I'd go mad. Maybe that was what was wrong with Auntie Em; too many days hunkered down in the house, listening to nature prove what powerless, feckless things we all were. If it had driven her quietly crazy, I couldn't find it in my heart to blame her. I didn't want to spend the next five years of my life cooped up in a four-room farmhouse with her, either, but I didn't blame her for going stark raving mad. No one should be expected to stand up under that malignant onslaught, day after day, year after year.

I certainly wasn't going to.

I had actually been *waiting* for a good storm, thinking it would slow Uncle Henry down should he decide to come looking for me, and I was pretty positive he would. Not out of love, exactly. He often looked at me, as I imagine he had looked at my mother, as if I were some odd specimen from the moon; like he couldn't quite figure out who or what I was, but damned if he didn't keep on trying.

No, he'd come after me out of some sense of perverse duty that only Uncle Henry, and maybe my crazy Auntie Em, fully understood. It was the same sense of duty that had made him come get me in the first place—a completely misplaced sense of responsibility invoked simply because we shared the same blood.

But he also had a nearly infernal sense of responsibility to the farm, and I figured if he had to choose between the two of us, he would stay with the farm until the storm passed, and make sure all the pigs and cows and chickens (chickens were forever getting carried off by the wind, the idiots) and roofs and walls and fences survived, before he came after me.

It was as if the farm were his master, and he its loyal servant.

So I packed up my things in a small bundle and waited until the hot furious blowing was well underway, black clouds boiling up as if they were waves that would soon bury us completely under a wall of water from which there was no escape.

I could hear them talking to each other outside the house. "Henry, clapboard the shrapnel!" screamed Auntie Em. "I will, Em, as soon as I get these shutters buttoned up!"

And when everyone was busy running around like a bunch of frightened geese, I made my escape out a window and ran like hell for the nearest neighbor's house, where there was a bicycle I could use to make my getaway.

The neighbor's place was a good two miles away, but I was young and fast, and made it nearly a third of the way there before the sky turned an ugly puke green and lightning started to flash out of those clouds with a deadly intensity that made my hair stand on end. There was a blast and a crash that nearly knocked me off my feet, and my heart gave a thump as big as a bass drum, then started racing like a hare at a dogfight.

There wasn't a piece of shelter in sight closer than Uncle Henry's farm, and despite my earlier resolve to get the hell out of there regardless of what it took, I turned on my heel and raced back, even faster than I had run away.

I got as far as one of the old sheds when I saw the malevolent tentacle of the cyclone reach down and slam into the earth like a poison fist.

I would have peed my pants, but my entire body froze. I was nearing the main house, but nowhere close enough to make it before the cyclone cut between us. And then, as if sensing me, the entire thing twitched, shifted and headed my way.

It broke my momentary paralysis, seeing that gargantuan tower of filthy air and debris hurtling toward me, and I turned and ran, not directly away from it, because it seemed a hundred times faster than me, but at an angle, hoping to dodge out of its way.

I saw a small shed that Uncle Henry used for storing tools and equipment, and made for it, so fast I was almost flying myself.

And still the cyclone came.

The wind was almost unbearable, so loud I couldn't hear it anymore, just felt it vibrating my entire body. My hair was whipping around my face and neck until I felt half choked and could hardly see, and the air was full of flying junk that battered at me like fists.

I made it to the shed and wasted precious minutes fumbling the door open against the fury of the storm.

Then I was inside and the sudden decrease in sound and air pressure made my ears ring and my head spin.

The shed shifted and groaned as if every timber was being wrenched apart. It shook and swayed, and there was a huge, wrenching snap and my ears popped and the pressure inside the shed changed. The bottom dropped out from under my feet, although I could still see the floor right *there* under my shoes. Something hard smacked me in the elbow, and I ducked down under a table to avoid being hit by any other of the shed's contents, which were flying and flailing in the tiny room as if they'd suddenly come alive.

From under the table I whimpered in fear. I wasn't sure exactly what was happening, but I was sure it was wrong, wrong, wrong. The word 'airborne' crossed my mind.

I crossed myself, although I'm sure that would have offended Uncle Henry right to the soles of his Lutheran work boots, and began to pray.

43

"God", I said, trying not to blubber so loudly that he couldn't make out the words if he were listening, "please get me out of this shit storm and away from this Godforsaken asshole-of-the-universe place called Kansas, and I swear, I'll do . . . "

At that moment, something large and hard flew up and hit me in the head, making my head feel like I was inside a huge bell that had just been struck by the world's largest gong. That's the last I remembered for quite a while.

I was just coming to, with a splitting headache, when there was a huge thud and the shed slammed into the ground. The entire structure started collapsing on top of me, with shredded wood hurtling past like so much shrapnel, and dirt and debris flung up into the air and in my face. Coughing, I struggled out from under the table, shoving away chunks of roof and wall, and emerged into a bright, sunny day that had me blinking my stinging eyes in wonder. Gone were the gloomy sepia-toned vistas of Kansas. Here the sky was bright blue, the clouds a fluffy white, the grass a brilliant green. Birds were singing, and my heart skipped a beat as I realized that while I might not be in New Orleans, this had to be a hell of a lot closer to it than anyplace in Kansas could ever be. I stepped away from the remains of the shed and turned slowly, as my head was still throbbing, trying to take in my new surroundings. "Eh hm," said a voice behind me. "I, Glinda the Good, would like to welcome you to Oz. I have summoned you here on this very important occasion--"
"Oh, bullshit," said another voice. "You haven't summoned anyone anywhere, and you know it."

I turned, and saw two women. One was tall and willowy, with curves in all the right places under a skin-tight silk gown that would have made Felicity proud, and the other was a short, stacked broad with dark hair and pale green skin.
"Of course I summoned her here, you old toad," said the pretty blonde. "What the hell are you talking about?" The wand thingamajig that she was holding twitched threateningly.

44

The shorter woman was wearing a clinging, low-cut black number, boobs pushed up and out in ways a teenage girl could only dream of, a cloud of midnight dark hair piled up in loose curls on her head. She had a tattoo of a man's face on one bare shoulder, with the words 'hopeless romantic' etched underneath. Her eyes were lined with kohl and her lashes impossibly long on those pale, pale green cheeks.

The woman in black snorted. "You are so full of shit, Glinda. And I suppose you're going to pretend this is all part of some great plan of yours to--"

ZAP!

She never got to finish her sentence. A bolt of lightning flew out of the blonde's wand, and the short broad went flying through the air, landing on the ground with an ominous thwacking noise.

I looked uncertainly at the blond woman. Glinda.

"Did you kill her?"

"Certainly not, but she's gonna have a hell of a hangover tomorrow. Fortunately," Glinda continued, patting her hair to make sure it was unmussed, "she won't remember a thing. Suspect, maybe, but remember, no. Now, help me get her over here in the middle of this junk. She'll think your building fell on her."

"Uh, I don't know ... " I started, pretty sure we were breaking some kind of law, although I couldn't imagine which law covered zapping someone with a magic wand.

"If you help me, I'll give you her shoes," said the blond persuasively. "They're brand new. And her memory should be wiped for ... oh ... the last two days or so. Highly likely she won't remember them at all."

I looked. Toady was wearing a very nice pair of silver, kitten-heeled pumps, which beat the hell out of the cheap flats I had on. "Okay," I decided. "If I can have her bag, too. It matches. But what about her wallet?"

The blond sighed. "Kid, you remind me of me. If she has any money on her, we split it fifty-fifty, okay? We don't have that much time. Are you gonna stand there and gawk, or you gonna help me?"

45

'Helping' turned out to be 'doing all the heavy lifting', but the shoes were pretty cool and the green broad had a wallet containing nine silver coins and a dried lizard skin. I ended up with two silver and Glinda kept seven, but since I didn't know if the wand was still loaded, I didn't argue with her math.

We had just finished when there was a rustling in the bushes nearby.

"Oh, shit, the Munchkins are here," said Glinda. "Let me do all the talking, okay, kid?"

I was happy to agree, as I had no idea who, or what, the Munchkins might be.

It turned out that the Munchkins were a bunch of very small people I would have thought were kids, except for the beards and mustaches. They had some of the wildest hair I'd ever seen, waxed and teased and twirled and piled up on their heads like surreal sculptures. And that was just the men. They shoved one of the guys forward, eying the horizontal green woman uneasily the whole time, and he politely asked Glinda if there had been some kind of accident.

"You guessed it, shorty," said Glinda. "Big accident. This other witch fell out of the sky in her flying house and knocked Nessa there out cold. Might want to dig up some aspirin before she comes around." She pointed dramatically at me with her wand.

"Hey!"

Before I could say anything in my own defense, the little man stepped back to confer with his buddies.

"You're gonna try to pin the rap on me for this?"

"What rap? It was an accident. You and I are the only ones who know different. Toady's not gonna remember."

"You said you summoned me. So even if my shed had bonked her, it would still be your fault, not mine."

She sighed and gave me a smile that I was pretty sure was as fake as all that pretty blonde hair. "Yeah. Summoned you right to Oz. What do you think so far, kid? Beautiful, huh? Lots of nature, cute little animals, got you those shoes. That bag. Not bad at all."

46

"But what did you summon me *for*? And does that mean you're gonna send me back?"

She looked slightly embarrassed. "Well, okay, maybe I didn't summon you so much as make the best of a serendipitous opportunity."

"What's that mean?"

"Means you appeared out of nowhere, kid, and I used the surprise to get in a shot at Toady over there."

"So now what do I do?"

While we were talking, the Munchkins had approached again, and now one stepped up and gave me a lascivious look. "You could stay with us if you want to. Plenty of room at my house."

"I don't even know who you guys are, anyway. Part of a traveling circus or something?"

"We're the Munchkins, babe. Part of the Grimoire Guild, to be exact."

"What's a grim whore?"

"Grimoire. *Grimoire*," he said, pronouncing it slowly, like that would help me get the meaning. I shook my head and he sighed.

"Grimoire is a magical text. Teaches you how to make spells and magical amulets and things."

"So you guys do magic?"

"No. We're printers," he replied. "We print up the books and sell them to libraries and private readers."

"That doesn't sound very exciting. Why don't you learn the magic in the books and do something yourselves?"

He gave me a surly look. "Don't get smart with me, girly. I've got a dictionary here, and I'm not afraid to use it."

"I'm not trying to get smart."

"Obviously."

"Hey. That's low. But I was just curious is all. Why just publish about it, when you could be doing it?"

"We also serve who only print and distribute. But, seriously? Munchkins can't do magic. Not in our DNA. Not the spell kind, anyway, although the old lady says that I'm pretty magical in the sack department, if you get my drift. But only the witches and wizards in Oz can do magic, and that means beanpoles like you and Glinda. And the Wicked Witch of the East, there."

He crouched down so he could look up the fallen witch's dress. "Hey, guys! Beaver shot! Who's got the camera? Oh . . . wait. That's just black lace. Still, a photo op's a photo op."

"That's not very nice," I observed.

"We do the *Ozculator*, too. Weekly tabloid. Not so highbrow, but it pays the rent."

Glinda, who'd been following the exchange with interest, offered to hold the light so they could get a better shot.

I waited impatiently until the photo shoot was complete and the Munchkins faded back into the bushes, taking their camera with them.

Then I turned back to Glinda.

"You really have no idea what I'm doing here, do you?"

"Not a clue, kid."

"How am I supposed to survive? What do I do?"

She looked thoughtful. "I could use a good assistant. You interested in a job?"

"Maybe. What would I be doing?"

"A little of this, a little of that. I need someone to go to the Emerald City and collect on a little wager for me, for example. You get the guy to cough up the dough, and I'll cut you in for ten percent."

"Ten percent of how much?"

"A thousand silver. That's a lot of dough here, kid. What do you say?"

Nothing better was looming on the horizon. I nodded. "Okay, I'll play. Now tell me, how do I get to this 'Emerald City,' and who am I looking for when I get there?"

"That's easy, kid. See that road there? The one with the yellow brick? Just follow it right on out of town. It only goes one place. The Emerald City. And when you get there, just ask anybody for the Wizard. He won't be hard to find."

I got an uneasy feeling. "Wizard? Like in *magical wizard*? Does he have one of those zappity wand things?"

"Well, maybe, but he'd never use it on a kid, kid. That's the beauty of it. Just take the road to the Emerald City, like I told you, and ask for the wizard. The Wizard of Oz. Then cry a little, if you have to. It'll be a piece of cake."

Chapter Seven
Get it in writing

There was complete silence in the Baum's kitchen as I stopped talking. I took a gulp of coffee gone cold, surreptitiously trying to gauge their various reactions.

The look on Frank's face was wonderful. I didn't know if he totally believed me, but he looked delighted and amazed, a lot like the way a kid looks when you tell them a really good story. Maud was harder to read; she would have made a hell of a poker player.

Matilda was stone still for a full minute, looking off at the ceiling with an inscrutable expression. Then she tipped her face back down to look at me, and broke into a huge laugh, braying like a donkey and stomping her feet. "Frank, she gasped out, when she had control of herself again, "if you don't write this all down, you're an idiot. It's the best story I've heard in years. If the rest of it is as good as the beginning, you've got a genuine novel on your hands." She wiped tears of laughter from her eyes as she spoke, and I gave her a tentative smile. I wasn't sure exactly why she found the whole thing so funny, but she liked it, so I figured that was basically a thumbs up.

"Go on, Dorothy," said Maud. "I want to hear what happened next."

"Please," said Frank. "And Matilda is right. Would you mind if I took a few notes?"

I shook my head. "Nope, it's your turn. I don't mind if you take notes when I start back up again, but I've talked enough for a while. Finish telling me what happened when you went to boarding school."

"I could do that," said Frank.

"Oh, I love that story," chimed in Maud.

"Very well, then. Perhaps some more coffee, first, Maudie, dear?"

Maud stood up and bustled over to the stove, while I stretched in my seat and Frank got out fresh cream and sugar to doctor it with.

Before Frank could pick up the thread of his story, there was a thunderous knock on the door. Maud frowned and went to answer it, pulling the heavy wooden door open with a jerk.

"Keep it down," she said, in an unfriendly voice.

"My apologies, friends and neighbors," was the booming retort, as a huge, mountain of a man pushed his way in past her. I was impressed. Anyone who could push their way past Maud was no ninety-seven pound weakling, for sure.

As he entered the room, I saw he was entirely bald, with a golden tan and a shiny, egg-shaped head, set atop a neck that was as broad as my waist. His shoulders were wider than the door frame, and he had to stoop and turn sideways to fit himself through. Once inside, he scanned the room with small, sharp eyes that glittered when they landed on me.

He raised his left hand, which held a cracked leather Bible, and pointed it at me. "I heard there was some trouble here, brother," he boomed. Apparently, the 'sisters' weren't worth including. "I heard that in all Christian charity, you reached out your hand to two Jezebels of the night, and I came to warn you they will turn on you like vipers from the pit. Save yourself, and cast these demons from your home, lest you too be corrupted by their abominations and cast down into the fiery depths of hell itself!"

As he hollered, I could see him looking around for the other 'whore'. He had me pegged, but he couldn't figure out where 'Frannie' had gotten to.

Maud and Frank were just blinking at him, Frank with his jaw dropped nearly to his chest, but Matilda leaped into action, hopping out of her chair and advancing on the preacher with the empty coffee pot clutched in her fist like a weapon.

"What on earth are you thinking, barging into this house and spouting off all that religious gobbledygook? You turn around and march right back out of here, or I'm going to give you a conk in the noggin that'll give you martyr status in three counties, you smarmy son-of-a-bitch!"

The preacher blinked in surprise, and so did I. Matilda was half the size of her hermaphrodite daughter, but she sure sounded sincere.

Light glittered off the preacher's bald dome.

Frank rose to his feet and stood by his mother-in-law's side, and Maud joined them, presenting a united front. Frank smiled at me reassuringly. "Matilda doesn't care much for religion. Feels like it's the Christians that hold women down."

Ah. I'd heard that some suffragettes took exception to all that Christian stuff about women obeying their men and doing what they were told and all. Myself, I had nothing against religious folks as individuals; hell, some of my best friends were religious... well, okay, actually, I couldn't think of a single person I knew and liked that was, but theoretically, I thought they were alright as long as they weren't hanging out in big groups speaking in tongues and threatening to burn people at the stake.

This guy, though, seemed like he could already be contemplating what I'd look like medium-rare.

The preacher drew himself up, until his head nearly scraped the ceiling. "Madam!" he boomed. "In the name of ... in the name of ... of ... of ... " Inexplicably, his speech got slower and slower, as did his theatrical hand gestures. He gurgled once more, managed to say, "blastonomy," in a ponderous voice, and then he ground to a stop altogether, and stood frozen in the kitchen, the hand holding the Bible extended toward Matilda like a threat. For a moment there, at the end, he had sounded a little like Auntie Em.

We all looked at him, then at each other, waiting for something to happen. After several minutes passed, when the preacher still hadn't moved, Frank stepped forward hesitantly. "Mister? Are you okay?"

The preacher didn't blink, didn't even seem to be breathing. Frank reached up and slapped his face, lightly, trying to bring him around.

"Ow! His face is as hard as a rock!" said Frank. Puzzled, he looked at his stinging hand, then at the preacher, then reached up and rapped his knuckles against the frozen man's forehead.

There was a hollow ringing sound.

"What the Sam Hill is going on?" said Matilda.

Realization dawned. I sighed. "He's not a real man at all. He's a mechanical man. Created by the firm of Smith and Tinker in Oz. I've seen their work before."

"A mechanical *man*?" cried Matilda. "I've never heard of such a thing."

Frank gave him another resounding whack in the forehead that made the preacher's body ring like a gong. "You've got to admit that he's not a regular man," he pointed out.

He slowly circled the preacher, poking and prodding from every angle. When he had completed his circuit without provoking a response from his subject, Frank put his hands in his pockets and rocked back on his heels, looking thoughtful. "This is entirely outside anything I've ever seen, too, Matilda, although I did see some gadgets at the Chicago World's Fair a few years ago that seemed constructed along these same lines. About the way a lizard is constructed along the same lines as a flame-breathing dragon, I guess, but seems as if the same principles might be involved."

I scowled at the preacher. It was nice to have some corroboration of my story, but I didn't like his presence here one bit, and had no idea what to do about it. "I apologize for his coming into your kitchen like this. I have no idea why he's here."

"It's not your fault, said Maud. "You didn't tell the big lummox to come here, did you? He must belong to someone, somewhere. Can we get the owner to haul him away?"

"The original owners are gone," I said regretfully. "One died and one went to the moon, but apparently someone is continuing their work and not for the better. If I'm right, you'll find a works somewhere on him that needs winding up, and hopefully, a key."

"Why would you want to wind him back up when he's so horrible?" said Maud.

"Because he probably weighs a ton," I pointed out. "If we don't wind him up and convince him to leave under his own power, we're going to have to cart him out of here, then find somewhere to hide him."

"How do you *convince* a wind-up toy to do anything?" said Matilda.

"He's not a wind-up toy, exactly," I said. "He really is a man, even though he's made of metal. With all the thoughts and feelings, and he can change his mind, although from what I've heard, they tend to be rather dogmatic."

"I'd rather reason with him than try to carry him," said Frank, and got busy looking for the works and the key.

"I think I found it," he said, after a bare minute's search, and yanked up the back of the black broadcloth jacket and plain white shirt the preacher was wearing. I stepped around, and sure enough, in the middle of the mechanical man's back was a brass plate with a spot for a key to be inserted. The plate was inscribed with directions for winding him back up.

> *CLOCKWORK PREACHER:*
> *Talks, walks, thinks*
> *Does everything but live and forgive*
> *Turn key once for talking; twice for action;*
> *three times for thinking*

"Well, *that's* the problem," I said. "He was wound for talking and walking, but somebody forgot to wind him for thinking, too."

"Sounds like a lot of preachers I've run across," said Matilda darkly.

"Now all we have to do is find the key," I said, patting down the preacher's pockets.

Before I could find it, another figure slipped through the half-open kitchen door.

"No need, no need," said a wizened little man with huge whiskers and ancient pinstriped pants. "I've got it right here."

"Who are you?" I asked.

"I'm Garbanzo Tinker."

"Tinker of Tinker and Smith? The inventor?" I said. "I thought you had climbed to the moon and pulled your ladder up after you, never to be seen again."

He gave me a cross look. "What can climb up can climb down, you know. I got lonely. And I missed things. Like cheese. I had been told the moon was made entirely of green cheese, but that turned out not to be true. Why do people lie about things like that?" His whiskers quivered in indignation and self-pity. "I don't know," I replied. "I think they just make up stories because they're fun. I don't think anyone actually expected a person to go there and try to live, just because of a story. But we have more important problems right now. Can you wind up your mechanical man and get him out of here? I don't think the Baums want him permanently installed in their kitchens, and I don't want to listen to him anymore."

"He's a fine specimen," objected the little man, as he looked through his pockets for the wind-up key.

Matilda took a step towards him, brandishing the coffee pot.

"Oh, look, it's right here!" he said, eying her nervously as he pulled a large brass key on a chain out from around his neck.

He set to winding, with much huffing and puffing and straining. Maud stepped up and took over when the little man started running out of breath. He relinquished the task readily enough, but stayed close as Maud turned the key mightily. "Not too hard, now," he cautioned. "If you wind him too tight, all sorts of things could go wrong."

Maud gave him a baleful look and kept turning.

"That's enough," he cried a minute later, but it was too late. Maud gave the key one last turn, and there was a sproinging, clunking noise and the preacher's entire body shuddered in a way that was fearful to see. From deep inside the behemoth came a horrible grinding and clanking.

"Too tight, too tight," moaned the little man, hopping up and down on one foot. "Look what you've done!"

Another titanic shudder, and I ducked behind a chair as the clinking and clanking rose to a head-splitting pitch.

There was a moment of complete silence.

Ping!

A tiny gear shot out of the mechanical man's left ear and flew across the kitchen, landing in the middle of the chocolate cake.

We all looked from the gear to the preacher and held our breaths.

Its eyes blinked. Slowly, the hand holding the Bible came down, and the preacher turned his great head and looked at Tinker. "Master?"

"Yes, Bellows, I'm right here. Give me a moment to sort things out."

Tinker hopped over to take the gear gingerly out of the thick chocolate frosting that cushioned it, and wiped it off with a dishtowel, examining it dubiously. Then he shrugged and put the extraneous gear in his pocket.

The metal preacher began to rock back and forth.

"Bellows, what are you doing?" said Tinker.

The metal man blinked. "Thinking, Master Tinker," he said. "I have ruminated on a number of the premises I previously held true, and find that the logic is not only flawed, but that I have a great need to remonstrate with others to correct these various errors of thought until all agree with my new-found wisdom. The idea, for example, that man has a spirit—or 'soul' if you will, that transcends the purely utilitarian function of survival in order to procreate and thereby to continue the species is an idea for which there is no empirical evidence with which to support it." As he spoke, he grew louder and louder, as if he stood at the pulpit of a cavernous church rather than in the Baum's tidy kitchen, and soon his voice had gotten to such a volume that it was impossible to talk over him.

Being mechanical, he didn't have to stop for breath, and we waited helplessly as he went on and on in the same vein, before we realized he had no intention of stopping. Finally, Tinker peered indignantly at Bellows and began shouting himself. I couldn't hear what he was saying, but I could read his lips. "Bellows, stop that at once!"

Bellows just looked at him helplessly, as if torn between wanting to obey and his desire to declaim his new-found truths. He closed his mouth, but it popped open again immediately. This time he was even louder than before, if that were possible. "Any idea for which there is no empirical evidence cannot be true. What we perceive of as consciousness is just the result of accumulated functional homunculatic nodes of . . ."

Tinker looked furious. "You're supposed to be a preacher, not a thinker!" He turned to Maud. "Madam, may I use your poker?"

"I beg your pardon?" shouted Maud, taking her fingers out of her ears, as Bellows continued to, well, bellow.

"I said," repeated Tinker at the top of his lungs, "I need to use your poker!" He pointed at the collection of cast iron implements leaning against the fireplace brick.

Maud nodded.

Tinker picked up the poker and swung it like a railroad pick at Bellows' shiny pate.

There was a ringing sound that set the mechanical man's entire body vibrating, and the mechanical man attempted unsuccessfully to ward off the blow. He almost stopped talking, but regrouped and went on.

"Just like magic, consciousness is a superstition that does not, in reality, exist," Bellows yelled. "It is the banal belief of those who cannot accept the reality of their own animal nature, and therefore adopt the ludicrous belief system that there is more to life than survival of the fittest in order to live long enough to fulfill the ultimate role of all living things—to perpetuate their own species. There is no other meaning to life and any other contention is pure bunk."

Tinker swung the poker. Again, the mechanical man attempted to avoid the blow, but his movements were clumsy and slow. The poker made a dent a good four inches long in Bellows' head, but the erstwhile preacher ranted on.

"Do you think that's good for him?" yelled Maud.

"Oh, sure," Tinker hollered back as Bellows explained how happiness was also an illusion. "Nothing like a good knock on the head with a hard object to smack the common sense out of a person.

Can't have a good preacher with a lick of common sense." He gave Bellows an expectant look, poker waving about like a flagpole.

"In the ultimate analysis, man is no different than the flatworm, except that while man presumes himself superior to the flatworm, the flatworm does not have the effrontery to presume himself better than man." Bellows said loudly.

"It's all Smith's fault," shouted Tinker. "Crazy old coot. He worked on the brain and the heart, while I worked on the body. Every time I think I've got all the bugs out, Bellows starts thinking for himself and trying to make sense again," the inventor shouted.

Considering that under Bellows' brand of logic, he himself shouldn't exist at all seemed to be a major flaw in Bellows' thinking to me, but neither Tinker nor Bellows seemed bothered by it one bit.

Bam! went the poker. *Bam! Bam! Bam!*

The wall of sound emanating from Bellows stopped. The silence made my ears ring.

"Thank God," said Matilda, after a full minute passed with no further noise. "My head hurts."

"Maybe he needs this after all," said Tinker, pulling the extra gear back out of his pocket. He used his handkerchief to wipe off a few more flecks of chocolate frosting. Apparently satisfied by the results of his inspection, Tinker climbed up on a chair and proceeded to use the poker like a ramrod to guide the runaway gear back into place through one of Bellows' overlarge ears. "Never doubt that highly complex mechanical equipment can be fixed by the proper application of a good whack or two," he said, giving the now silent Bellows a satisfied look. "Same with children."

"You come near my children, I'm going to give you a good whack," said Maud.

"Of course, not having children myself, that's only a theory," said the inventor. He took a small eyeglass out of his pocket and peered into Bellows' ear. "Bellows," he said, "Say something."

Bellows eyed the poker nervously, but obliged. "Hellfire and damnation eternal on those who doubt the word of the Lord."

58

A look of relief crossed the mechanical man's face as Tinker set down the poker. I didn't blame him. Bellows' once smooth and shiny head now had a dozen dints and dings. If Tinker whacked him like that whenever he tried to make sense, no wonder even his best thinking seemed like so much silliness.

"Well, that's that," said Tinker. "Now, to get on with the business that brought me here." He climbed down off the chair and pointed a gnarled finger at me. "Are you Dorothy Gale?"

"I am."

"Glinda wanted me to find you. She says she needs you in Oz, and she'll be looking for you, you-know-where, to summon you back."

Chapter Eight
Revolt, Revolution, Something Like That

Now, that was what I'd been waiting to hear. Glinda, wanting me back in Oz. I took a second to preen mentally, and pat myself on the back. She *needed* me. I sat back in my chair and actually smiled at Tinker. He blushed and wiggled his eyebrows at me. It looked like two caterpillars trying to do the hula.

"Yeah, she seemed pretty shook up. Especially after that firebombing thing."

"What? Firebombing?" I got a sinking feeling in the pit of my stomach. "What's going on in Oz?"

He waved a small hand. "Oh, something with the Munchkins, I think. Revolt, revolution. Something like that."

"A revolution in Oz? Are you serious?"

The nervous look returned. "Come, Bellows, we must away."

The mechanical man tilted his head down to look at his master. "Does that mean we're going home?"

"That's right, Bellows. It's time for us to leave these good folks. Come with me."

"Bellows?" said Maud.

"It certainly fits," I pointed out. She nodded.

Dejectedly, the tiny inventor and his gargantuan companion walked back out the door.

"Wait," said Frank.

"Wait?" I asked.

"Are you crazy, Frank?" said Matilda.

"Wait," said Frank firmly. "We don't have any cheese, but we have some excellent chocolate cake. Would you like a slice before you go?" The inventor and his mechanical man turned around, the inventor with a hopeful look on his face.

"I do not eat," said the preacher. "I am programmed to pretend to do so at potlucks, as part of my function, but I do not actually need food. A few drops of oil here and there, and my gears work just fine."

"Fool, he meant me!" said the inventor. "I suppose I could force myself to eat a piece of cake, just to be hospitable. No cheese, huh?"

"No cheese," said Maud, giving him a queer look.

"Well, alright," he said, hopping up onto a chair.

Soon, the inventor was working his way through a generous slice of cake, and slurping coffee out of one of Maud's mugs.

"But why build a phony preacher, of all things?" said Matilda, as we watched Garbanzo Tinker fork cake into his mouth. "The real ones are phony enough."

He swallowed. "When I was on the moon, I got bored. So I built myself a giant telescope to observe the earth with. Now, here's a funny thing. Telescopes, as scientific objects, can't see Oz, which is basically magical in nature. So all I could see was your bit of the world. And the preoccupation of you mundanes with religion was absolutely fascinating. Everywhere I turned my telescope, I saw churches, temples, basilicas, mosques, you name it. I saw preachers, and priests and monks and rabbis and holy men of every shape and size. I saw singing, and chanting, and preaching and twirling and jumping and all sorts of things. And I started to wonder what it would be like to have some of that religion stuff in Oz."

"Horrible," I said. "Absolutely horrible. That's what it would be like. What's the matter with you?"

He shrugged, and chased crumbs around his plate with his fork. "I thought it would be a fun experiment. Oz is so . . . so undisciplined. And religion is such a great organizing force. People in Oz just run around willy-nilly, doing whatever comes into their heads. There's no fear of the devil - there's not even any devils. Poo! Some moralizing would do everybody good!"

"You have Utopia in your grasp, and you want to ruin it for . . . an experiment? You are a crazy little man, you know that?" said Maud.

I got a sinking feeling. "Where's this telescope now?"

"I left it on the moon," he said. "Why?"

"Oh, nothing," I replied. For some reason, I didn't feel any

61

better.

"It's completely safe, if that's what you're worried about," Garbanzo said. "I left the ladder set up so the Munchkins could go back and forth and check on it for me."

"You're letting the Munchkins look through it?" I asked, alarmed.

"No, I'm letting them watch it for me. Totally different."

"Well, I guess that's okay then."

"Of course, it's all set up. I suppose if they wanted to, they could look through it," he continued. "But it won't do them any good. Funny thing about watching the earth from the moon—you can only see the future."

"What?" I said, finding a source for my relentless feeling of alarm.

"Something wrong with the lens, I suppose. Everything I see through the lens is set . . . oh . . . about seventy years in your mundane future. I'll have to work on that if I ever go back up there. In the meantime, the Munchkins are paying me a dime a climb on my ladder, so I've got no plans to take it down any time soon."

"How many Munchkins have paid you to go up there?" I asked.

"Well, all of them, I think. Give or take one or two, maybe."

"Has it occurred to you that letting the Munchkins look into earth's future could have anything to do with the revolt Glinda is dealing with?" I asked.

"No, can't say it has."

"Maud's right. You are crazy."

"It's not the first time I've heard *that*," he replied nonchalantly. "Do you have any more cake?"

Maud handed him the platter that held the last slice, while Frank asked him questions about his inventions and the town he lived in.

"Evna, in the land of Ev," the little man, explained, while Frank took notes.

I sat and pondered what I'd heard—Tinker's telescope that could see into the future, revolt amongst the Munchkins, Glinda sending Tinker to tell me she needed me back in Oz. What the hell was going on?

Tinker had just finished explaining to Frank about the cruel King Evoldo, who sold his wife and ten children to the Nome King in exchange for a long life, when the air went still and the inventor's voice went tinny and distant.

"Uh, oh," he said in a small voice.

The preacher looked around with interest. "Are we going back home now, master?"

"I believe so, Bellows."

The space around the pair seemed to stretch, then there was a quick, snapping noise and they both disappeared.

"Well!" said Frank.

"Well, indeed!" said Maud in disgust. "He took one of my good forks with him. Where'd he go?"

"Back to the land of Ev," I said, and sighed.

"Isn't that where you want to go?" asked Frank. "Why didn't you go with him?"

"It's close to where I want to go—right next door, in a manner of speaking. But I can't. It takes a special kind of magic to get a plain old regular person to Oz—or to Ev. Otherwise, we'd be falling into it all the time, because it's all around us. People from there can cross over to here, especially around me, because I've been there before, and a little bit of it stays with me, no matter what. But they can't stay very long, and pretty soon, they get snapped back to where they belong."

"But Tinker said someone wanted you to go back. She was going to summon you. How does that work?"

"There's a place in Kansas where the membrane between Oz and our world is very thin and porous. It just happened to be the spot where Uncle Henry had built his shed. If I can get back there, Glinda can pull me through. That's where I was trying to get back to when I got arrested."

Matilda looked at me thoughtfully. "Does this happen to you a lot?"

"What? Getting a message Glinda wants me back in Oz? No,

that's the first time, actually."

"No, I meant more like having Ozian's popping in and out of the world right around you."

"Oh, that. More than you would believe. It makes life weird. Interesting, but weird."

"I'll be damned," said Maud. "It's all true."

"Pretty much."

Frank grinned at me. "Tell us more."

"Oh, no. Not yet. You promised you'd tell me some more of your story first."

Reluctantly, he nodded. "It's not as exciting as your story, by a long shot, but I did promise. Okay, here goes." Drawing a breath, he began.

"After that night, I never saw Nick again. I left for boarding school the very next day, the welts from my father's belt still oozing blood ... "

Chapter Nine
Frank: The Nightmare

I arrived at Peekskill Military Academy on a Monday afternoon, in the pouring rain. Prior to this, I had been schooled by a succession of governesses, so my understanding of school of any kind was mostly theoretical. But I was reasonably sure that the ruler-straight rows of young men I saw lined up on the lawns, drenched to the skin, were not part of the normal school experience.

Still shocked and preoccupied by my brief and unconsummated tryst with Nick, as well as my brutal expulsion from home, I didn't recognize it as the portent it was. The next two years would be bumpy ones.

I was put in a cramped room with two other students. We each had a narrow, hard cot with a thin blanket, two drawers apiece in an aging dresser, and shared a desk for homework. My roommates were Will, a thin, gawky boy who at fourteen was already six feet tall and looked like he'd been stretched on a rack for every inch; and Tom, a chunky blond youth who had been sent to military school when his mother remarried and his new stepfather decided that her coddled son needed to be made into a 'real man'.

Depression crawled around in our room like a chilly miasma.

The next morning, I was awakened from bed before dawn by a blast from some damnable horn that sounded right outside our window. At the urging of my roommates, I clambered into the clothes I had been given the day before, and scrambled to join the other boys lining up outside in the darkling air.

An instructor soon singled me out. "You there! You're the new boy, correct?"

"Yes, sir," I said, standing stiffly as I saw the other boys were doing.

"You're damn puny, you know that, son?"

He looked at me with contempt, as if my small stature were

somehow the result of an inferior nature which he could determine on sight.

"Yes, sir."

"We'll work that out of you. You look like a pussy, son. Like this fellow next to you. Pussy Willow. Isn't that right, Pussy Willow?"

At my side, Will looked straight ahead, his expression betraying no hint of his thoughts and feelings.

"Gentlemen, today, in honor of our new student, we will do double the calisthenics we normally do before breakfast, just to show him what's expected of the cadets we are training at the Peekskill Military Academy. For the next two hours, you are going to be breaking your shriveled little nuts to show him what our standards are around here. After breakfast, please be sure to thank your new friend for that. Now, we're going to start out with a little run, just to warm up. Five miles. Cadets . . . "

And so it went. By the end of our two hours of exercise, I was exhausted, muddy, and starving. To the instructor's surprise, I managed to keep up—after all, I was a country boy, and running, climbing, fighting and riding were a daily experience for me. Tom and Will fared less well, but when I stopped once to try and help Tom to his feet after a fall, he gave me a baleful look and motioned me on. "Are you trying to make him notice me?" he hissed in my surprised face. "I'll have to do it all over again if he sees me needing help." After that, I left Tom to his own devices.

I don't know how many 'real men' they were managing to churn out from our fearful, alienated ranks, but if they had been exporting raw terror and total confusion instead, they would have made a fortune.

Each day began the same way—before sunrise, with calisthenics outdoors, regardless of the weather. We were rained on, half-frozen with snow and sleet, buffeted by high winds and occasionally blistered by the sun. We were randomly singled out for verbal abuse of the rankest nature. When the calisthenics portion of the morning was over, we raced to dress in our uniforms. After, and only after, we successfully passed morning inspection, were we allowed to eat breakfast and proceed with our lessons.

It took about a week before the bully boys got me alone. Tom and Will had warned me about them, but one morning I found myself trapped in the showers with four bulky young brutes between myself and the door.

Their leader was a dark-haired, muscle-bound boy named Chess, who grabbed me by the shoulder and threw me with bruising force against a clammy stone wall.

"Well, if it isn't the puny little momma's boy who got us all two hours of calisthenics last week. What you got to say for yourself, you little pussy baby?"

There seemed to be a heavy reliance on the word 'pussy' as an insult in the Peekskill Military Academy.

Chess didn't really seem to be expecting a response, so I didn't say anything, just tried to feint past him and escape. It didn't work, and I ended up being slammed back against the wall a second time.

There are few feelings worse than standing naked and alone against a contingent of bigger, stronger fellows, especially when you can see the shark-cold blood lust in their eyes. I cupped my hands protectively over my genitals and resolved to show as little weakness as I could. Weakness and fear, I knew, were like catnip to bullies, but I was sure this was going to be bad. *Bad.*

"I hear they put you in with the other losers—the kids that got sent here because nobody didn't want them anymore. How come your family didn't want you no more, kid?"

I just looked at him, miserable. Appalling grammar aside, what he said was true—after catching me on my knees with Nick's cock in my mouth, my family didn't want me anymore. I still had the stripes on my back to prove it.

"That's it, isn't it?" crowed Chess, reading my face. "They didn't want you anymore, did they, poor little babsy-wabsy?"

The rest of the boys hooted with laughter.

"What did you do, country boy? Get caught fucking the family sheep?"

I stared straight ahead.

Chess grabbed my arms and wrenched my hands away from my genitals. "No, it wasn't that," he said. "You don't have enough of a dick to fuck anything. I bet daddy got mad cause he caught you trying to suck some milk off mommy's titties. That it, pussy baby? You still trying to get a little milk off mommy's titties and daddy caught you?"

He doubled over with laughter and I made another break for it, but the boys behind him caught me.

"Clive, go fetch my ink and quill," said Chess, as he looked at me, struggling on the stone floor, while the other boys held me down. "I think we need to do something to let the rest of the school know exactly what kind of pussy-baby we're dealing with here."

When Clive got back, Chess proceeded to write the words "pussy-baby" and "mommy's boy" over and over in indelible ink on every inch of my skin, taking pleasure in scraping the quill into my tender flesh.

After it was over, he motioned for the other boys to release me, and stood, surveying his handiwork with satisfaction, as I lay, breathing hard and trying not to cry, on the cold stone floor of the showers.

He gave me a grin. "Now everybody will know what you been up to back on the farm, boy."

I kicked out with my foot and caught him in the balls.

They beat the shit out of me after that, but it was worth it.

I didn't make it to breakfast that morning, spending the time bleeding and scrubbing ink off my skin with the harsh lye soap they kept in the showers, but I was on time for classes, and for dinner, and for calisthenics the next morning. I didn't get all the ink off, but enough so that I looked badly bruised rather than badly bullied. And bruises were a dime a dozen at Peekskill. I hated Chess with a force that overrode everything else—pain, hunger, exhaustion, fear. I didn't know how I was going to get revenge, but I'd find a way. Paying Chess back had become my life's mission.

Have you ever heard of paraldehyde? It is used in the treatment of seizures, and since I had a history of them, the school nurse decided to keep some in stock. Paraldehyde is a particularly vile liquid, and a powerful sedative, and a spoonful or so would easily knock a boy of my size out for the night.

Shortly before Christmas, I came up with a far better use for it. During the holidays, most of the boys went home, but an unwanted few of us stayed on, forming a select group of rejects and orphans. Interestingly, but perhaps not such a surprise, Chess and his gang were among those who were left to languish at school. He covered it up, of course, with a lot of bluster and balderdash about how his father had been called to Europe on some important business for the president, but no one really believed him, any more than they believed Will when he said his father was too sick to come fetch him that year, or Tom when he told us that his grandmother's untimely death prevented the family from sending for him.

All in all, we were a sad bunch, and the threat of Chess acting out his humiliation on any or all of us hung over our heads like a sharpened blade. I was doing my usual reconnoiter of the showers one morning—making sure the coast was clear before entering— when I heard Chess and his goons talking about having hidden a jug of brandy away in the stables for later, during the instructors' Christmas feast. I snuck away, pondering what I had heard, and then came up with an idea.

Later that day, I feigned an illness, and was sent to the infirmary, where I was put to bed with a poultice on my head and many disapproving looks from the nurse. Being between sessions, however, he could not rightly accuse me of trying to excuse myself from anything, so with some head scratching, he advised me to keep the blankets tight around me and left me to my own devices.

At dinner time, it was a simple matter to filch a bottle of paraldehyde from his well-stocked shelves and slip into the stables, find the hidden jug of brandy, and substitute part of its contents with my medicine.

I beat the nurse back in plenty of time, and spent my afternoon quietly in bed, watching him putter around, mixing noxious concoctions for the various pestilences and plagues likely to beset our school at any time.

When it was time for the feast, the nurse approached me to eject me from his rooms, but I had made preparations of my own, which included slipping myself a small amount of syrup of ipecac, also courtesy of his well-stocked shelves. When he bid me open my mouth for my nightly dose, I obliged by vomiting copiously all over him, myself and the bedclothes.

To say he was dismayed was an understatement.

In his haste to get the mess cleaned up and escape to the Christmas feast, the nurse forgot all about sending me back to my own rooms, where I would have lost my alibi, and I was left alone, smothered in fresh blankets, as he hurried on his way to the laundry with my stinking bedclothes. His idea of solicitousness was to issue dire warnings about what would happen if I ruined any more linens in his absence.

I waited until I was sure he was gone, then slipped out to the stables to observe the results of my labors.

Sure enough, Chess and his four buffoons were all passed out in the stables, the jug of doctored brandy between them. Smiling to myself, moving swiftly, I yanked the breeches of each boy down to his knees. When I came to Chess, I couldn't resist laughing. At least one source of his anger was now apparent. If I'd been so poorly endowed, I'd have been enraged as well.

That done, I cornered one of the sheep the school kept for its supply of mutton and wool, and tied a lead to it, bringing it back into the stable and tying it in such a manner that its purpose in being there could scarcely be mistaken. Then I returned to the infirmary, satisfied with a night's work well done, itching to see what the morning would bring.

I didn't have long to wait.

It seemed like my head had barely touched the pillow, when a good deal of bellowing and shouting roused me. I glanced round the infirmary, and saw my nurse, blinking sleepily as he lifted his head from the pillow. "Here, boy, what's all the commotion?"

"I don't know, but it sounds like it's coming from the stables," I said, slipping out of bed. He was too sleepy to make note of my miraculous recovery, and followed me as I ran from the infirmary to see what all the commotion was about.

In the stable, the tableau was exactly as I had left it, with the exception of the large and appalled crowd now gathered to observe. All five boys were passed out with a jug of brandy nestled in the straw between them, pants down to their ankles, members shriveled and dangling in the cold winter air, a bound sheep in front of them bleating piteously, all four legs secured as it presented its sheepy ass to its apparent ravagers.

That paraldehyde is wondrous stuff. Several of our illustrious instructors were shouting at the boys to wake up, and even now, Chess was beginning to stir. He forced his heavy lids open just as our Commanding Officer arrived on the scene.

"Wha? Whathehell?" Chess mumbled, attempting to sit up, looking around him blearily.

The Commander took one look at the scene—half naked cadets, alcohol, a spread-eagled sheep, and summed it up quite eloquently. "Officers," he addressed his staff. "Get this mess cleaned up and prepare for court martial. If their fathers complain, suggest the Navy." Without another word, he swept out.

And, except for watching them pack up and leave, that was the last I saw of Chess and his band of merry men.

Chapter Ten
Babe in Boyland

There was a crashing noise from over our heads, followed by peals of wild laughter, and I jumped, but Maud just sighed and said, "the boys are up," as if that explained it all, and headed out of the room.

"Our sons," explained Frank as she departed. "Frankie, Bobby and Harry."

In a few minutes, Maud was back with three angelic-looking little boys in tow. The oldest one, nearly as tall as a Munchkin, took one look at me and gave a whistle. "Hot stuff!" he said happily. "Is she the new teacher?"

Maud smacked him on the back of the head and he quickly rearranged the smirk on his face into the expression of a choirboy looking at pictures of saints.

"Daddy," said the next biggest. "Why is she wearing your dress?"

"Chore time," said Maud firmly. "Frank, will you take the boys out and see to the animals while I get supper ready? I'll need a chicken. That old hen with the feathers missing out of her tail, I think. She hasn't laid an egg in two weeks." She quickly shooed them out the door, the littlest one riding on Frank's shoulders. They ducked in unison going out the door, the very picture of father-son camaraderie.

"I think I might wander upstairs and freshen up while the boys are outside," said Matilda. "How long 'til dinner?"

Maud considered. "Chicken and dumplings, so about two hours?"

"Send Frank up to get me, not those little marauders. Last time they caught me napping, they glued my knees together."

"Will do, Mom," said Maud.

We watched her leave. "They glued her knees together? Really?'

Maud grinned. "Yes they did. And I should tell you, 'nap' is a euphemism for 'have a few snorts and pass out', so when she came to and couldn't get her legs apart, for a couple of minutes, she was convinced Judgment Day had come after all and God had taken away her privates for her sins. You should have heard her scream. Took us nearly half an hour and a gallon of hot water to steam her legs apart. By then, she'd peed her pants twice. Ruined a pair of perfectly good knickers."

Just then, Frank came in with the unfortunate chicken. He'd already removed the head and pulled the guts out, so Maud scalded it and then plucked the feathers while I chopped carrots, potatoes and onions under her watchful eye.

While the chicken and vegetables were simmering in a pot, Maud whipped up a batch of dumplings. I watched her for a moment, then decided to broach the subject that I had been considering ever since Frank told me about her.

"So, what's it like to be part man and part woman?"

She shrugged. "It can be hard. I haven't had it as tough as Frank, because Mother was behind me no matter what; but still, the only place for me in society is in a freak show, so I could never just be myself. It's hard, always hiding who and what you are."

"When did you find out you were different?"

"Mother was always honest with me. I can't remember not knowing I was special. But it took me a while to understand why I always had to be a girl in public. Mother took her best guess when I was still quite young as to which gender I would pass for most easily."

Maud waved a floury hand at herself vaguely. "As you can see, she guessed wrong, but by the time she realized, it was too late. Family, friends, everyone knew me as female. When I finally figured out that I wasn't like other girls at all, it was horrible. I locked myself in my room and cried for a week. My mother spent hours outside my bedroom door trying to explain to me that it was for my own protection, but I didn't want to hear it."

Sitting down at the table across from me, Maud sighed. "Finally, I snuck out of my bedroom window and went to my best friend's house and told her. She didn't believe me at first, and demanded that

73

I show her. When I did, she laughed so loud that her parents came running. They took one look and started screaming for the police, saying I was trying to rape their little girl—I was ten, for Christ's sake! I ran back home and told my mother that she was right and I was wrong. Then I told her what had happened. It cost our family hundreds of dollars to hush the whole mess up, and my mother paid for my former friend's family to move far, far away. I never argued with her about it again."

"That's awful, Maud. I feel so sad for you."

Our eyes met and she smiled. "You have a good heart, Dorothy, and an open mind."

"So do you, Maud, or you never would have let me come back here with you and Frank."

"Oh, pish tosh," she said, standing up and going back to the stove, where she commenced spooning dumpling batter on top of the stewed chicken and sliding the pan into the oven. "Did I mention that I won five trophies in my wrestling days?"

I whistled admiringly.

"I have a scrapbook, too. Want to see?"

Companionably, we adjourned to the parlor so I could leaf through Maud's wrestling scrapbook.

Over dinner, the oldest boy ogled my bodice, while the younger two regaled us with their recent adventures in the barn. From the sounds of it, it was lucky that both boys and livestock had emerged unscathed.

"Are you going to be visiting for very long, Miss Dorothy?" asked Frank Jr. "You can sleep in my bed if you like. I'd be glad to sleep on the sofa *if* you want me to," he added with a very mature leer.

"Actually, I'm just passing through," I said, snapping my fingers at eye level to get his focus off my boobs for a second. "I'm trying to get back home."

"Why don't you take her, Daddy?" asked the same kid who had sussed out the fact that I was wearing one of his father's dresses.

"Yes, Frank, why don't you?" asked Maud. "That's a wonderful idea, Bobbie!"

"You think so?" asked Frank. "Could you two ladies spare me for a couple of weeks?"

"Absolutely," said Matilda. "I can fill in for you at the paper. I'm a damn find editorialist, if I do say so myself."

Frank winced, but kept his thoughts to himself on that one.

"And I'm sure Archie can keep things under control at the store for a couple of weeks," said Maud. "Do it, Frank. Dorothy needs you."

He grinned and turned to me. "How about it, Dorothy. Would you like a ride home?"

I jumped out of my chair and hugged Maud and Frank. "Really? Oh, really? That would be so wonderful! Oh, do you mean it? Thank you, thank you, thank you!"

The littlest one, who had been relatively quiet up to this point, looked up and pointed a spoon dripping with gravy at Frank. "Go bye-bye, Toto!" he said enthusiastically.

"Toto?" I said.

Maud nodded. "That's his nickname for Frank. Never has called him Daddy."

"Okay, then," I replied, giving Maud and Frank another hug. "Toto, take me to Kansas. Please."

We determined to leave early the next morning, so the rest of the evening was taken up with planning and packing what we would need to travel the four hundred and some odd miles back to my hometown. Frank went into town to raid his store for non-perishables, and Maud churned out biscuits and salted beef we could eat on the way.

Much to little Frankie's disappointment, I opted to spend the night on the sofa instead of tucked into his bed, which had some suspiciously spotted sheets. Twice I woke up to find him leering over me and sent him, none too politely, back to his own room.

Twice I was woken up by a jitterbug ball in the corner, so all in all, I was ready for about a gallon of hot coffee once everyone was up.

Maud happily obliged. We gathered at the kitchen table for another one of Maud's big breakfasts, this one of shirred eggs and pork chops with oatmeal on the side, topped with honey and fresh butter.

I promised to tell Frank the rest of my tale during the trip, and he promised to write it all down so that he could relay it to Maud and Matilda when he returned. Maud presented him with a brand new pencil and pad of paper to use for that purpose, and Frank ceremoniously sharpened the pencil to a fine point with his pocketknife while Maud packed our vittles basket.

After some consideration, Frank and I had both decided to travel as men, to cut down on possible trouble as we went. I was wearing a pair of Frank's denim pants and a plain cotton shirt, a loose vest and jacket over the top to hide my cleavage. My hair was tucked up under a weather-beaten hat, and I looked like a derelict farm hand if ever I'd seen one. To avoid the appearance that we'd have anything anyone would want, Frank was dressed similarly, and we used the second best wagon and old tack on the horse, a sturdy but middle-aged gelding called High Boy.

Even faded denim didn't deter Frank's oldest son; I had to remove Little Frankie's hands from my ass several times when we were all hugging goodbye, and genially threatened to break his fingers if I ever caught them in proximity to any part of my anatomy ever again.

He gave me an innocent look and a smile, like the world-class pervert he was probably going to grow into. I patted his cheek. "I mean that, Frankie. With all my heart." He just beamed at me.

I sighed and headed for the wagon.

Once we were both aboard, supplies strapped in and covered with a heavy oilcloth, horse hitched and stamping impatiently in the cold morning air, goodbyes said and kisses given, Frank chucked the reins and we embarked on the long, dusty road that would lead us to Kansas.

When the Baum farmhouse had disappeared in the distance, Frank nudged me with his elbow. "You know how to drive this buggy?"

"Sure. I lived with Uncle Henry for nearly a year. How come?"

"Because I want to get out my pencil and paper and start taking notes while you tell me what happened after you went in search of the Wizard of Oz."

I took the reins while he dug out his writing supplies, and when he was ready, I picked up the thread of my story. "The chance to make a little money sounded good, so I agreed to go collect Glinda's bet money from the Wizard. With my pack on my back and my new shoes on my feet, I set off on the Yellow Brick Road . . . "

Chapter Eleven
Dorothy: On the Road

It took me a little while to get used to navigating the bricks while wearing heels, but before too long I got the hang of it, and was swinging on down the road, pack on my back, sun overhead, enjoying the greenery and the music of the birds and the breeze in the leaves and the burbling brook that ran alongside the path.

Occasionally, a squirrel or a bunny would make itself known, head peeking out from the brush inquisitively as I passed by. After a few minutes, I noticed they were hopping and darting out to the road and following behind me, one or two at first, then more and more. A trio of chipmunks joined in. A particularly brave squirrel ran ahead of the pack to peep up my skirt, then darted back into the ranks of his comrades, to the accompaniment of what sounded suspiciously like rodent laughter.

After this happened several times, I turned and put my hands on my hips. The little army of buck-toothed beasts stopped and looked at me. I gave them my best glare.

"Hey! Are you guys looking up my dress?"

One of the squirrels nodded, while several of his buddies started laughing so hard they actually fell over. A couple of the rabbits started thumping their feet enthusiastically.

"Well, you better cut it out, or I'll knock you into next week, I swear!"

This statement caused more mirth, as a suspicious draft hit my fanny. I whirled around to find that two bold little hares had sneaked up behind me and were using their ears to lift up the hem of my dress for a better look.

I swung at them with my backpack, and sent one flying into the bushes, where he lay for a minute, smiling dizzily. I shook a fist at the rest of them. "There's plenty more where that came from, you degenerates! Go get your freak on with your own species!"

Slowly, one of the squirrels tiptoed forward with a grape clutched between his paws and held it up to me with a tentative smile.

"What? Are you saying you want to trade me food for a look at my ya-ya? Is that it?"

He nodded and extended the grape. It was juicy looking and plump, a deep, delicious purple.

I sighed. "Got any peanuts?"

I must say, once I got used to the idea, traveling with a bunch of rodents wasn't so bad. They kept me topped up with nuts and berries, and carrots, too, so I didn't have to worry about food. When I got tired that night, they helped me find a nice sheltered spot to sleep, and then tucked themselves in all around me, so I had a warm, living fur blanket to keep away the chill of the night. I tried not to dwell on how much they were enjoying themselves, and fell asleep thinking of ways I could increase my rates if they were going to be copping feels all night.

The next morning, I was taking care of business under a tree, after I'd made my little fuzzy entourage promise not to look. I thought I heard some muffled giggling from overhead, and stood up abruptly, banging my head on something hard.

"Hey! What the fu-- Ow!" I said, rubbing the spot where I'd conked myself.

"Hey yourself," replied a hoarse, masculine voice. "Stop banging the cage, sweetheart. You're making me seasick."

I stepped back and looked up. In front of me was a gaunt, filthy man inside an iron cage that had been suspended from a thick tree branch. He was clad in tattered clothes and was so thin and disreputable he looked more like a scarecrow than a man. His hair was long and shaggy, a dense blue-black that hung over his face and almost covered a long thin scar that ran from his left eyebrow down to his jaw.

"Oh, my God! What are you doing up there?"

"What does it look like you stupid git? I'm a prisoner. Why don't you be a sport and let me out of here?"

"Well, for one thing, you just called me stupid."

He gave me what I'm sure he thought was a charming smile, but as he obviously hadn't been maintaining his dental hygiene, it made him look even more like a serial killer than he had before.

"Sorry, beautiful. It just popped out. You startled me."

"You didn't answer my question. What are you doing up there?"

"Oh. This. That rotten bitch Glinda—wait, you wouldn't happen to be a friend of Glinda's, would you?"

"You mean Glinda the Good Witch of the North?"

He sighed. "Well, I guess that answers that. Okay, I admit, Glinda and I had a little tiff, and she put me up here. But then she must have got busy, because I'm sure she didn't mean to leave me up here until I starved to death. So why don't you be a good girl and do your friend Glinda a favor and get me down, huh? I bet she'll thank you for it later."

Above his head, several squirrels had materialized and were shaking their heads violently in the negative.

"What did she catch you doing?"

"Well, actually . . . You heard of a woman named Nessa?"

"Short, green, nice rack?"

He grinned. "That would be her. Glinda caught me . . . ah . . . playing hide the wand with Nessa and her twin sister, if you get my drift."

I studied him. He did have a certain roguish charm, under all the dirt and grime. And I'd already seen Glinda's temper at work. Hothead was an understatement. And this was her ex? I felt a surge of pity. Plus, I figured it wouldn't hurt to learn everything I could about my new boss.

"I'm on my way to the Emerald City to collect on a gambling debt someone owes her. I could use a little muscle. What do you say?"

"Collect from who?"

"The Wizard?"

"Of Oz?" He burst into laughter. "Good luck with that. Hope you have a few tricks hidden under your skirt."

80

"Unless you've got cash, what I have under my skirt is none of your damn business. Look, you want to help, or you want to stay up in that cage, eating leaves?"

"I don't eat leaves," he said indignantly.

"They're stuck in your teeth," I said. Not to mention that every branch within arm's reach of the cage had been stripped bare. "In or out. Hurry up. I've got places to go." Above his head, a squirrel put his paws together, pleadingly, and shook his head in an emphatic 'no.'

"Anything is better than this cage," he said. "Even going to the Emerald City on a wild Winkie chase. Besides, maybe while I'm there I can get him to take a look inside my head and help me figure out why I'm attracted to these gorgeous psycho dames like Glinda."

"I already know the answer to that. You have a brain the size of a pea, and it's located inside your cock."

"That's funny," he said. "I always thought brains were located in a person's head. Maybe I can get him to take it out and put it where it belongs. By the way, did you know there's a rabbit looking up your skirt?"

I put down my pack and fished out my Bowie knife in its beat-up leather sheath, then tucked my skirt around my knees so I could shimmy up the tree. "You don't know the half of it. I'm Dorothy, by the way. What's your name?"

"Pleased to meet you, Dorothy," he said, watching as I climbed up the tree and out on the limb so I could saw through the rope that held his cage up in the air. "They call me Scar, because of this," he continued, sweeping back the hair on the left side of his face so I could get a better look. It was old and puckered, a thin white slash in his tanned skin, visible even through the dark beard that covered the lower half of his face.

I had cut through most of the rope when it finally gave, unraveling rapidly and sending the cage plummeting down to the ground, where it crashed against a rock and sprang open. For a guy who was half-starved, Scar moved with surprising agility to escape his prison. When he was standing on his own two feet, free at last, he gave me another one of those cocky grins.

"But my real name is John. John Crow. That's why she locked me up in a damn birdcage. Crow—crow. Get it? Like the bird."

"Got it," I said. "Now, how about you hop in that creek and scrub off some of that crud before we get on our way. I don't want to get knocked off my feet by the smell every time I get downwind of you."

"You got any food on you?"

"Bath first, food after," I said firmly.

He grumbled, but he went, and I lent him my knife so he could scrape the beard off his face. While he was gone, I got my little rodent army to gather up enough nuts and berries to feed two men.

He returned shortly, clean and smooth-shaven, and I could see why Glinda had gone for him. It took him about five minutes to devour the food, and then he pronounced himself ready to travel.

It was still morning when we got back on the road, and we'd gone several miles when I spotted a scarecrow in a nearby cornfield.

"Look, Scar," I said. "Even that scarecrow is better dressed than you are. Maybe you should trade places with him. Instead of a scarecrow, they could have a *Scar*crow."

"Very funny," he replied. "But you're right. His clothes are better than mine. Hang on a second."

In a flash, he was over the split rail fence, and had ripped his tattered clothes off. One of the bunnies whistled appreciatively as the sight of his bare ass. I didn't blame him. It was a really, really nice ass.

He had the plain black shirt and black work pants stripped off the scarecrow before you could say, 'bi-questioning', and took the shoes and hat for good measure. By the time he was back at my side, he looked more like an adventurous man-about-town than the pitiful prisoner he had been that morning, and I was feeling a lot more confident about the job I had to do when we reached Oz.

"Hey," he said, as we started walking. "There's some pervert chipmunk sneaking looks at your butt."

"I know," I said with a sigh. "Want a blackberry?"

Chapter Twelve
Dorothy: Brule County Blues

Frank and I made it as far as Chamberlain, South Dakota that first day, but we were too late to catch the afternoon ferry across the Mississippi, so we boarded the horses for the evening at the local stable and got a room at the Starlight Hotel. Chamberlain was a bustling town, and it boasted two more hotels besides the Starlight, half-a-dozen saloons, a feed store and two dry goods emporiums, and an honest-to-God bathhouse. The ferry service ran from dawn to dusk, so once High Boy was seen to, we headed out to find a restaurant where we could grab a hot dinner and make an early night of it.

The man at the hotel recommended Edie's diner, where we got split pea soup, thick slices of buttered bread, and liver with fried onions. We shared a table with half-a-dozen other men, so our conversation was limited to topics like the recent weather, crop prospects and gossip about the local whores. For the most part, I kept my mouth shut and listened; I had pretty much talked myself out during the day; Frank was quiet, too, so I let him be and contented myself with filling my belly and trying to think like a man.

We picked up a good pint of Irish to take back to our room, and settled in comfortably. Frank and I tossed down a few shots, and once we were both good and loose, I kicked back on the bed and reminded Frank that it was time for him to pick up the thread of his narrative.

"Come on," I said, prodding him with my foot. "I talked all day today. Now, it's your turn. Tell me what happened after you got rid of those rotten bullies at your school. Did things get better after that?"

"For a while," he said, looking off absently as if the grubby walls were of vast interest to him. "For a while, things got better. Another new boy joined us, and I fell in love the moment I saw him. His name was Renfield Brown, but everyone called him Renny . . . "

A look of sadness came over his face, and he leaned back against the headboard and closed his eyes for so long I thought maybe he'd fallen asleep.

Finally, though, he stirred and gave me a look filled with sadness.

"Tell me, Dorothy, have you ever met someone so evil that they scarce seemed human to you?"

I shook my head. "No. I've met people I didn't like, and I've met people who didn't like me much, such as that principal I told you about. But no one that was just pure evil like in a book or a play. Why? Have you?"

He sighed and closed his eyes again. I waited as patiently as I could.

After a long silence, he sat forward, looking at me earnestly. "I have, Dorothy. I met a man so purely evil that he corrupted everything he touched. It was a long time ago, but it's still hard for me to talk about."

"Frank, if it hurts, you don't have to tell me. We can talk about something else."

"No," he said. "I want to talk about it. Maud is the only one I've ever told about this. His name was Humbert Gulch. But the story really starts with Renny Brown . . . "

Chapter Thirteen
Frank: Out of the Frying Pan...

... Renny Brown was the handsomest youth I'd ever seen. Unlike Nick, who would be forever scarred by the war, Renny was perfect in every aspect, with smooth, pale skin that stretched taut over impressive muscle, a head full of thick, curly hair that gave him just the right dash of reckless insouciance. He had innocent blue eyes and a generous mouth that was nearly always curved up in a smile. And, oh, was he popular! Everyone loved Renny. Even the instructors were infatuated with him—he had a way about him that just made you feel like a better person in his presence. He was everything a fine young man should be. Kind, generous, brave, honest and smart. And from the first moment our eyes met, I knew that on some fundamental level, he was just like me. And yet he was all that was manly and wholesome.

In one sense, this was extremely puzzling to me, and in another quite reassuring. After all, if Renny was such a paragon, and he felt as I did, could I really be so bad? On the other hand, I trembled with desire to know how he reconciled his public persona with his hidden desires and motives—was there some secret he could share with me that would help me reach a truce with those warring impulses inside of me?

One day we found ourselves on the same work detail in the yards, and I was so excited to finally have the opportunity to talk to him alone that I could hardly figure out what to say. After starting and stopping half-a-dozen times, he finally gave me a sidelong smile and said, "it's okay, Frank. You can go ahead and say it."

"You favor men instead of women, too?"

He laughed. "And would deny it if you ever said so in public. But I recognized you as a kindred spirit as soon as I saw you. You've gone to fewer pains to hide your nature than I have. But let's not pretend with each other—it would be such a relief not to have to pretend, just once in a while!"

There was a world of sadness in his tone, and I had to know more. "Why do you pretend if it pains you so?"

That earned me a frown. "My father is a general, from a long line of military men. My grandfather once shot a man under his command who was caught daring to do what we talk about. What do you think my family would do if they knew? I would be disinherited, banished, abandoned."

I didn't say anything, remembering the last scene with my father.

Renny laid a hand on my shoulder, and the heat from his palm warmed me to my toes. "I can see you know something of which I speak. Your eyes have grief in them."

I nodded.

"I intend to toe the line and make my father and grandfather proud of me in every way. I will graduate from this academy and go on to a fine university, from there to an honorable military service. I will marry and produce the grandchildren my father yearns for. And when he dies, I will cheerfully collect my inheritance and carry on the pretense to my own grave, upholding the family name and honor, while I do my best to never give in to the devilish desires that try to corrupt and damn me."

His speech shocked me. This was *Renny*, for God's sake! Without ever before having exchanged a meaningful word, I had elevated him to the status of personal hero. Surely, if Renny could not find a way to make this alright in some way, there was not a way to be found. I was seized with despair. "Why would you bury your true self like this?" I asked, daring to hope I had misunderstood him somehow.

"Because it is the right thing to do," he said, seriously, looking me in the eye. "The world is not made for such as you and I, Frank. We are abominations, freaks of nature. We must learn to subjugate or exorcise our unnatural urges and desires to the manner in which God intended us to function. Nothing more and nothing less. Do you understand what I'm saying to you?"

I squinted up at him. His lips were saying one thing, but I thought

86

I saw something more in his eyes. Maybe it was his use of the word 'exorcise'. Whatever it was, I was quick to seize the opportunity I thought was presenting itself, my despair of mere seconds ago already discarded. "I'm not sure, Renny. Maybe you could meet me in the stables later and explain it to me some more?"

When he gave me a slow, reluctant smile that made his eyes crinkle at the corners, I knew he was mine. Thus began the single most painful—and most glorious—period of my life.

Renny and I met whenever we could find the time and opportunity, which wasn't often. It was school policy to manage the lives of its students from daybreak until lights out. Physically, Renny was a gorgeous, if not particularly imaginative, lover, and the thrill of the forbidden, coupled with Renny's own oft-voiced certainty that what we were doing was damnably wrong, sufficed to keep me stirred up with a mixture of longing and dreadful anticipation that one day soon his love would be taken away from me.

The effects of two years of military school had left their mark on me. While I would never be a beloved, popular boy like Renny, nor as tall and compelling in body, I had developed well for my size, and was known for my speed and agility, as well as having a rather deadly eye with a rifle or arrow. I'll never forget the words spoken to me by my marksmanship instructor, after I cleaned the field during a long-range firing competition. "Frank," he said, clapping me on the back, "You're a hell of a shooter. If you weren't such a sarcastic, insubordinate son-of-a-bitch, you'd be a hell of an army man. As it is, I'm not even sure the Navy would take you."

That and a handful of blue ribbons were the most praise I ever received at Peekskill.

My idyllic emotional joy ride with Renny came to an abrupt and unexpected end when we were joined mid-semester by a new instructor. Along with a proficiency in mathematics, grammar, history, battle strategy and geography, we were expected, oddly enough, to spend one full hour per day in the study of the Christian

Bible. Or perhaps it was not so incomprehensible. Murder is ever easier if the conscience of the murderer is soothed by the religion of his compatriots.

Humbert Gulch. Even now, his name makes my stomach clutch with dread and anger.

He was a tall, emaciated crow of a man, with limp, flaxen hair and burning green eyes. He dressed in simple black, which some might have considered a mark of modesty, but which I suspected was a calculated choice to keep his audience's focus on his pale, sharp-boned face and mesmerizing voice.

He joined the staff just after Christmas, our previous religious instructor having been dismissed when evidence of his fling with one of the cooks became irrefutable in the most prosaic of ways—a seven-pound baby boy who looked—and sounded—remarkably like his father.

In addition to leading the Sunday morning service, it was Mr. Gulch's duty to instruct us in religion as part of our regular curriculum. No good war could be fought without an underpinning of Christian authority and sanction, I believe was the thought.

Of course, during our recent civil war, both sides had claimed the religious right, and thousands upon thousands were senselessly slaughtered anyway, on both sides. I don't think having God on your side during a battle means as much as our fearless generals believe it does.

Regardless of my cynical attitude toward religion and its place in a military school, however, Christian instruction was a regular part of our day, every day, right after lunch, when the sound of one of the surprisingly frisky Chaplain Digbert's droning lectures had previously been guaranteed to put all but the most fervent into a sound sleep.

After listening to one of our junior mathematics instructors fumble through Digbert's notes for two weeks while a new teacher was frantically sought, I expected more of the same on the introduction of Mr. Gulch.

For just a moment, as the tall, thin man stepped forward, I

thought him bland—a milquetoast stick figure with an anesthetic's build and a moralist's ineffectual and faded personality. Then he raised his head from its modest downcast position on that skinny neck, and those blazing green eyes swept us.

Their electrifying arc came to rest, it seemed, for just a moment on Renny, handsome and ripe as a fresh peach a few seats away from me.

A feeling of unease rippled through me as Gulch raised one hand in salutation at the front of our classroom. He had a Bible clutched in his spidery fingers, I noted, although this was supposed to be a mere introduction.

A smile as sharp as shattered glass flashed across his face. "My new students," he began in a silky voice. "I am delighted to meet you all. Delighted to be entrusted with the shaping of your fine young souls. For those of you who have already strayed far down the path of sin and decay, I am grateful to have this opportunity to offer you redemption for your evil deeds, mercy through repentance, confession and penitence."

I snorted quietly to myself—we were all still in our teen years. How many sins did he think we could have fit in? But it was impossible to dismiss him. He was authoritative, a commanding presence in our classroom, his voice a sword. To my left, I could see Renny, sitting ramrod straight, eyes wide and fixed on our new instructor.

Behind Gulch, the mathematics instructor who had been filling in shifted on his feet, eager to be done with his task and back to doing complex calculations.

Professor Gulch was an ordained Methodist minister, and as such was chosen to guide us in all matters spiritual and scriptural. Unlike most of our instructors, who simply oozed vitality and good health, Professor Gulch was a thin, bloodless man, much given to brooding. He would frequently interrupt his own dry lectures to spend a few minutes raining warnings of hellfire and brimstone down on our youthful heads if we should ever reject our collective role as God's pure warriors to indulge in such soldierly pleasures as alcohol, gambling and loose women.

So graphic were his descriptions of these vices that I'm sure he lured more to the side of the devil than he ever dissuaded, but none of us ever attempted to point out the error of his ways to him; Professor Gulch did not invite criticism, helpful or otherwise. I simply sat in the back and tried to escape his notice. There was something about him that made me extremely uncomfortable, though I was loath to put my finger on it.

Every day, Renny seemed more enthralled with Professor Gulch. He was also becoming less and less willing to meet with me for our private trysts late at night. It started when he began objecting to the use of my paraldehyde to drug our roommates so we could slip out together unnoticed.

"What do you mean, you don't think it's *right?*" I was incredulous.

"I don't know," Renny said, rubbing the back of his neck and avoiding my eyes. "What if it's bad for them or something?"

"They've been giving it to me for years—has anything bad happened to me?"

"No, but you have seizures. I've seen you. Maybe it's different for you."

One. I'd had one seizure at the school, during an oral exam at the end of last semester. It had been witnessed by half the staff, and my entire class, to my everlasting embarrassment.

I took Renny's hand and stood directly in front of him, so that he couldn't help but look at me. "Are you telling me you don't want to meet with me anymore?"

"No," he said, blushing. "I mean, maybe. I don't know. The things Professor Gulch says, Frankie—he makes me want to be a better person. A good person. He makes Hell seem *real*, you know? I don't want to go to hell. Do you? Maybe we should stop. Put the sins of the flesh behind us. All that stuff. What do you think?"

I was crushed, because I had just realized a fundamental difference between Renny and myself—I was in love. Totally, hopelessly, head-over-heels in love with tall, muscular, handsome, popular Renny. I would have married him if I could, taken him before God and man as my partner, my pride, my lover. I loved his smell, his taste, the way his eyes crinkled when he smiled, the dimples in his ass.

Renny, on the other hand, loved *boys*. He loved the physical sensation, he felt the lust, the pull, the urgent desire to mate—but he did not love *me*. He would miss the sheer physical pleasure of making wild, sweaty love in the dark. But would he miss *me*? I had my doubts. Sure, I was a friend. I knew him better than most, because I knew his darkest secret. But would he miss me any more than any of the other young men of his acquaintance? Maybe not.

From the way he was eying me now, perhaps he would even be glad if I were to disappear somehow, taking the memory of our secret love away with me like it had never been.

I whirled away and stalked across the barn to throw myself in a pile of hay. "Fine, then," I said, betrayed and hurt. "If that's all I mean to you. Just go."

He hesitated at the door. "It really will be better this way, Frank. It's the right thing to do. It's what God wants us to do."

"Go!" I shrieked. Then I buried my head in my arms so I wouldn't have to look at the relief on his face as he left.

After he was gone, I cried in the dark for hours.

Class with Professor Gulch became a torture. Renny would sit, back straight, eyes shining. Sucking up every word the professor uttered as if it were a divine pronouncement. I slouched in the back of the room, trying to avoid notice and doing my best to keep a sneer off my face.

The love of my life had abandoned me without a backward glance, apparently, and over the course of the next few months, I watched with dismay as he became Professor Gulch's prize pupil. He followed the professor around like a puppy, and began spouting scripture with a zeal that was frightening in its intensity.

Feeling lovesick and forlorn, I took to slinking along behind them at a discrete distance. Occasionally, I would give my roommates a paraldehyde mickey and slip out to wander the campus in the dark, peering through the window of Renny's cabin so that I could stare at his sleeping form and torment myself with unrequited love.

One night, I decided to stop by Renny's room and peek in at my former lover, and found to my amazement that he was missing from his bed.

This was unimaginable to me. Had he been taken ill? Had he been sent home for some reason? Had he . . . had he been lying to me about his spiritual conversion and found another lover?

My heart pounded in my chest as I considered this last, my breath harsh and rasping in my own ears. Who could it be?

Gulch!

Abandoning all sense of discretion, I raced across the moonlight quadrangle to the teachers' quarters, making a beeline for the one modest cabin from whose windows light still leaked. I thrust myself up into the window to see a most horrifying sight.

Renny, on his knees in front of the professor, shirt off, gold skin gleaming in the unholy lantern light. Professor Gulch looked like a demon from hell in the flicker and glow, a Bible clutched in one hand, and his other twisted painfully in Renny's hair.

Through the inch or so of space between the bottom of the window and the sill, I could hear Gulch's mesmerizing voice battering at my handsome young lover.

"To be saved you must confess! Do you want to be saved Renfield?"

"I do!" replied Renny in a fervent voice that made my heart sink.

"Then confess your sins to me and be free of them! Have you engaged in carnal sin?"

"I have," replied Renny. The hand twisting in his hair tugged painfully.

"Have you engaged in carnal sin with another man, violating the laws of nature and of God?"

I held my breath. Gulch's eyes glittered.

"I . . . have," said Renny in whisper I could barely hear.

"Show me what you've done! Show me every sin!" exclaimed Gulch, jerking Renny's head.

"Sir?" said Renny, looking up at him.

"Show me. Demonstrate to me this sin you've committed!"

Hesitantly, Renny reached out a hand toward the buckle of Gulch's belt. He paused and said, "sir?" one more time, as if asking permission.

"Show me, sinner!" thundered Gulch, and Renny obediently undid Professor Gulch's trousers and took the inflamed member housed therein, putting it between his lips as if it were a holy wafer.

I couldn't believe my eyes. Nor could I tear them away.

Gulch's hips pumped, and he dropped the Bible to clutch Renny's fair hair with both hands, thrusting his cock into the younger man's mouth.

When he came, I shuddered also. An involuntary movement of horror and lust and disgust mixed.

"Now you have revealed your soul to me, and with penance, you may be cleansed, sinner," said Gulch as he restored his clothing. "Do you feel the cleansing power of confession moving through you?"

Renny looked up at him adoringly. "I do!"

Gulch turned and picked up a coil of rope and I realized that it was a horsewhip.

As Renny knelt obediently, Gulch's semen still glistening on one fair cheek, the professor uncoiled the whip and began flailing Renny's back with a wiry arm. The blows shook Renny's form and welts began to form, but Renny remained passively at Gulch's feet as the beating went on.

As the blows marred that perfect golden back, I could stand it no more. I grabbed the window and shoved it open, jumping through to grab the whip from Gulch's upraised hand.

"You demon! How dare you strike Renny! You are the one who needs a beating, you foul, perverted, lying bastard!"

Before I could turn the whip on its owner, Renny jumped up and grabbed me from behind.

"Frank! Frank, stop it! He's helping me—he's saving me from my sins! What are you doing?"

Gulch drew himself up to his full height and pointed a finger at me. "You are the demon, you little abomination! You will be damned to hell for all eternity for your sins and seductions, you succubus of the devil!"

The look in his eyes was triumphant. I could feel Renny's arms around me like steel bands, preventing my struggles, keeping me from ripping Gulch's eyes out with my bare fingers. It was more than I could stand. I screamed, a sound of pure rage and pain.

The sound must have penetrated the furthest reaches of the camp, because other instructors, and then students, began to pour through the door, shouting, jostling to see what or who was being slaughtered in Gulch's cabin.

No animal, just me. The sound was the sound of my soul being ripped out.

As his audience grew and settled, Gulch turned to them as if he were giving a command performance. "I have found the source of sin within our midst. This young man has been sowing the seeds of Sodom, sent by Satan to corrupt and condemn these fine young men we are tasked with protecting. Who knows how many he has corrupted?"

On the other side of the room, I could see one of my roommates, blinking and stuporous, eying me with revulsion. Infinitely more painful was the sight of Renny, returning to stand at Gulch's side.

There was a stirring at the door and the crowd gave way to make room for the headmaster. "What's going on in here? What's all this ruckus?"

Gulch pointed at me. "We have found a homosexual, a male prostitute, a foul pervert among us. He has been attempting to seduce and practice his foul lusts on our students. May the wrath of God fall upon you, you disgusting animal."

The headmaster goggled and looked at me, and I felt a fine cold sweat break out all over my body. My muscles convulsed and I could feel my bones grate with the force of the convulsion that was sweeping me up. "God, please not now," I thought, but he was deaf to my pleas.

Maybe Gulch was right, and God had damned me, too, because

that was all I remembered until I woke up in the infirmary and was told I was being shipped back home as soon as the morning train arrived.

Chapter Fourteen
Dorothy: River Ride

After Frank finished his tale, I fell asleep still thinking about him, Renny and Humbert Gulch.

I assume Frank fell asleep, too, poor dear, but I don't recall another thing until there was a knock on our door and a deep voice announced that we had one hour until the first ferry of the morning departed.

We scrambled into our clothes and went to check on the horse. Once he was hooked up to the wagon, we headed back to Edie's for scalding hot coffee and flapjacks.

The Mississippi was smooth as glass that morning, all silver and rose under the early morning sun. On the banks, the trees were green and cool, and trout tickled the surface of the river, sending out tiny ripples as they looked for tasty bugs.

The ferry was a huge, creaky old thing, and listed alarmingly as it was loaded, but I was the only one who seemed to notice, so I did my best to look as bored and impatient as everyone else crowding the bow. I jumped when the steam engine roared to life, making a rough-looking old man next to me burst into laughter. Miffed, I moved away, and spent the rest of the trip soothing High Boy and marveling at the lush beauty of the Mississippi Valley as we slid through the water.

After we debarked we found the road broad and well traveled, with quite a bit of traffic, and twice we picked up men on foot and carried them with us for a way. It wasn't until we set up camp for the night that we were well and truly alone.

Frank had spotted a handy creek, so we decided to take advantage of the convenience, and we made camp while the sun was fairly well up in the sky. We were out in the middle of nowhere, most of the day's traffic having siphoned off to other roads and other destinations. I gathered wood while Frank set up camp, then we tossed dried beef into a bubbling pot for stew.

Once all our domestic chores were taken care of and our bellies were full, Frank pulled out a second pint he had acquired in Chamberlain and asked if I was ready to resume my tale.

"Hopefully, it will be something a little lighter than the one I shared with you last night," he said, half apologetically.

I thought about what happened after Scar and I set off to find the wizard. "Definitely. That's one of the things I love about Oz. There's no one like your Humbert Gulch there. Glinda would make toast out of a scoundrel like that in two notes."

He smiled. "That would be something I'd like to see—Humbert Gulch getting a good zap from Glinda's wand and having that scrawny ass of his knocked right into next week."

"It was awhile before I saw Glinda again," I said. "As a matter of fact, I met quite a few of Oz's other residents before I saw that pretty witch again . . ."

Chapter Fifteen
Dorothy: The Queen of the Forest

By Scar's estimate, we were still about a day out of the Emerald City, and the yellow brick road had become sadly neglected by whatever sort of road maintenance crew was supposed to take care of it. We were passing through a particularly overgrown and weedy section when a strange man jumped out of the bushes at us, wearing nothing but a glittering banana hammock and a threatening look. He brandished a club and growled like a madman, bearing great pointed white teeth.

Scar pulled out the Bowie knife I had lent him earlier, while I grabbed my pack in one hand and hefted it as menacingly as I could.

For a tense second, the two men faced off, then suddenly Scar relaxed and shoved the knife back into its sheath. "Well, well, well. Look what the cat dragged in." He turned to me, amusement on his face. "Relax, Dorothy, it's only Fucking Leon."

The man who had jumped out at us scowled. "Scar? I should have known. The only travelers I see on this road for two weeks are even broker than I am. And don't call me Fucking Leon. I *hate* that. It's *Leon*. Just Leon."

If he didn't look so pissed off, he would have been kinda cute. He had a thick halo of short golden hair, a broad nose in an exotic, high-cheekboned face, and bright golden eyes with odd, slitted pupils. He had the faintest suggestion of a harelip. He must have felt me looking at him, because he snapped his heels together and gave me a short bow. "At your service, doll face."

I curtsied. "Back at you. I'm Dorothy."

"You know, there's a squirrel with his nose up your skirt?"

Scar gave the squirrel a hearty kick that sent him flying through the air. I winced when I heard the little guy come crashing down a moment later.

"So," said Leon. "What are you guys up to? Headed to the Emerald City?"

"Yeah," answered Scar. "Gonna collect on a little debt for my girl Glinda."

"You two back together? I thought she washed her hands of you after she caught you, Nessa and Elfa in the sack."

Scar grinned. "What can I say? I'm a hard guy to replace."

"Yeah, without a couple of D batteries," said Leon with a snicker.

"Batteries?" I said, pronouncing the word carefully. "I don't get it. What are those?"

Leon gave me a knowing look. "You're not from here, are you?"

Scar looked interested. "When *are* you from?"

"When?" I was getting more confused by the second.

"Yes, *when*," Leon said.

"Oz isn't bound by the same time frame as your mundane world, cutie," added Scar. "We connect at a variety of 'whens', just like we connect at a variety of 'wheres'."

"Oh," I said, trying to sound like I understood what he was talking about. "It's June of 1883. Or, at least it was when I left."

I frowned. If their connection to time and place was as tenuous as Crow seemed to think, when was it now? If I returned to the world I had been born in, would I return to the same time, or would I be thrust forward or backward to some other year?

On the other hand, why would I ever want to go back? I gave a mental shrug. I had been in Oz about two seconds before deciding that it beat Kansas by about a mile. Looking down, I admired my new footwear. Plus, the shoes were to die for.

We walked for a few minutes, then Scar turned his attention to our new companion. "What about you, Leon? Sunk to mugging strangers to keep yourself in catnip?"

Leon's odd gold eyes glittered. "Why, you holding?"

"No, but if you need some quick cash, you could tag along with us."

"Who's gonna pay him?" I asked. "Not me."

"Come on, Dorothy. Oz is a slippery bastard. We go in the front, you're gonna need someone to watch the back door so he doesn't slide out."

"You're gonna go try to shake Oz down? Count me out," said Leon, turning and heading back into the shrubbery.

"Yeah, go on, you scaredy cat," said Scar. He went on, loud enough for Leon to hear. "You know why we call him Fucking Leon, Dorothy? Because he's *that* guy - you know the one? The guy that tells you he'll be by on Tuesday with the money he owes you and he shows up two weeks later broke and hung over and checking your couch cushions for change when you're out of the room. He's the guy that says for a hundred smackaroos he can cop you an ounce of great shit, and he comes back with a dime bag of oregano and the cops right behind him. He's the guy who says he's got your back, and then at the first sign of an AK47, he--"

"You're an asshole, Scar. You know that?" said Leon, who had turned around and looked like he might cry any minute.

"And you're a chicken-shit, two-bit, fuck-faced, no-nuts queer, Leon."

"That's harsh," I said, elbowing Scar in the ribs.

"I'm not a queer; I'm a drag queen," said Leon with great dignity. He dug a card out of his pocket and handed it to me.

Leona Rent
Musical Extravaganza
She Sings! She Dances! She has Hourly Rates!
Now appearing at:

In the blank space at the bottom of the card, someone had neatly hand lettered 'The *Kit-Kat Club, Green Light District, Emerald City*'.

"Wow," I said, impressed. "You're an entertainer?"

He bowed again, while Scar snorted. "If you call strutting around in a sequined G-string and yowling old show tunes at the top of your lungs entertaining."

100

"I've gotten damn good reviews," said Leon defensively.

"If you're doing so damn good, how come you're out here, trying to shake down tourists, instead of living it up on all the money you're raking in? Which was a joke, by the way, because we both know you'd turn tail and run at the first sign your target was going to fight back."

Leon gave a watery sniff. "I would not! And I was invited out after a show for a carriage ride by a couple of out-of-towners. They promised me the moon, then dragged me out here in the middle of nowhere, and gave me the old 'fuck or walk' line. I thought that was the whole idea, but when I stripped and they found out I was really a guy, they dumped me and took off. Do you believe that? They really thought I was a broad," he finished, with an odd mix of pride and distress.

Scar gave me an inpatient look. "Come on, Dorothy. Let's stop wasting our time. Leon's a con man, a hustler, a grifter. He's no good for the kind of job we're on, anyways. The best he could do would be to talk Oz to death. Or, even worse, sing to him. Hey, Leon. Maybe you should come with us and ask Oz to grow you some balls."

"That's really cold," I said.

"No, really. He has no balls. He had himself fixed because he couldn't fit all his junk under the G-string."

"You're kidding."

"I most certainly am not. Look."

I looked at Leon, who was blushing like a beet. He nodded sheepishly.

"Oh. Well. That's a horse of a different color. Are you . . . doesn't that make you a . . . what do you call yourself, then?"

"A eunuch," said Scar. Leon gave me a weak grin. "Dorothy, you ready to go?"

"Wait, wait," said Leon. "Please let me go back with you? I hate it out here in the woods alone. It's cold. And scary. I think the animals don't like me. Please, please?"

"Sure," I said. "Of course you can go with us."

"Oh, thank you, Dorothy. You won't regret this. I promise. Wait two seconds while I get my bag." He darted back into the woods.

Scar looked both resigned and exasperated. "Oh, the animals don't like me. I'm shunned by beavers and porcupines everywhere," he said in a falsetto, then continued in his normal voice. "He puts a move on me, I'm gonna bust him right upside his head, you got that, Dorothy? You keep your little pet on a leash if you want me to leave his head on his shoulders."

Before I could answer, Leon came bursting back out of the bushes wearing a somewhat worse-for-the-wear evening gown in a startling chartreuse, draped in a molting feather boa and hauling an oversized purse that looked like it could have concealed a small pony. He'd put on a great, flowing blond wig that cascaded down the back of his head like a lion's mane. He trotted up to us and stopped in front of Scar with a pretty pout. "Scar, could you be a gentleman and carry my bag for me? I'd do it myself, but it's *so* heavy."

Leon batted his eyelashes and pouted some more. Scar shot me a look and pushed past, striding away in the direction of the Emerald City.

"Oh, well," said Leon. "Can't blame a girl for trying, can you?" We set off after Scar.

Chapter Sixteen
Dorothy: Under the Starry Sky

"That fellow, Leon," Frank began, somewhat hesitantly. "At first, I thought maybe he and I were ... alike. But really, he had his ... man goods ... *removed*? That just seems so *wrong*."

"It's his equipment. What's wrong with that? I mean, if he doesn't want them, why *not* get rid of them?"

Poor Frank. He actually reached between his legs and cupped his nuts protectively, giving a small shudder.

"It's just so extreme. I mean, sure, I feel like a woman, I think of myself as a woman, but I accept what I was born with. And it feels good. Why get rid of the whole package just because it wasn't what I hoped was under the Christmas tree? Those bells still jingle, regardless of what shape the clacker is."

"Some people care more about the shape of the clacker than ringing the bells, I guess."

"I guess," he said, not sounding convinced.

Chapter Seventeen
Dorothy: On to Oz

We came back out of the woods and traveled for several days through easy country on the broad brick road, a route that was lined with lush farmland and friendly farm folk. At least, the farmers were pretty friendly. I can't say as much about their families—they took one look at Scar and locked their wives and daughters up tight, then one look at Leon and did the same with their sons.

Still, we managed to have a good time everywhere we stopped, until we hit the bottom lands, and the terrain and the weather changed all at once.

From cool, sweet pines and craggy hills interspersed with fertile valleys, we emerged into a great plain, thick with flowers. In the distance, we could trace the path of the yellow brick road as it wound its way to the gates of a mammoth gray city that towered over countryside like a crusty old king with flowers strewn at his feet.

We all stopped to take a long look. "Is that the Emerald City?" I asked, not sure what the joke was. "That doesn't look green to me."

Scar whistled under his breath. "What the hell's been going on here, Leon?"

Leon shrugged. "Same old shit, different day. Things got a little tighter since you took off with Glinda, Scar. It's an election year, and Oz is putting on the dog a little bit to impress folks. Soon as the election's over, things will go back to normal."

Scar nodded, but looked doubtful. When we passed a billboard that proclaimed, "Emerald City—Our Way or Leave," he scowled and flipped his middle finger at the stern-looking gentleman pictured there in heavy dark robes, scowling down at passersby through small round glasses.

"Is that the Wizard of Oz?" I asked, not sure how I felt about trying to collect money from a man who looked so . . . so *scary*.

"Yes," said Leon. "But he's really not like his picture. It's all props. In real life, those glasses are rose-colored."

I didn't know if that was supposed to reassure me or not, but I decided it was a good thing I'd let Scar out of his cage.

When the road finally plunged into the field of flowers, Scar let out a whoop and bolted forward at a lope. Leon, an eager look on his face, took off right behind him, so I had little choice but to hike up my skirts and sprint after them. I think one of the rabbits fainted.

"Hey, wait up," I called after them. "Are you guys going to run all the way there? Cause I think that city is farther away than it looks."

Scar turned and gave me a grin over his shoulder. "We're not racing to get to the city, sweetheart. We're just half-a-mile from Tito's House of Thai. Come on!"

By now, I'd caught up with him, and he linked arms with me and tugged me along.

"I don't know," I said, as we skimmed down the road. "I don't really care for foreign food. And it's not even lunchtime yet. Do they have anything American on the menu?"

Scar rolled his eyes and poked me in the ribs. "It's not a restaurant, silly girl. Look around you! Don't you know what this is?" With his free hand, he made a sweeping gesture at the riot of colorful flowers surrounding us.

"Duh, flowers," I replied, indignantly. Did he think I was an idiot?

"You're an idiot," he said cheerfully. "These aren't just flowers, they're coca-poppy flowers."

"So?" I replied, stung.

"Flowers of the Gods," said Leon, who had stopped to catch his breath and was sniffing the air appreciatively. "The Party Gods."

"I don't get it."

Scar rolled his eyes. "You will, soon enough. See, there's a group of Munchkins . . ."

" . . . called the Lotus Lover's Guild," chimed in Leon.

"I thought you said they were coca-poppies," I said darkly.

"They are," said Scar impatiently. "That's just the name of the guild. Pay attention."

"When the coca-poppies are ready to pop, the Lotus Lover's Guild catches the happy dust, packages and sells it."

"They sell *happy* dust? From popped coca-poppies? For what? To give to happy maids?" I was still miffed about the 'idiot' comment.

They both stopped and turned to stare at me, mouths open.

"Oh, girl," Leon finally managed.

"She's a happy-dust virgin," said Scar.

"Oh, *girl*," said Leon again. Then they grabbed my elbows and yanked me like a doll the rest of the way to Tito's House of Thai.

Chapter Eighteen
Dorothy: Tito's Place

Smack in the middle of the coca-poppy fields was a large, ramshackle house that served as headquarters for the entire Lotus Lovers' operation. It was brightly painted, mostly in shades of purple, red and orange, and combined at least a dozen styles of architecture in such a haphazard style that I was completely charmed. Cupolas and turrets and balconies jutted off improbably from every direction, and the whole thing looked like it could easily house a hundred Munchkins.

Behind the main building was a large barn, which Scar said was the processing plant, where they turned the happy dust into *smoke*. I still didn't get it, but Tito's House of Thai had a cheerful look to it and I suspected that if nothing else I could get a hot bath and a home-cooked meal, so I didn't argue.

A giggly young Munchkin woman dressed in lavender opened the door of the farmhouse when Scar knocked, and gave us an appraising look before inviting us in and putting us in a side parlor while she went to fetch Tito. While we waited, Scar made Leon turn his bag inside out looking for anything that they could trade for happy dust, but all they came up with was some costume jewelry and a handful of brightly wrapped French letters, of the same brand that Lilly used to buy by the caseload for the girls at Walnut Hall.

Tito, the head of the Lotus Lover's Guild, was a chubby, obliging fellow with rolls of fat covered in baggy drawstring pants and a loose, hooded fleece shirt the color of old bubblegum. He was mildly interested in the French letters, but then Scar had a brainstorm and pointed out that we had enough fresh rabbit with us to feed Tito's entire guild for a week. I hesitated for about one second while I thought about what a bunch of little pervs they all were, then happily agreed.

Tito, who didn't look like he missed many meals, wanted to know just how fresh, and Scar led him to the window, where my rodent fan club sat patiently waiting for me to reappear.

"You sure you can catch them?" said Tito.

"Deal on delivery only," said Scar.

They haggled out a price which didn't mean much to me—I wasn't even sure what a gram was, for Pete's sake, much less why one should be worth three rabbits. But Scar and Tito both ended up looking satisfied and pleased with themselves. When Tito heard I'd never tried happy dust before, he offered to give us a tour of the 'dust works'.

We started the tour by going up the stairs in a nearby turret and stepping out onto a balcony overlooking one of the extensive coca-poppy fields. The rows of brightly colored flowers were being tended by a team of lively looking female Munchkins wearing nothing but face masks, rubber gloves and a substance I was told was called 'Happy Wrap'—a clear, shiny fabric of some kind that clung to every curve and dimple.

"It's to keep the happy dust off their skin," said Tito casually, as if he were so used to the sight of a couple of acres of jiggling naked women that he no longer noticed. "It's also good for wrapping leftovers so the whole family can watch them decompose slowly in the fridge."

Leon didn't appear too impressed by the naked Munchkin women either, but Scar had the same slack-jawed, glazed over look on his face that I felt on my own.

I took another look at my companions—Tito looked like he'd eaten so many jelly donuts he was in danger of turning into one, and his skin and hair had a permanently greasy look. Sweat stains darkened his shirt under his arms and along his expansive belly. Scar, at least, was tall and muscled, but he was all angles and edges and . . . well . . . scarred. His face was covered with stubble, his nails were dirty and ragged, and the clothes he was wearing were the ones he had stolen from a scarecrow.

Leon was Leon.

It was then that it struck me for the first time that while boys had their uses, I *really* preferred girls—*a lot*.

The women below us were skipping back and forth between the flowers, looking for blossoms that were ready to burst and shoot out a small cloud of happy dust, Tito explained. Their job was to clip the blossoms and capture them in little airtight bags just before the explosion, so that none of the happy dust escaped into the open air. To that purpose, each was armed with a gleaming pair of silver clippers and what looked like a large drawstring purse made out of the same see-through fabric that covered their bodies.

Occasionally, a pod of happy dust would explode and one of the nearby women would give a happy wiggle and then pass out cold, to be hauled off by a crew of Munchkin men wearing heavy yellow outfits that looked like beekeepers' suits. The head coverings were made of the same thick fabric, with only a small glass visor for them to see through.

"Golden Retrievers," said Tito, when I asked. "Sometimes, no matter how good you wrap 'em, someone gets a hole in their Happy Wrap, and they get a dose. The Retrievers go in and extract 'em. We hose 'em off, toss 'em on a cot in one of our happy rooms to sleep it off, and in a couple of days they're fine. Of course, we dock their pay for the down time. And the buzz. It's a business, not a charity."

After we looked our fill at the bouncing Munchkin maidens running back and forth clipping blossoms for all they were worth and deftly catching them in their shiny bags, Tito took us to the barn to see what happened next.

In the barn, bags full of popped coca-poppy pods were emptied into giant sifters, which separated the chaff from the happy dust. Once that was done, the happy dust was pushed together and pressed into bricks, which were then sold to happy dust lovers throughout Oz.

In no time at all, Tito and Scar concluded the deal for our fee. When they had it all worked out, I walked to the front door and stepped out on the porch, making sure to flash a little leg when I went down the steps. "Oh, there you are," I said, smiling sweetly as a crowd of rabbits and squirrels materialized at my feet. The fact that they were all looking up my skirt only made it easier. "We're all taking hot baths after our trip, and I thought you fellows might like one, too."

Now I was getting a few doubtful looks. I headed to the back of the house, where the kitchen was located. "The thing is, I really, *really* like my men clean." More doubtful looks. Rabbits are so stupid. "I mean you guys. If you ever want a chance of getting a paw up my skirt, you need baths. Every single one of you. Are we clear?"

Finally, they started nodding. I fanned out my skirt to give them a better look—after all, since their lechery was leading them to their doom, they might as well get one last good peek—and opened the kitchen door. "Right in here, gentlemen. I mean, gentle-rabbits. Squirrels too. Seriously. No bath, you'll never lay a paw on me. Got it?"

They grumbled, but marched right into the pot. I slipped out of the kitchen just as one of the cooks grinned evilly and clapped on the lid. *Men.* And the only thing worse than normal human men were the hare-brained ones.

When I rejoined the guys, Scar was quizzing Tito on the changes that had been happening in the Emerald City.

Tito looked uncomfortable.

"Look, it's like this: Oz started sending me these letters saying that sin sells, and he was right. Since he closed us down in town and made happy dust illegal in Emerald City, our profits have tripled—hell, they've quadrupled! Sure, now we have kickbacks and payoffs and once in a while we gotta bond one of our delivery boys out of jail, but what the hell? Profit's a profit in my book. Same with the sex clubs and the pay-for-play."

Tito's eyes skittered toward Leon and swept over his red-sequined gown. "You know your place got raided a couple of days ago, right? Locked down tight as a drum, from what I heard."

Leon looked shocked. "They closed down the Kit-Kat Club? But Oz used to love that place—he was a regular back in the day! How could he close it down? For what?"

Tito held up his hand and rubbed his thumb and fingers together. "It's all about the cash, sweetheart. Heard the Kit-Kat Club couldn't come up with the kibble to buy off the local coppers."

Scar sneered. "I'd like to see some of those coppers try to shut me down."

Tito looked at him soberly. "I wouldn't risk it if I were you, Scar. Half the people are committing so-called criminal acts, and the other half are running around trying to catch 'em."

"And all that gray paint?"

"The Wizard said no one would take the EC seriously if it was painted some candy-ass green color."

"Why the hell does anyone need to take the Emerald City seriously? This is Oz, for fuck's sake."

Tito shrugged again. "I don't know, man. Wiz got some kind of bug up his ass, and all of a sudden it was 'don't do this,' and 'can't do that,' and he had that nutty inventor yakking at him all the time, and pretty soon, there was one of those brass preachers on every other street corner. Now it's no drinking, no happy dust, no screwing around, and work, work, work. Everybody wears suits, nobody smiles."

With a visible effort, Tito replaced the dour look on his face with a smile. "But they sure all want what I have, now. Which brings us to the purpose of your visit. For the very fine number of pelts and the squirrel and rabbit stew that you've donated, we're prepared to offer you a Happy Room with all the amenities, for two full days. How's that sound? Doesn't include any Happy Gals to party with, but I figured with Leon being Leon, and you bringing a companion with you . . . "

"Yeah, yeah," said Scar. "Never cared for your Happy Girls too much. They never struck me as being as happy about their work as you thought they were."

Tito laid a small bag full of happy dust on the table in front of us, along with a pipe and box of matches, then stood up.

"You're not going to stick around?" I asked.

"No, darling. Duty calls. Besides, I'm allergic. Happy dust is not for Tito. I have to find my happiness some other way." He leered at me in a way that gave me a pretty good idea of what he thought a good time was.

"It seems a little weird—I mean, here you are, devoting your whole life to making happy dust for other people, and you can't enjoy it yourself."

His eyes glittered. "Yeah, ain't that a shame."

Then he was gone, and Scar was measuring out a careful pinch of happy dust into the pipe. "Okay, who goes first?"

It was a good thing Tito gave us two full days in a Happy Room, because it was that long before I swam hazily to the gritty surface of real life and realized that I hadn't moved a muscle since the pipe had first been handed to me. Literally. The cheeks of my ass were numb. Sprawled next to me were my fellow travelers, Scar and Leon. When I glanced around, trying to blink the crust out of my eyes, I saw Tito himself, wearing a bright suit with super-wide lapels.

"Well, hello there, chicletta," he said, giving me a lazy smile. "How you doin' this morning?"

I blinked some more and glanced around the room. "Is it morning? It's hard to tell with the windows all covered up like that," I croaked out. God, was my throat dry.

"Figure of speech, doll face." He offered me a glass of water, then snapped his fingers. A rail-thin Munchkin woman slowly stood and made her way to the windows, where she tugged lethargically on a drapery pull until the curtains opened and sunshine flooded the room.

"Hey!" exclaimed Scar, throwing an arm over his face. His speech was muddled, and he hadn't shaved or showered in two days. He looked nearly as bad as the day I'd let him out of his cage.

Leon didn't even stir, laying in a puddle of what looked like cat piss. He'd taken off his wig and was using it like a pillow under his cheek.

Shakily, I stood up, and gave Leon a shove with my foot. He moaned and rolled away from the light. I pulled back my foot to give him another, harder kick, but Tito reached out a meaty palm and stopped me.

"You gotta be gentle with the kitty, sister," he rumbled out, snapping his fingers again. Sighing, the skinny woman went out and came back with a plate of tuna. She placed it on the floor in front of Leon and stepped away.

"I don't see ... " I began, but Tito shushed me and pointed at Leon, whose nose had begun to twitch.

"Two days with no chow, and the kitty's getting hungry," said Tito with a chortle.

"Oh, my God, what's that smell?" said Scar, sitting up.

"Tuna or you, depending," I said, wrinkling up my nose. "We have work to do. I promised Glinda I'd collect on that debt for her. We've spent two days here. Time to get on the road again."

He moaned, but remained upright. I turned to Tito. "Is there someplace here we could get cleaned up and grab some fresh clothes?"

The pudgy Munchkin exchanged looks with the woman while he fingered a thick gold chain around his neck. She gave Leon a sour look, but nodded.

"Sure," said Tito. "Leda can show you the way. Don't know that we have any spare clothes around, but if you stay long enough to take a shower and grab some breakfast, Leda will get your own clothes washed and dried for you."

We had to actually pry Leon off of the floor—he'd gotten stuck in a sticky spot that didn't want to give him back, and I had to slide Scar's knife underneath him at one point to finish the job. When I was done, he was upright, with a small bald patch on his left hip.

I took one last look around the room we'd spent the last two days in. In the sunlight, which I now realized was rather dim after all, coming through windows caked with dust and grit, the place looked dirty and disreputable, with aging pillows, empty beer cans and overflowing ashtrays scattered in equal measure across a filthy floor. I was starving, my hair was matted, and I think I'd dragged my dress through the puddle of Leon's stinky piss.

113

But my mouth tasted like flowers and my brain still had a soft and warm fuzz between it and the rest of the world. Could have been worse, I suppose. After all, what if Tito hadn't been willing to accept his weight in rodents for a trade?

And speaking of rodents, was that rabbit stew I smelled on the crisp morning air?

Smiling, I headed for the shower.

Chapter Nineteen
Dorothy: Out of the Dream Shack

Leda wasn't much of a laundress, if I do say so myself. Our clothes were clean enough, but still damp, and with that scrunchy stiff feel of laundry that got stuck in a wad in front of a fireplace instead of being hung on a line to dry.

Still, everyone smelled decent, and I was reasonably sure there weren't any fleas or lice on any of us, our bellies were full, and we still had a good half a day of sunshine in front of us when we headed out of Tito's.

Scar had even shaved again, looking at least half-way reputable.

We were traveling down a particularly overgrown section of road, boxed in by high, rocky embankments on either side of the road, gnarled tree roots escaping from the thin, crumbling dirt as if to reach out and grab us as we passed.

I caught a flicker of motion out of the corner of my eye.

Then another and another. At first, I thought it was just one of the few rabbits or squirrels still foolhardy enough to try and follow us after the Great Rodent Massacre in Tito's kitchen. As the day wound on, though, I realized that it was something or someone else altogether.

Finally, I sidled over to Scar and muttered to him out of the side of my mouth, "Scar, I think someone is up there, following--"

"I know," he interrupted. "Ignore it. Don't look."

"Will that keep it from attacking us?"

"Probably not, but maybe we can delay it until we reach an area of the road where we're not so boxed in."

Too late. As if they had heard us, half a dozen graceful forms dropped from the embankments above to surround us front and back. What I had mistaken for one forest creature was a small troop of extremely well-endowed females that appeared to be the same species as Leon.

"Halt!" said a commanding but thoroughly feminine voice.

We stopped immediately. Even if I hadn't been inclined to obey the speaker, the arrows and spears pointed at my vital organs would have brought me up short. The newcomers had a vaguely militaristic look to them; their hair was cropped short and their clothes were strictly utilitarian, slim trousers and tunics the same color as the trees and shrubs and earth that surrounded us. Not to mention the multitude of weapons they all sported.

One of our captors stepped forward and lifted up the hem of Leon's dress with her spear. "Nice shoes, Leon."

"Celione? Celione, is that you? Oh, thank God," babbled Leon. "I thought we were goners for sure!"

She snorted and poked him with her spear a little higher up. You could hear his teeth click together audibly as he choked back whatever he was going to say next.

"You're not out of the woods yet, baby," Celione purred. "Where you all coming from?"

Leon frowned. "Tito's. Why? Were you looking for us?"

Celione shook her head and stretched her mouth in what might have been a smile. Or a sneer. Or a preparatory step in taking a great big bite out of him with those long, sharp teeth. Behind her, the other women tittered.

"Leon, nobody in her right mind is looking for *you*. You are an even bigger fool than I always thought you were."

Leon gaped, clearly wounded, and Scar stepped forward. "Ladies, ladies, ladies. Look, you interested in Tito's? Just so happens we have a little happy dust right here, if that's what you're looking for. All we want is safe passage so that we can get to the Emerald City. What do you say?"

He had a sincere smile on his face, his arms were open wide in invitation.

He was tied to a tree in less time than it took him to lose that charming smile.

Leon and I joined him shortly.

"Now," said Celione, when we were secured. "Where's the happy

116

dust?"

"Hey, you didn't have to tie us up for that," said Scar. "There's enough for all of us."

Celione sauntered over to Scar and put her face close to his chest, taking a deep breath. "I can smell it on you, Scar. It's... geez, did you let Leda wash your clothes? That detergent *stinks!* But it's... here!" she finished triumphantly, sticking her hand into one of his pockets and fishing out a plastic baggie generously filled with white powder. She waved it in the air and the other KittyCat Dolls gathered round, eyes shining.

"Hey, you're going to share that with us, right?" said Leon. "There's enough for all of us, Celione."

She laughed. "Oh, we're not going to *use* it, Leon. We're going to destroy it."

"What?" he said, shocked.

Scar thunked the back of his head against the tree and groaned. "I should have known it," he muttered. "Muchkinolics."

"What's that?" I asked.

"They're people who used to be hooked on dust, and kicked it. Now they spend all their time running around trying to get everybody else to give it up and making them read some stupid book."

The discussion about who exactly was going to be entrusted with destroying the happy dust seemed to be taking an inordinately long time. I decided to change the subject. "Leon, you know the leader, right? What's up with her?"

He sniffed, and I guessed he was still pouting about Celione's earlier comments. "I know all of them," he said. "They belonged to the hottest stage act in the Emerald City for a while, The KittyCat Dolls. Singing, dancing, a little burlesque, a little bit vaudeville. The guys ate it up. So did some of the girls, if the rumors were true. They used to come into the club I was starring at, them and their entourage, buying lots of drinks, heckling the performers..."

By *performers*, I had a sneaking suspicion he meant *himself*, but it seemed like the wrong time to bring it up.

Celione and another woman seemed to have won the argument

117

about destroying the dust, and I saw them take off at a trot to perform their task, while the rest of the group watched.

"So what happened?" I asked. "How did they get from being the darlings of the Emerald City theatre set to playing Robin Hood and her Merry Fems out here in the wild?"

"I'm not sure," said Leon. "I heard rumors, of course, that the success had gone to their heads, that the parties were getting wilder and wilder, that the girls had started turning on each other, each one claiming that she was the real reason they were a success . . . "

"Bullshit," said a voice over my shoulder. "It was all the happy dust." While we'd been taking among ourselves, the other women in Celione's group had finished whatever debate they'd been having and were now shamelessly eavesdropping on our conversation.

"I beg your pardon?" I said politely.

"Happy dust," responded the woman, sauntering closer. "We were doing great, the best years of our careers in front of us, when one of Tito's stooges started offering us happy dust to get through our performances with a little extra oomph."

Just then, Celione and the other woman reappeared, looking at lot . . . happier than they had been when they left. They sure must have liked destroying all that dust.

Celione wiped her nose on her sleeve and jumped into the conversation. Her eyes were glowing a bright, fiery green. "Kitrina's right." she said. "At first it was all sunlight and roses, fun and games, catnip and ice cream. But eventually we started to need more and more, and the cost started to go up and up. And up and up. And--"

"Celione!" snapped the Doll who had helped Celione destroy the happy dust. She wore a name tag that spelled out *Kitney* in sparkly pink letters. "Sorry, she gets a little OCD when she talks about the dust," the woman continued apologetically.

Celione wiped her nose again and went on. "So, the price started to go up, and eventually, we ran a tab we couldn't cover. Then Tito offered us a little side deal to help pay what we owed him. At first it was just hanging out, being 'nice' to some of Tito's special clients. The high rollers. Then it turned into doing a little work in the fields, helping out on the production line. Pretty soon, we were out there slaving away in the hot sun, wearing nothing but happy wrap and waiting to collect our cut at the end of the day so we could catch a buzz, pass out and then wake up and do it all over again. One minute we were rolling in catnip, the next minute we were shoveling the kitty litter."

"That sounds awful," I exclaimed.

"Oh, that's not the worst of it," said Kitney.

"It got worse," Celione agreed. "Because if you do enough happy dust, eventually, you stop caring about anything else. You stop even remembering there's anything else to care about. You know how long I spent at Tito's, working off my debt?" Celione demanded. "I was there for nearly two years. I forgot what I was working for! Every day, I'd slave away for that fat bastard, then collect my little baggie of happy dust at the end of my shift, and forget I had a life to get back to. Two years! Two stinking, miserable, disgusting, depraved, rotten--"

"Celione!" said Kitney, giving her a nudge.

"Anyway, I was there for two years, and I'd be there still, if it hadn't been for the early frost."

"Early frost?" asked Leon.

"The early frost," intoned Celione's followers in a creepy, harmonized monotone.

"We were out in the field," said Celione, "When all of a sudden, a cold front set in and it started to snow. All of the coca-poppies froze on the stem, unpopped. No cut for us that night. It was the first time I'd had a clear head since I arrived. I rounded up the rest of the girls and we made a break for it. And we've been living here in the wild ever since, doing our best to stop any further shipments of happy dust from getting to Emerald City."

The others nodded and shook their bows and spears in what I assumed was the general direction of Tito's House of Thai.

"Well," I said, uncertainly. "That certainly explains . . . some of it. Does Tito know about this? Because he never mentioned it to us."

"Of course the fat little bastard knows about us," spat Celione, eyes taking on a fanatical look. "He's worried sick, anxious and twitchy, heart pounding as he thinks of how trapped he is, like a rat cornered in a sinking ship, shivering and scurrying around in circles--"

Kitney put her arm around Celione's shoulders. "Honey, you need to sit down for a minute and chillax or something."

I turned my head to exchange a look with Scar.

"We also practice this groovy 12-step program," said Kitrina. "We came up with it ourselves. It's kind of loosely based on Munchkinolics Anonymous, you know, but with our own little twists."

"Like what?" I asked. Scar didn't seem to care for Munchkinolics Anonymous, but it sounded kind of interesting to me.

"Well, for one thing, we have our own book," said Kitrina. "We call it the *Big Book of Crack Cats*. It's got pictures of us all in our happy-dust chic period. Want to see how it works?"

"Sure," I said.

From out of a satchel, she produced a large, heavy-looking blue book. Behind me, I could hear Scar groan in disgust.

The woman walked up to him and held the book out, then without warning, began beating him over the head and shoulders with it, all the while shrieking, "Don't use happy dust! Don't get high! Don't snort it, don't smoke it, don't drink it!" All at the top of her lungs.

"Oh, oh, hey, don't do that!" I called, but there wasn't much I could do, being all tied up. After a few minutes, her arm got tired, and she stopped, amid the applause of her sisters.

"See," she said to me, "That's how it works. We have a seventy-five percent success rate. At least, among those who survive the bludgeoning."

"Yeah, I see that," I said. "Have you ever considered oh, I don't know reading it to people instead?"

She looked at me uncertainly. "*Reading* it to people?"

"Or showing them the pictures. You know. As opposed to beating them with it."

The woman shook her head. "We're not really readers. Sometimes we look at pictures with people afterward, if they're not too concussed. We have to make do with the tools we got." She nudged Scar, who looked like he was starting to come around. "You feeling any more sober yet?"

He winced. "Yeah, I think I see the light. Sober as a judge, that's me. Where do I sign up for one of those books?"

She beamed at him. "That's great! And it only took one session."

She whirled to face me and raised the book.

"I, uh, I already got it, just from watching you beat Scar!" I said. "I don't even need to get hit with the book!"

"I've never heard of anyone getting it that quick before," she said, pleased.

"Get what?" asked Leon.

I shook my head and tried not to listen while the girls 12-stepped him. One chapter at a time.

Even though we'd all been beaten into sobriety, the former KittyCat Dolls refused to untie us, "until the first 24 hours is up. That's the hardest part. After, we'll give you a pretty token and everything," explained Katrina. But they made us a nice lunch and hunkered down to tell us a little more about their lives in the forest seeking to undo the wrongs perpetrated against them by Tito.

It sounded like a drag, hanging around in the trees, no running water, waiting to beat unsuspecting travelers with their big picture book. The pictures weren't really that good, either. Mostly of them wearing their show clothes, with longer hair and lots more makeup, looking very pale and terminally bored. I mean, they were hot and all, but how many glamor shots can you look at before the sight of Tanorexic® Blush and Lip Stain makes you want to hurl?

"You know, have you ever thought of going to the source?" I finally asked.

"Going to the source?" repeated Celione. "I don't get it."

"I mean, instead of waylaying random passersby, taking their happy dust and bludgeoning them senseless, why not go after Tito himself? He's the one that got you hooked, exploited you, and ruined your careers, right?"

"Ah . . . Dorothy?" said Scar, shaking his head at me frantically.

"Go after Tito?" said Celione. I was starting to wonder if she had a hearing problem.

"Yeah. I mean, you take away a customer here or there, what does he care, really? He can always find more, just like he found you girls, right? But if you convert him . . . "

"Wow," said Celione. "I think I like it! Go after Tito! We could burn his whole fucking operation down! Torch the fields, the house. We could torch him along with his whole rotten operation . . . " She jumped to her feet and waved her spear in the air. "Burn that motherfucker! Burn! Burn! Burnburnburn--"

"Celione!" said Katrina. I breathed a sigh of relief. She'd get Celione calmed down and explain the difference between changing his mind and cleaning his clock.

"What?"

"You're a genius! I'll get the torches."

"Hey," I called, as they prepared to go to war against Tito and his happy dust. "Can you guys untie us first? Please?"

Despite the fact that it had been my idea to begin with . . . well, except for the burning, maiming and killing part, we were left tied up, with nothing to do but listen to Scar point out how many different ways we would probably end up getting screwed out of this.

"They go after Tito and succeed, no more happy dust. Every happy dust junkie in Oz will hate us," Scar hissed at me as he thrashed helplessly at his ropes. "And if Celione and her girls fail, and Tito captures them and puts them back to work, we'll stay out here tied to this tree until we die from hunger and thirst. Unless Tito finds out whose idea it was—then I'm pretty sure we'll be in for some really serious torture before he turns us into happy dust slaves."

Across the clearing, I noticed a cute, furry bunny peeping out at us. I shifted my position so he got a better look at my legs. "Maybe not," I said, giving the bunny an encouraging smile. He smiled back, and hopped a little closer, and I noticed he had a nice, sharp set of pearly white teeth. Perfect for munching carrots or cutting through the ropes that we were tied to our trees with. Now if I could just get him to set us free before Celione and her 12-step commandos returned.

Thank God for horny rabbits. He had us freed in no time. I almost felt bad when Leon decided to gobble him up for a snack before we hit the road. Almost. Rabbit hickeys sting like hell.

Chapter Twenty
Dorothy: In the Clutches of the Coppers

The closer we got to the Emerald City, the more dire billboards we came across, warning that just about everything from booze to yodeling was against the law. It must have been somebody's full-time job just thinking of things to arrest people for. And every billboard carried an image of the Wizard, looking more sour and dour from one picture to the next. Underneath the Wizard, in small letters, were invariably inscribed "This Message was Brought to You by the Emerald City Social Club."

You could tell Scar didn't like it one bit, and by the time we got to the gates of Emerald City, he was ready to go off on the first person who looked at him funny. Leon just got more and more worried, and nearly yanked the pouf off his tail, twisting it like worry beads as we walked—until he saw a billboard that said, "Tail Yanking is Punishable by Fine and/or Jail", and showed an old, toothless, rheumy-eyed lion man being hauled away by a bunch of stern looking cops in gray uniforms. Leon stopped dead when he saw it, and hastily dropped his tail.

"Hey, isn't that your Uncle Rufie?" asked Scar.

Leon looked closer and then nodded. "Sure looks like it. Never could keep his hands off his tail. Wonder why they made him look so decrepit?"

I raised a hand against the sun overhead and looked more closely at the billboard. Sure enough, at least a couple of those missing teeth weren't really missing—they'd been blacked out. And that mangy mane of hair looked suspiciously like a bad hairpiece.

"Do you get the feeling we're being watched?" said Leon nervously.

Now that Leon had mentioned it, I realized there was a brooding quality to the air that suggested *something* was out there watching us. And not something friendly. But no matter how hard I looked, I couldn't see anything out of the ordinary. Besides, who could it be? The Emerald City Social Club? A chill trailed up my spine. Their name sounded so friendly, but their billboards were so scary.

Something about that just didn't add up—why would a group call themselves something that sounded as fun as the Emerald City Social Club, and then pass laws outlawing just about every type of fun there was?

I got the answer at the next billboard—or, at least, the excuse. "The Emerald City Social Club Wants YOU to be Safe and Legal during your Visit to the Emerald City," it proclaimed in big letters. There was a picture underneath of a bunch of men and women that made Uncle Henry and Auntie Em look like party *animals*.

When Scar got a look, he was outraged. Apparently, many of the current members of the Emerald City Social Club were his old running buddies. "Those . . . those hypocrites," he sputtered. "Some of these guys *invented* the stuff they're passing laws against now!" He pointed. "There's Bob the Boffer, and Slutty Sal, and Huffin' Harry, for fuck's sake."

"They want people to be safe," I said. "You have to admit, all these things they've passed laws against can cause people harm."

"Yodeling?" Scar retorted.

"Okay, maybe not yodeling. But nearly everything else."

Leon patted his arm. "Maybe they've just . . . grown up."

Scar scowled. "I'm pretty sure that's medically impossible for Harry, now."

"See," I pointed out. "If there'd been a law against whatever caused that, maybe he'd be okay now. There had to be some reason for them all to change so drastically," I said. "Maybe they converted?"

"To what?" asked Scar bitterly. "The Society of People with Massive Sticks Up Their Asses?"

A thought struck me. "No, to the Emerald City Social Club. Either of you have any idea what kind of club it actually is?"

"I think I can answer that," said a new and melodious voice. A man made entirely of brass, with wheels instead of legs, rolled out from behind the billboard we'd been staring at.

125

"Who the hell are you?" demanded Scar. Leon quivered.

"I, my profane friend, am Chamberlain Hammer, of the Sect of the Socially Appropriate. And since you are not yet within city limits, I'll overlook your use of obscene language, defamation of the sterling reputations of our illustrious founders, general disrespect and . . . incredibly poor personal hygiene," he finished with a nearly human grimace of distaste.

"Yeah, yeah, yeah," said Scar. "Like I give a shit about your opinion."

Actually, he was starting to smell a little rank again, but it seemed like the wrong time to mention it.

"Young man, your frivolous disregard for the rules and sensibilities of the citizens of the Emerald City is beginning to wear on me. Tell me, what is your business with our fine city, anyway?"

"We're going to see the Wizard on a matter of great personal importance," I said, stepping between the brass man and Scar before things could get any worse. "The Good Witch Glinda sent us."

The brass man rolled back a few paces. "Glinda? Glinda the Good? Last time she was here, she barely escaped being tarred and feathered, young woman. It was only the forbearance of our kind, forgiving and most Wondrous Wizard of Oz that she was allowed to escape with just a warning."

Scar snorted with laughter. "The day that you and your mob can pin Glinda down long enough to tar and feather her is the day she's been knocked unconscious by a two-ton bat before you get within a mile—and I wouldn't want to be there when she wakes up. Even the Wizard couldn't pull that off."

The brass man's eyes did a good imitation of a glare, but his voice was mild as he said, "What's the nature of your business with the Wizard?"

"We could tell you, but then the Wizard would have to deactivate you," said Leon. "You wouldn't want us to blow—er, disclose his confidential business, would you?"

I thought that was exactly what the brass man wanted, but he made a show of considering the matter carefully before he reluctantly conceded that perhaps he should allow us to proceed without breaching his boss's privacy.

"I'll just get an escort for you," he said, and blew on a brass whistle before we could decline. From out of nowhere came a squad of the gray-clad coppers that had been featured so prominently in all the Emerald City Social Club billboards. They crowded around, forcing us together, and I had a suspicious feeling that if the Wizard didn't agree with the importance of our errand, Hammer and his coppers weren't going to let us leave the Emerald City as easily as we had talked our way in.

"Take them to the Immaculation Station first," instructed the brass man. "They need to be presentable before they see the Wizard." The coppers saluted in unity, and the brass man rolled away, leaving us to cover the final mile or so to the Emerald City in the company of our grim and cheerless escort.

Emerald City was the dreariest place—outside the bone-dry plains of Kansas—that I had ever seen. The buildings were painted a thick, gloppy, unrelieved gray. The inhabitants were likewise cloaked in gray, except for the ones that wore black. They rushed joylessly about on tasks I assume were both very important and very distasteful, judging by the sour looks everyone wore. The coppers were given a wide, respectful berth, and Leon, Scar and I were ignored completely.

I wondered if there was a law against gawking at strangers.

The Immaculation Station turned out to be a big, dreary warehouse of a place where we were marched through to be scrubbed, sprayed, starched and dressed in clothing that was guaranteed not to offend, titillate or encourage lewd or lascivious thought of any kind. There were so many buttons and buckles and layers and zippers that even if I had wanted to do something naughty, I don't think I could have stripped down for it without a can-opener and two assistants. The only thing I got to keep was my shoes, which, by virtue of being silver, met the requirements, more or less.

"No babushka?" said Scar sourly when I was led back to the room where he and Leon were waiting. Like the rest of the citizens of the

Emerald City, they were clothed in plain gray shirts and trousers, with bowlers jammed firmly on their heads and plain leather shoes to complete the non-look.

"Oh, we don't insist on babushkas here, young man," said the dour matron who had supervised my reinvention as a forty-year-old spinster. She gave him a baleful look and then tugged painfully hard on my tightly braided hair. "*Yet.* You can wait here for the Wizard. He'll send somebody when he's ready to see you." Then she turned on her heel and stomped out, and we were alone together for the first time since we'd been ambushed by the brass man and his coppers.

Scar leaned back on one of the lumpy couches and rested his head on his hands. "Might as well get comfortable," he said. "I have a feeling this is going to take a while."

Like any bureaucrat worth his salt, the wizard kept us waiting. And waiting. And waiting. There seemed to be an endless trail of servants in and out of the room we were cooling our heels in. We passed the time with the help of the small packet of happy dust that Scar had brought with him from Tito's, and which he had hidden God knows where when Celione and her group of Recovery Marauders had grabbed us. Finally, I got tired of sitting around, and remembered one of the many useful lessons I had been taught by Lilly at Walnut Hall.

"Do you have such a thing as newspapers here?" I asked one of the servants, who had come in to dust and tidy.

He nodded. "We do, ma'am. Two of them. *The Ozian*, and the *Green Sheet*."

"So, tell me, which one do you think would pay more for a story about the Wizard's unpaid gambling debts?"

"I . . . I'll go let the Wizard know you want to see him *now*," said the servant, suddenly nervous. Without another word, he fled out the door.

We were ushered into the wizard's presence in less than thirty minutes. When our escort came to get us, Scar whistled admiringly. "Dorothy, I don't know what you said to that guy, but it sure worked.

What was it?"

I grinned. "I suggested that the citizens of this dismal berg might enjoy reading about the Wizard's gambling debts over their morning coffee. I think he must have agreed with me." Then I sashayed out the door and down the hall to finally meet the Wizard.

The Wizard's office was a large, cold room, all done in white and shades of gray, and it seemed like it took forever to cross the long tiled floor and approach the desk. My heels clicked loudly on the marble as we walked, so the Wizard must have known we were there, but he remained with his back to us in a big leather chair until we had reached the desk and Scar slapped a hand on the dark polished wood.

"Damn it, Wiz, we're not the rubes. Cut the crap and turn around and talk to us."

Slowly, the chair rotated until I got my first view of the Wizard of Oz.

Except, he wasn't a wizard at all. He was Tito, from Tito's House of Thai. And he was looking a little the worse for wear. Actually, he was looking like he'd been beaten extensively around the head and shoulders with a large book. I eased back a step and tried to look innocent.

"Hey, look what the cats spit out," said Scar. "What the hell are you doing here? Where's the Wiz?"

Tito smiled, but he didn't look particularly happy to see us. "The Wizard is indisposed. He asked me to fill in for him, since I suddenly find myself out of work." He spared a glare for me, and I knew that Celione had blabbed my role in her assault on the House of Thai. "That's all you need to know. Now, tell me, what the hell are *you* doing here? Planning to take down the Emerald City, too?"

"Oh, no," said Scar. "I'm not wasting my time listening to you flap your gums, Tito. I mean, we're friends and all, but I want to talk to the Wizard, or I'm going to march right the hell out of here and start screaming from the rooftops that this is all some big scam, and that you and your boys have knocked off the Wizard and taken his place."

Tito glared at Scar. Scar glared back. I wasn't so sure Scar had it wrong—maybe Tito had bumped off the Wizard. From facing doors, two brass men rolled in.

"Meet my friends, Citizen Anvil and Citizen Tongs," said Tito.

Scar snorted. "I hope their balls are detachable," he said. "Because I'm gonna give them back to you on a platter real soon, and if they don't come off easy, that's definitely going to leave a mark."

Scar looked ready to kick some serious brass, and a crafty expression crossed Tito's face. You could practically see the wheels turning. "Suppose I tell you the Wizard put me in charge while he went off on a little . . . vacation?"

"Tito, I believe you about as much as I believe that when Elfa says, 'as much fun as a barrel full of monkeys,' the monkeys are having a good time being stuffed in that little barrel of hers."

There was a moment of silence as we all worked that one out.

Scar turned on his heel, nearly mowing Leon and I over in the process. "Come on, Dorothy, let's get out of here and start telling people that they've been taking orders from a bullshit artist and his brass thugs."

"Wait," said Tito. "One more step and I'll call the guards and have you thrown in the same cell that the Wizard's in. Then you can confer, confab and otherwise hobnob with that weak-minded pantywaist until my nose falls off." Tito's nose was puffy, and a little crooked, but it didn't look like it was planning to part with his face any time soon. Not good.

Slowly, Scar turned back around. "So you've got him stashed here, huh? But I don't think you're going to stick us in with him. If you were going to throw us in jail, you would have already done it. You can't, can you? Too many people saw us come in here, demanding to talk to the Wizard. If we disappear too, people really will start talking. You can't have that, can you? He's a looney charlatan, but people love him. If they knew you had him locked up somewhere, you'd have a riot on your hands."

Tito made a restless gesture with one hand, and I knew Scar had it figured out. Maybe not all the details, but the big picture for sure. "Look, I won the EC fair and square in a card game," Tito said. "I just don't think it's the right time for all our happy citizens to know that yet. You know? So we're hanging onto him a little while. Like insurance, you know? No harm done. He's happy as a Winkie right now, playing cards and smoking cigars. It's not like he's tried to leave and we stopped him or anything."

Something else occurred to me. "It's more than just that," I said, stepping forward. "You want something from us, don't you? What is it?"

"There *is* this one thing," said one of the brass men. Anvil. "We should have taken care of it before we put the Wizard away for safekeeping, but we didn't know."

He sounded almost plaintive.

"Know what?" asked Leon, getting bolder now that it was clear we weren't going to be tarred and feathered immediately.

Tito sighed and sagged a little. "This has been a . . . negotiating issue between me and my boys for a while, now. They've come to the conclusion that you're the only one who can help them, Dorothy."

"Why me?" I asked, puzzled.

"You got one over on Nessa, for one thing," said Tito. "And Glinda seems to have your back. Then there was the fact that you somehow managed to organize the KittyCat Dolls and take over my happy dust operation." For a moment, his face darkened.

"Take over? I thought they were going to rehabilitate you." I said. "What happened?"

Tito glared. "Put a bunch of crazy catwomen in a factory full of happy dust, whaddaya think happened? They all relapsed, flipped out, and went commando on my ass. Next thing I know, Celione was parked at my desk, shouting orders, and I was being shoved out the door with a warning not to come back unless I wanted a spear shoved up my ass. Although she did allow me to maintain my lucrative Emerald City franchise. She couldn't blast me out of here with a stick of dynamite, and she knew it."

"I don't get it," I said. "If you're in charge here, now, why is everything so uptight? I would have thought you'd be having the world's biggest party."

"Nah," said Scar. "Make it too easy and the price goes down."

"It's a quantity versus quality issue," said Tito. "I thought a lot about how to position myself to be of the utmost service to the good people of the EC."

Scar sneered. "And by 'of utmost service', you mean 'squeeze out every dime'."

Tito nodded and gave a self-satisfied grin. "Been doing a hell of a good job at it, too. If I do say so myself. But let's get back to the point. My boys here want your help, Dorothy. And if I don't get it for them, they're gonna walk out on this operation and leave me high and dry."

"Why don't you tell us what you want, and then we'll decide if we want to help," Scar said.

Tito nodded. "It's kind of a long story, but it starts like this: As I mentioned, I won the EC off the Wizard in a game of poker. But I wasn't the first person he'd lost big to. Apparently, the Wizard has a bit of a gambling problem."

Scar smiled. "Apparently."

Tito nodded. "And apparently, shortly before we won the right to rule the EC, he had gone to a poker game over at Elfa's place, and ended up losing... losing something important to my boys here that they had entrusted to him. We want that something back. Dorothy, we want you to go over to Elfa's and get back what that stupid Wizard lost. If you do, I may be able to forgive the fact that you put Celione up to doing a hostile takeover of my happy dust operation."

"That wasn't really my fault," I reminded him. "I suggested she talk to you, not wreck the place. And the torches were totally not my idea."

Tito gave me a skeptical look.

"If we're going to get 'it' back for you, we're going to have to know what 'it' is," said Leon, reasonably.

Anvil made a peculiar sighing noise. Tongs rolled restlessly back and forth. "It's not our fault."

"What's not?" asked Scar.

"The way we were made. We were supposed to be as lifelike as possible, but at the same time, our builder wanted our parts to be detachable for easy maintenance and repair. We were told that it was time for our quarterly maintenance check, and they'd been sent back to the factory for a lube and oil. But they were still waiting to be shipped, and Oz used them as stakes in a game of seven-car stud."

"Okay," said Scar, sounding a little impatient. "I'm with you so far. Hell, the squirrels would be with you so far, and they marched right into a stew pot. Now what the hell did he gamble away?"

More sighing. I think if a mechanical man could have blushed, this one would have.

"Our penises."

"What?" I said, sure I must have heard wrong.

Scar burst into laughter and Leon tittered. The brass men hung their heads.

"Oh, I think you heard exactly right, Dorothy," said Scar. "And it certainly explains what's been going on here."

"Oh, no you don't," said Leon. "Don't blame this on their being clipped. I don't have one either, and I never passed a law in my life!"

"Yeah," said Tito. "I was the one who had the idea for the whole anti-vice thing. And mine's still right where it should be. I just want my boys happy. They're working hard for me. And what's the fun of all this repression if the guys at the top don't get to break all the rules they're making? Just because my boys are made of metal doesn't mean they don't have feelings." He looked at the moping brass men. "I don't want to be surrounded by a bunch of depressed, whiny guys in brass suits. I got this new gang, I'm in the big chair, I want to have a little fun, you know?"

I nodded. He had a point.

"So," Scar continued. "Why exactly would Elfa want a couple of dozen metal penises, anyway?"

Tongs muttered something I couldn't make out.

"What? Speak up," said Leon. "I can't hear a thing you're saying."

The brass man looked up and glared. "I said, they still work."

I admit, my jaw dropped. "You mean . . ."

He nodded. "That's right. Turns out they really do have a mind of their own. And we all know a completely operational dick in the hand is worth two mounted to a metal frame, weighted with copper balls and accompanied by a bad personality and a constant scent of motor oil."

The brass men all nodded. You could hear their heads rattle. Sure sounded like somebody had a screw loose.

I forced myself to shut my mouth. The possibilities were certainly . . . intriguing. I began to see why Elfa had considered them worth having.

"And what better way to insure a market for pleasure, than to lock it all up tight as a drum and make people so miserable they'd pay anything for a little fun," said Tito brightly.

"So you find out that your gang's pipes aren't actually getting cleaned—they're all Elfa's now, and her and her band of laughing lesbians are doing the Wizard knows what with them--"

"Actually, I think I have a pretty good idea of what's being done with them," said Anvil glumly. "Once we get 'em back, we're gonna clean 'em really, *really* well . . ."

"Yeah, yeah," said Scar. "But you gotta know that Elfa's not just gonna give those up."

"Oh, we know that. We've already tried," said the bronze man. "But we believe you three could do it."

"You'll have to turn the kingdom back over to the Wizard," said Scar. "That's the only way I'd even consider it. The EC goes back to normal. You can still run your business, but give the EC back. This is too fucking weird."

"No way," exclaimed Tito, but the brass men rolled threateningly close to him, and he piped down.

"Scar, are you *crazy*?" hissed Leon. "Elfa's gonna make kitty curry out of me, and just because real scarecrows have a stick up their asses doesn't mean you're going to like one up yours."

Scar waved an arm at the room around him. "Leon, look at this place. You seriously want the Emerald City turned into the Big Gray Shitbox for eternity?"

Scar put his hands on the desk and leaned forward until he was almost nose to nose with Tito. "Decide. We haven't got all day. We get your dicks back, and you give the Emerald City back to the Wizard. Deal?"

Tito looked at his fellows. One by one, they nodded. Finally, he looked back at us.

"Deal," he said firmly. "You put their dicks back in their hands, and the Emerald City—and the Wizard—are yours. As long as my business goes on, untouched. Do what you want with the rest of it. Politics isn't all it's cracked up to be anyways."

Chapter Twenty-One
Dorothy: Elfa's Place

We got directions from Tongs and provisions from Anvil. The directions were simple but sucky—head off in the direction of the scary looking forest, and then keep going in the direction of unremitting evil until Elfa's minions find us and take us prisoner.

The provisions weren't much better. A lot of chewy bread and dried fruit. No meat, no dairy. I wondered if they were on the forbidden list, like nearly everything else seemed to be.

Tito'd laid a new stash of happy dust on us . . . and just polished off a healthy chunk of it when we reached the forest, so at first I thought maybe I was having a mild hallucination.

Then I heard Leon giggle, and I realized he was seeing it, too.

It was the trees. What had looked like pinecones and fruit from a distance turned out to be ball gags and fuzzy handcuffs on closer inspection. From bushes underfoot sprang whip ferns and cock ring flowers. I saw a fairy ring of mushrooms that looked an awful lot like . . . well, mushrooms kinda look like that anyways, I guess, so that was nothing unusual, but mushrooms aren't usually that fleshy pink color.

"Ah," said Scar. "The Fetish Forest. Just like I remembered it."

A breeze kicked up and the branches overhead rubbed together, making a noise suspiciously like muffled giggling.

Out of the side of his mouth, he said quietly. "The things that live in the Fetish Forest are mostly nice, but they can get pretty naughty. If they start getting out of hand, just talk dirty to 'em. They love that."

"Okay," I said, uncertainly. I liked a good time as much as the next girl, but those whips looked like they could sting.

"I can handle that," said Leon. "Comes from years of dealing with hecklers. I'm a master of the salacious double entendre. If anything pops up, just let me do the talking." He grinned. "See?"

Leon walked into the forest with a proud swish of his tail. And off we went, through the Fetish Forest, in search of Elfa, the Wicked Witch of the West. Whips and cuffs and ball-gags—oh my!

We walked for a couple of days without anything remarkable happening. It was just after noon on the third day when we heard a great flapping of wings and a horde of flying monkeys in fancy red jackets descended from the skies and landed in our path.

"Oh, shit," said Scar. "It's the Mounties."

"The Mounties?" I asked. "Why are they called that? They're on foot—er—wing."

"You'll see," said Leon glumly.

On the ground, the monkeys didn't look so graceful—they had that weird knuckle-crunching walk that all simians have, but they were quick, and in a minute, we were face-to-face with their leader.

"Halt," he said. "Who goes there?"

Scar sighed. "Isn't that a little corny, Mel?"

The lead monkey shrugged. "It works if you work it, Scar. Long time no see. How's it hanging?"

"Little further to the left than it used to, but that ain't nobody's business but mine, Melvin."

The monkey grinned. "If you say so, Scar. Seems to me you used to make it everybody's business. Now, tell me, who's this luscious young lady you have with you?"

I gave him a short curtsey. "I'm Dorothy, Sir."

"Not you—you're a little young for my taste, jail bait. I mean this hubba-hubba hottie hiding behind you."

Scar and I both turned to look at Leon, who had jumped back into his wig and sequined red dress the second we escaped the Emerald City.

"Him?"

"Him?"

"Her," corrected Mel, sticking out his really remarkable tongue and licking his eyebrows.

"That's Leon, the drag queen," said Scar. "Look, we want to see

Elfa. Can you . . . oh, damn, there he goes," he finished in a mutter.

Melvin was kneeling in front of Leon, clutching one of the drag queen's hands in both of his. "Gorgeous, gorgeous lady, I don't care what your plumbing says, your eyes tell me you're all woman. Have you ever done it with a flying monkey? We're really . . . agile," he said, licking his eyebrows with that long, long tongue again.

Leon tittered and blushed but didn't pull his hand away.

"They don't call 'em Mounties for nothin'," said Scar. "Starting to get the drift?"

I nodded. The rest of the group had pressed closer, and I had to slap somebody's hand off my butt. One of the female monkeys began stroking Scar's hair and rubbing against him suggestively.

A pint-sized Mountie started humping my thigh, and I shook him off in disgust. "Hey, I get good money for that, buddy. You wanna play, you gotta pay!"

He just grinned and eased on over toward Leon.

"Dorothy's right!" Scar said.

"You mean, you charge for it now?" asked the female Mountie, looking intrigued.

"No, I don't charge for it. I mean, we have business. *Business*. With Elfa. You guys gonna take us to her, or what? Cause if you're just here to screw around, screw each other. We have more serious things to do."

He would have looked more credible if he weren't sporting a massive hard-on where the monkey girl was rubbing against him. He still sounded pretty impressive, though, and the Mounties paused to confer among themselves.

Finally, Mel nodded. "You really know how to take the fun out of things, you know that, Scar?" He motioned to the other Mounties. "Come on guys, everybody grab something—and I don't mean T & A. Ready?"

And that's how I ended up flying through the sky, being groped by a troop of flying Mounties, on the way to Elfa's castle.

Once we were in the air, we made good time, and before long

I could see Elfa's castle in the distance. It was a sprawling affair, all white and gold and shining in the sun. After we landed safely in the courtyard, I gave the monkey who had been carrying my left leg a good slap on the nose. "Next time, keep your hands where they belong, bozo!"

He gave me a pout and shambled away.

"Well, look what the cat dragged in," said a sultry voice somewhere behind me. A curvaceous green bombshell, twin to the witch that Glinda and I had rolled back in Munchkinland, sauntered out and trailed the business end of a magic wand across Scar's chest. Then she slanted a glance at Leon. "And the cat who dragged him. Thanks, Leon. You can collect your kibble from the treasury. They're waiting for you."

Scar looked thunderous. "Leon? You fuck-faced traitor! You were working for Elfa all along? I'm gonna run into you again, pal, if it takes the rest of my life, and when I do, I'm going to use your guts to tune my guitar, I swear on--"

"Now, now," said Elfa, and made a motion with her wand that caused Scar's mouth to snap shut. I could see his jaw working, but his lips weren't letting the sounds out. "It's not Leon's fault that he likes to take good care of all nine of those lives of his. I wanted to see you again, Scar. That's all." She made a sexy little pout and thrust her cleavage at him, and even though his jaw was still working, I could see he was having trouble keeping his eyes on her face instead of those lush green boobs.

I'm pretty sure Elfa noticed the same thing, because she gave a small, self-satisfied smirk before she glanced my way. "And you must be Dorothy." She looked down at my feet, where Nessa's pretty silver heels sparkled and glimmered in the afternoon sun. "Nice shoes."

I wasn't sure if she knew the whole shoe story, so I kept my mouth shut. Stepping closer, she ran the tip of her wand along my jaw and tilted my head up, examining my face from both sides. "Aren't you just the yummiest little snack?" she said, and pressed those full, moist lips to mine. I could feel my toes curl.

Then she stepped back. "And unfortunately, much too young for the likes of me. Never mind, there are plenty of things for you to do here while you finish growing up, beautiful. Melvin!" She snapped her fingers and the head Mountie approached. "Take her down to the kitchens and find her an apron and a mop. She can get busy on the banquet hall floors while I take Scar to my chambers for a little ... questioning."

"Mopping? Really?" I said. "I'm too young for hanky-panky, but I'm old enough to clean up after a troop of libidinous monkeys? I'm older than I look—really. Lots older." It didn't do any good. Without another glance, Elfa sashayed off, with several of the Mounties tugging a struggling Scar along behind her.

"Gee, Dorothy, I'm sorry about how things turned out," said Leon. He really did look regretful. "But I'm getting a little long in the tooth, and a guy can't go on doing what I do forever. I needed to think about my future."

"That's okay, Leon," I said with a sigh. "I hope it turns out the way you want it to."

"Thanks, Dorothy," he said, "Try and talk to Scar, for me, will you?"

I nodded, then Melvin took my arm and led me off to the kitchens.

The work was hard, but no worse than any other work that I'd done. So I scrubbed, and mopped and polished and fetched and carried, waiting for a chance to talk with Scar and make plans to get the hell out of there.

I'd only been at it a couple of days when Melvin led me into a big room full of beds and couches, all of them tumbled and disarrayed. Scattered around the room, along with scores of lopsided pillows and wrinkled blankets, were the very items we had come to Elfa's castle to find: two dozen bulbous brass penises, looking a little the worse for wear. "What happened in here?" I asked Melvin.

He snickered. "If you have to ask, you're too young to know."

Then he waved an imperious arm around the room. "But you're not too young to clean this mess up. Get cracking."

I reached down to pick up one of the penises, but Melvin put out a hand to stop me. "It was a wild one last night. You might want to wear gloves," he said.

Obediently, I drew a pair of rubber gloves out of my cleaning cart and put them on before beginning to gather the brass men's members.

He watched as I put them into a sack. "What do I do with them now?"

"There's a boiler room in the dun—I mean, in the cellar. I'll show you where it is after you get all the sheets changed."

"I didn't know there was a dun—I mean, cellar, here," I said, thinking maybe this was where Scar was being kept. "Why do I need the boiler to clean the brass men's cocks?" I asked.

Melvin snorted. "The boiler supplies the hot water all through the castle. And there's a little machine right next to it called a steamer— we run Elfa's brassies through there after they've been used. Once that's done, you can polish them up and buff out the scratches."

I held up the one in my gloved hand for a closer look. "This one looks pretty bad. Are you sure a little buffing is gonna take care of it?"

He shrugged, already moving toward the door. "If not, we've got some Bondo and gold paint in a closet around here somewhere. Just make sure you sand it really smooth. Elfa hates it when she finds a rough edge."

I guess I would, too. Sighing, I got to work.

I saw Leon again before I saw Scar, and it was a very unhappy looking Leon that I ran into.

I had gone down into the cellar to run the brassies through the steamer, and got my first look at the boiler room. The boiler itself was a huge metal tub perched over a blistering fire, kept stoked by whichever Mounties Elfa was particularly displeased with at the moment. It looked a little bit like a gigantic still, with a huge cap on it from which several tubes protruded to carry off the water once it was hot.

The first day I was there, one of the Mounties had showed me how to place the brassies on a conveyor belt, then operate the mechanism that would take them through the steamer. "Takes about an hour, kid," he said sourly. "And I ain't no babysitter. Stay out of trouble down here."

Those brassies sure got a lot of use; I was down there running them through the steamer nearly every morning. They actually seemed to like the steamer, though, going in wilted and coming out raring to go. They also liked music, I learned. I frequently whistled while I worked, and the brassies would bop along merrily to whatever tune I was trilling at the time. As a matter of fact, they could be quite mesmerized if the music was right. After a while, I got to where I could get them to hop right behind me down to the cellar, and on and off the conveyor belt, just by whistling a tune they liked, which saved a lot of bending and stretching for me. And I never minded obliging them with a little music. It seemed to cheer us all up, although the Mounties looked at me funny when the whole little gang started bopping and hopping as they followed me from place to place.

While I was waiting for them to get steamed, I decided to wander around, looking into storage rooms and around corners, and found out that for a cellar, it was pretty darn roomy—and dank, and cobwebby, and lit with eerie flickering torchlight. One day, when I had just about given up hope of ever finding a clue to Scar's whereabouts, I stumbled across a shadowy stairway I had never noticed before leading down into the dark. I decided to give it a try.

I tiptoed down the flight of granite steps, each one darker and colder than the last, until finally I ended up in a long hallway lined with locked and barred cubicles. The nearer ones were empty, but I could hear sobbing coming from one of the cells further down the corridor, so I snuck down to see who was making all the racket.

And there sat Fucking Leon, sniveling into his tail. At least they had let him keep his wig and his makeup bag.

"Leon? What happened to you? I thought you were supposed to get a big reward for turning us over to Elfa," I said.

"Oh, Dorothy!" Leon got so excited when he saw me that he jumped to his feet and attempted to rush to the barred walls of his cell, but the chain tethered to one of his legs snapped taut and pulled him back. He landed in a forlorn heap on the floor. As I watched, he burst into tears.

I walked up to his cell and put my hands on the bars. "You didn't get your reward, did you?"

He shook his head miserably.

"You got put down here, instead?"

"She s-s-said she likes my v-v-voice," he hiccuped out between sobs. "Whenever she has company, she has the Mounties come drag me out to perform. Then I get put back here. Just like a dancing bear or something. And I h-h-hate dancing bears! S-s-showboats!"

"And have you learned a lesson from all this?"

He put his head in his paws and cried harder, looking at me through his thick fake lashes. "Oh, I have! I'll never betray my true friends again, no matter how much catnip I'm offered!" He gave me a tremulous smile.

I considered my options. Did I really think Fucking Leon had reformed? Maybe, maybe not. But he was highly motivated at the moment, and that might be as much as I could hope for. And I could use all the help I could get.

"Okay. I'll start looking around for a key to this dump and see if I can figure out how to get you out of here," I said. "Have you seen Scar? Is he down here somewhere, too?"

He snorted. "Scar? He's Elfa's precious little pet. He's been with Elfa whenever they had me up to perform. She keeps him on a leash, right at her side."

I blanched, thinking about how Scar was taking that.

"She makes this huge fuss over him, but he still hates my guts. He's at one of Elfa's orgies every night, gets the best food, sleeps on satin sheets, and still can't let bygones be bygones. Every time he sees me, he takes out an imaginary knife and throws it at me. Last time, he made me so nervous I nearly coughed up a hairball!"

The thought of a man-sized hairball nearly made me cough

something up, but if we were going to escape, Scar and Leon were going to have to make nice. "Okay, I'll talk to Scar," I said. "And when I come back down here with the keys, you be ready to move it, Leon. No screwing around. Got it?"

"Oh, yes!" he said. So I tiptoed back up the stairs to the boiler room, watching to make sure no one had observed me, and collected my nice, clean brassies.

Then I set out to discover where Scar was being kept.

Now that I knew what I was looking for, Scar wasn't that hard to find. I just followed the sounds of hot, heavy sex to Elfa's bedroom. The hard part was getting him alone.

There was a big cabinet for towels and bathrobes in Elfa's bathroom, which contained a jacuzzi big enough for Elfa and half-a-dozen Mounties. I took to hiding in the cabinet of the bathroom when I wasn't working, waiting for him to stumble in. It was the only place Elfa let him go by himself.

Finally, it worked. I heard the door open and peeked cautiously out of the cabinet—I'd seen enough Mountie butts in the last couple of weeks to last me a lifetime.

When I recognized him, I was elated. "Scar! Scar!" I whispered, stepping out of the cabinet. He gave me a groggy look and propped himself up against the wall with one hand.

"Sorothy? I mean, Dorothy?" he said.

"Scar, what's wrong?"

"Nothin'," he replied, but clearly something was going on.

"Scar, why are you talking like that? You sound like you're drunk or something!"

"S'maybe a little bit," he said. "Elfa's got the breast, you know. I mean, *best*." He corrected himself as laboriously as a child trying to pronounce a new word.

"Best what?"

"Monkey Lust. Dust. Whatever."

"What's monkey dust?"

He gave me a sloppy smile. "It's like happy dust, Sorothy. Sept

144

instead of making you mellow, it makes you horny."

I'd heard of stuff like that. You can't hang out in a whorehouse without hearing about all kinds of stuff to make weak members strong and quick members slow and tired members energetic. But I'd never heard of monkey dust before.

While I was musing, Scar raised a hand and pulled at the collar on his neck half-heartedly. The gesture nearly unbalanced him. He looked up at me, and made a face that I supposed he intended as a grin, but it was strangely simian, and a horrible suspicion crossed my mind.

"Scar." He was distracted now, and didn't look up at me. I grabbed his shirt and shook him. "Scar! Scar, where do the Mounties come from?"

He frowned. When he answered me, his voice sounded as if it came from a great distance. "Elfa makes them. With the monkey dust."

The more I saw and heard, the more that damn Elfa was pissing me off. Granted, I didn't think most of the Mounties had been stellar human beings to begin with, but to be turned into humping monkeys just to satisfy her libido—not to mention her ego?

That bitch was going down. I just had to figure out *how*.

Keeping the brassies clean gave me a great excuse for wandering around below the castle and keeping in touch with Leon. I also learned quite a bit about Bondo and touch-up paint.

There was a guard who made regular patrols past Leon's cell—I was lucky I had missed him the first time I went down there. He marched down the corridor to Leon's cell about four times an hour and had the key I needed to bust Leon out. Scar was going to be a little harder. The key to his collar was kept on a fine golden chain around Elfa's neck. I thought I might have been able to manage—if Scar were his old self. But in his current state of boozy rut, even if we could get him loose, how much would he actually hinder us in getting the hell out of there?

I began spending more time in the bathroom, hoping for another meeting. It was two days before I saw him again.

"Scar!"

"Sorothy? How the hell you do that? You have a room in there or something?" He peered blearily into the cabinet I had hopped out of.

"No, I was hiding in here, looking for you. Listen, Scar, this is important. We need to get out of here!"

"Get out of here? But I'm shtarting to like it here," he said. He pulled at the collar as he spoke.

"Scar! Focus up!—you're wearing a collar and being pranced around on a leash! It's that monkey dust that's making you think you like it!"

"I don't like it?"

"No! No you don't, not really. Look, you need to sober up, Scar. Stop doing the dust, before you end up like Melvin. You understand?"

"Stop. Doing. The. Dust." He nodded, then shook his head. "But I like the dust."

"No, you only think you like the dust. You want to end up a big, horny monkey?"

He squinted at me, and I could tell he was thinking about it.

"NO!" I said. "No, you don't want to be turned into a monkey, Scar! You have to stop doing Elfa's drugs, but you can't let her know, okay? You need to pretend you're still going along with everything. Do you understand?"

He squinted at me some more, and finally said, "Elfa's turning me into a monkey?"

"That's right."

"Being a monkey isn't good, is it?"

"No, it's not. If you weren't high on monkey dust, you'd hate this."

"Can't let Elfa know?"

"That's right, Scar! Can't let Elfa know."

He frowned. "But I like the dust."

There was a pounding on the door, and then shouting. It sounded

146

like Melvin. "Hey, Scar! You fall in or something? Hurry up!"

Despairing, I slipped back into the cabinet, placing my finger over my lips in a shushing gesture as I pulled the door closed.

"S'alright!" Scar called out irritably. "I'm coming."

He dropped his trousers to finish the business he had come in for, and I blanched. Scar had sprouted a tail.

Chapter Twenty-Two
Frank and Dorothy: Kansas

It was our fourth day on the road when Frank allowed that we were probably in Kansas by now. Kansas! As soon as he said it, the world seemed a little grayer. It never failed to amaze me that a place as colorful as Oz could intersect our world in a place as dull as Kansas. Or maybe it was that very contrast that made it possible. Oz was everything than Kansas was not, and vice-versa.

As we sat around the campfire that night, I asked Frank what happened when he returned to his family home following his expulsion from Peekskill Military Academy.

He laughed. "Well, it was quite a scandal, that's for sure. My father wouldn't even talk to me. He'd just tell my mother what he wanted me to know, even if I was in the same room—which wasn't very often. I stayed as far away from him as I could."

"Oh, Frank, that's awful," I said. I reached out and patted his hand.

He shrugged. "Life goes on. My father managed to hush up the worst of the scandal. All that the neighbors knew was that I'd had some kind of seizure and had to come home for my health. I kept to myself a lot. The whole thing with Renny had taken a lot out of me. I was a lot more naive then than I am now about the difference between lust and love. If a broken heart could have been fatal, I would have died back then, but it wasn't and I didn't, and eventually, I started to develop an interest in life again."

That made sense to me. With enough time, every hurt heals. "Did your father start talking to you again?"

"Not right away," Frank said, leaning back against his bedroll. In the firelight, his face looked dainty and sweet. "But eventually, I became interested in something that he was also interested in, and he decided I was worth communicating with again."

"What was that?" I said, sitting forward. "Business? Did you become a business man?"

"No," Frank said, smiling. "Better than that. I developed an interest in chickens."

Chapter Twenty-Three
Frank: The Fowlest Years

At first, I felt like a pariah within my family. Grief, anger, confusion, despair all swirled within me. Even if someone had reached out to me at that time, I don't think I would have been able to accept it. However, I was young, and despite my shock and despair, eventually, the hole in my heart began to heal—or at least, to grow a protective shell that allowed me to go on breathing and walking and, eventually, living again.

At the time, there was a great fascination with breeding fowl sweeping the nation. My father and brothers were quite interested in the subject, and I found myself becoming intrigued as well. By saving up the pocket money my mother gave me, I managed to purchase several pairs of Hamburg chickens, and they reproduced successfully enough to give me a show-piece flock. I became quite an authority on the subject of their care and breeding. Eventually, my father, ever the entrepreneur, became convinced that he could profit off the new craze, and he became willing to speak with me again as the presiding local expert on the subject.

He encouraged me to start a newsletter on the subject of raising chickens, with tips and strategies for managing them, as well as covering the latest developments in the field. It was quite popular, and soon my newsletter was in demand in an area far exceeding that of our little community.

Father went so far as to buy me my own printing press, to facilitate the copying and distribution of the paper. It was an event that transformed my life forever; it seemed as if the printer's ink entered my veins and fevered my brain. I came to appreciate for the first time my own talent for writing and research—I had always been good at it, but it had been considered more an oddity than a skill, within my family and community. At Peekskill, it was considered almost something to be ashamed of. But now, with the almighty press to give my words a definitive authority that only comes from mass-produced ink on paper, I was a lord of the printed word, a demi-God out of all proportion to a simple newsletter on the husbandry of fancy chickens. Out of such a haphazard beginning did I regain my interest in the world around me, in the promise of spring, in the glorious unknown future, in life itself. My life was saved by a passing interest in a fluffy pair of Hamburg chicks and a toy press.

Eventually, the national craze for chicken-breeding gave over to some new fad, and it was no longer a sufficiently profitable business to attract my father's interest. My own interest waned as well, as you might expect with a young man of my tender years. But whatever other pursuits might catch my eye, it was my love of writing and publishing that became the core of my renewed enthusiasm for life.

At about that time, I had an aunt and uncle who were quite active in our local theatre, which consisted mainly of popular plays being badly mangled by local farmers and their wives for the benefit of whatever friends and neighbors could be coerced into the audience. When I was first importuned to take on a role I was hard pressed to be talked into it, but they needed a young and handsome hero, and one that could memorize a fairly hefty chunk of dialogue at that.

I was not enthralled at the prospect of performing, until that moment when my foot first trod the stage in front of the several dozen locals that had been rounded up for the performance.

Magic! Delight! Euphoria!

I was dizzy with joy by the time the final curtain fell. Never had I heard a sweeter sound than the applause that rang in my ears that night—could any sound be as delightful as that of a crowd stamping and whistling for one more glimpse of the players who had transported them for a few moments from their miserable realities into the great and wonderful and infinite possibilities limited only by the imagination of the playwright?

Ah, the playwright!

It was not long before I began to write my own dramas, convinced that I could do as well as any of the playwrights that were popular at that time. And I turned out to be not at all bad, if I do say so myself. Soon, I was in demand, both as a performer and as a playwright.

As my aunt and uncle were both also heavily involved in the theatre, and as I was gaining a certain reputation as a success in the field, this created somewhat of a quandary for my father, who worshiped success, but who was naturally opposed to anything that reeked of the artistic and therefore effeminate.

While my heart might be dead to love, other parts of my anatomy certainly were not. I found the theatre a delightful place for dalliance. My exuberant libido was somewhat mortifying at first; after my experience with Renny, I had pictured myself as becoming a stoic martyr to my unrequited love, ever lonely, ever alone. I had not yet learned that love and lust were two different things; but I soon found a number of delightful tutors in the world of the theatre who were only too happy to educate me in the intricacies of both.

I was still riding that wave of success when I met Maud.

My sister Harriet was hosting a Christmas party, and she had invited me and several other cast members of our current play to round out the party. I was inclined to stay home; she had been hinting rather strongly that there was a young lady she wanted me to make the acquaintance of, reason enough to hibernate in my rooms with a good book.

"She's not the usual type of girl," Harriet insisted. "She's a very ... *handsome* young woman, Frank, but not the usual frilly, girly type. Maybe she would appeal to you, brother dear." She gave me a considering look as she spoke. I know my family was gradually becoming quite concerned over my failure to settle down and start a family of my own. My sister's attempt to find me a 'handsome' girl, rather than a pretty one, was as close as we had ever come to discussing my sexual proclivities. Her words only made me more determined to refuse her invitation.

I changed my mind, reluctantly, after I talked to Peter, a handsome young actor who had also been invited to the party to charm the young, single ladies who would be in attendance. Peter made his bread and butter playing the romantic lead on stage, and played it so well that few suspected he was a worshipper of Adonis rather than Aphrodite. Hence, he was highly in demand on the dinner party circuit whenever there were stray young ladies to be balanced out.

Peter was particularly insistent that I accompany him. His efforts were not without their effect. Peter's charms were many, even though he was more scoundrel than saint, as I had found out more than a year ago. Now we were simply friends, and I watched his amorous adventures with amusement and a spot of gratitude that I was no longer a part of them.

"Please, Frank," Peter said, giving me an appealing look. "Your cousin Josie and a scad of her college friends will be there. There's a young man she goes to school with, whom I believe is ripe for a few lessons in classical Greek, just the way I teach it." Peter gave me a naughty wink.

"And you want me to go along for what reason?"

"The regular rubes are impressed with stage actors, but these college kids are more--"

He paused, groping for the right word.

I obliged by giving him several. "Snobby? Elitist? Egalitarian?"

He winced. "Jeezus, Frank. You can be so harsh. I just think they'd be more impressed with an actual writer like you, than an actor like me. You know how it is."

I thought I knew exactly how it was. I had developed a sort of genial loathing for advanced education, considering it a waste of time for students who should be out in the wide world *doing* things rather than passively having knowledge poured into their heads. As such schooling was also a vast drain on the resources of befuddled parents who thought they were providing their progeny with opportunities rather than a place to shelter from the real world, I had come to the conclusion that college is the place for those who are not willing to actually work for a living.

However, I was more amused by Peter's attempt to woo his college student than I let on, and the thought of an evening spent being admired and fussed over by a gaggle of easily impressed youth was not without its attractions. In the end, I let Peter persuade me,

153

and putting on the finest coats we could scrounge up in the costume department, off we went.

The party was predictable, but enjoyable. Wine, small cakes, earnest conversations by aspiring philosophers and novelists who would soon be businessmen and bankers. I was called upon to read from my newest manuscript, a copy of which I just happened to have tucked in my greatcoat before leaving the theatre.

I excel at live readings, if I do say so myself—my time onstage has provided me the opportunity to develop and culture my voice, and I provided an energetic reading complete with well-developed vocal characterizations of all the parts included therein.

Afterward, a small throng coalesced around me, and I spent a pleasant hour giving forth my opinions to a group of admirers who didn't understand in the least that the primary difference between myself and them was that I was *doing* it, while they were taking *classes* about it.

The evening had started to wind down, and I was looking around to see how Peter was progressing with his college student, when my Aunt Josie, also in attendance, touched me on the arm and said, "Frank, I'd like to introduce you to someone." From her tone of voice, all sweetness and steel at the same time, I divined that my sister and my aunt were in cahoots in their matchmaking efforts on my behalf. I turned stiffly to acknowledge the young lady standing at my aunt's side.

My sister must have forewarned her about my attitude, because Aunt Josie kept a firm grip on my arm so I couldn't escape. "Frank, this is Maud Gage. You're going to love her!"

I turned and got my first look at Maud's stunning face. Strong and decisive, with a classic Roman nose, generous mouth, strong jaw. Her eyes were skeptical and intelligent, with large, thick lashes over sharp cheekbones and a pile of thick, dark curls atop her well-shaped head. She was tall—taller than me, with broad shoulders and slender hips that reminded me of the young military men that had surrounded me at Peekskill Military Academy.

I could actually feel my heart role over in my chest. In some indefinable way, her features mirrored the very best and finest of Renny's—that youthful confidence, the almost arrogant tilt of the head, saved from pomposity by the good-humored curve of those generous lips.

I picked my jaw up off the floor and offered my hand. "Miss Gage, consider yourself loved."

She took my hand in a firm grip and gave me a hearty shake. "Mr. Baum, I will hold you to that."

The party ended soon after, but through my cousin Josie, who went to the same school as Maud, I managed to keep in touch with this strangely alluring young woman.

Her attractiveness to me was as puzzling as it was compelling. I had never found a woman appealing to me before. Maud was different, though.

She had a fierce and fiery temper, Maud did. Not mean, but she was relentless in her need to set right the wrongs she saw before her. It's simply not within her make-up to walk away from a fight. The first time I saw her temper in action, we had popped into a bakery for fresh sweet rolls. There was no one in evidence in the storefront, but from the back came the sound of a piteous wailing and the whistling sound of a switch slicing the air. Without a second thought, Maud strode to the curtain that divided the front and rear sections of the store.

"What are you doing, you damnable bully?" Maud demanded in a furious voice.

I looked over her shoulder to see an enormous man clad in baker's whites holding a small boy in the air with one hand and wielding a switch with the other. The child was sobbing piteously and twisting his little body in the air, trying in vain to escape the beating.

Both baker and boy stopped dead when they saw Maud. Then the baker's lips drew back and he raised the switch threateningly. "Mind your own damn business, woman, before I give you a taste of the same thing."

Maud looked at him coldly for the barest second. Then she

cocked back a fist and delivered a punch that knocked the baker out cold with one blow.

The boy scrambled to avoid being crushed by the giant's fall.

We all regarded the baker in silence for a moment, as he lay stretched out on the floor. Then Maud knelt in front of the child. "Where's your mother?" she said, in a kindly tone.

After a moment's hesitation, the boy pointed shyly to the floor above us.

Rising, Maud turned to me briskly. "My guess is that she's in no better shape than the child. I'll go check on her, while you keep an eye on the baker."

I gave him a dubious glance. He was starting to rouse, and I wasn't sure if I could stop him if he were determined to escape, but I didn't want Maud to think me a coward, either.

She reached into her purse and pulled out a small derringer. Eying the baker, who was now looking at her evilly, she fired it into the wall behind him. He blanched as a small shower of plaster fell down on his head.

Maud passed the pistol to me. "If he moves, shoot him dead."

He never budged an inch while Maud went upstairs and returned shortly with a timid, dark-haired woman with a painful looking bruise covering most of her cheekbone. Her eyes were red and swollen from the tears that still tracked her cheeks, but her bag was packed and she had her chin up as she and her small son walked past the baker.

"You'll never lay a hand on this woman or child again," said Maud with satisfaction.

Then she ushered mother and son out the door. "We'll hail a cab," said Maud.

I waited until Maud had found a cab before relinquishing my guard on the baker, who watched sullenly, but made no protests. I noticed with no small degree of satisfaction that his face was beginning to bruise and swell where Maud had clobbered him. Soon, he'd have a face to match his wife's.

We whisked the frightened woman to a house established for just such a purpose—until I met Maud and her mother the suffragette, I hadn't even known such places existed. The look of gratitude and admiration she gave Maud on parting was truly heart-wrenching.

Maud's courage, her wholehearted defense of those smaller and weaker than herself, her lack of vanity—how many were her charms and how utterly admirable she was! No wonder I adored her!

And while I would not have believed before I met her that there was a woman on earth capable of stirring my ardor, I found that Maud exerted a strange pull on both my heart and my loins. I kept my hands to myself, not sure how to pursue a physical relationship outside the simple, earthy love of male-to-male companionship, but I grew increasingly intrigued by this unique and engaging woman. I was proud that she considered me her friend.

The more time we spent together, the more fine qualities in Maud I became aware of.

We became good friends—best friends, actually. Even with Renny, I had never felt such a closeness, such an easy companionship as I did with Maud. And still, there was a barrier between us. At some point, I realized that I was not the only one with reservations. Maud, too, was holding something back, and I wondered if it was because she sensed—or had somehow heard—about my proclivities for handsome young men.

As we had become more comfortable with each other, I had dropped my guard somewhat. It was certainly possible that she had correctly interpreted the reason my head would whip around at the sound of gay male laughter. And for my part, I wasn't sure where this relationship might be headed in the long term. Could a conventional marriage ever be in the cards for a man such as I? It would certainly please and relieve my father, but my theatre friends suggested that things would not be so simple.

"It's inconceivable, Frank!" exclaimed Peter one night, as we shared small neat whiskeys at a saloon near the theatre. "Men such as us don't change our ways—no more than a leopard changes its spots. You are deluding yourself if you think a time will not come when you revert to type. A woman can never satisfy all the passions that swell within you."

"You don't know that," I replied, rather desperately. I was becoming convinced that Maud was too dear a friend not to make a clean breast of things with, but I dreaded her reaction. Would she be horrified? Uncomprehending? Dear God, would she even know what I was talking about?

"Have you ever even kissed her?" asked Peter.

"No," I replied. "But I have been thinking about it."

Peter goggled at me. "You've been *thinking* about it? What if you hate it? What if you find you simply can't? You're putting all of your heart into a relationship that may be impossible for you to consummate. What if you proceed to your wedding night and find that when she removes her gown and is parading around in front of you in her unmentionables, you become . . . nauseous?"

"Nauseous?" I repeated doubtfully. "Really, Peter?"

He shuddered dramatically. "All that fleshy . . . flesh. Soft and doughy and . . . juicy. No muscle, no smooth, hard skin, wet where they should be dry . . . " He shuddered some more, and I patted him on the shoulder.

"For one thing, I don't think Maud is all that fleshy," I said. "She's as lean as a yearling. And secondly, it should be about the person, don't you think, not just the type?"

Peter nodded reluctantly, but he still looked dubious. Somehow, that helped to firm my resolve. I would speak with Maud on the morrow, and make a clean breast of it, so to speak. I would trust her excellent judgment and sophisticated understanding to determine our future course together.

She did not take the news at all as I expected. We were sitting in the parlor of her mother's house, and after I poured out my heart to her, including my desire to take our relationship to the next level, if she were willing, she simply sat back in her chair and stared at me blankly, for so long that I became uneasy.

"Maud? Maud, dear? I know this is a lot to contemplate all at once, but surely you suspected something? Tell me how you're feeling! Are you shocked, dismayed? Would you like me to depart and never darken your door again? Is there any chance that I might continue to see you? Would you even consider the continuance of our friendship? Maud?"

Finally, she stirred, and with a queer look in her eye, stood up and shut the parlor door, then turned to lean back against it.

"Maud?" I said once more, completely baffled.

"Frank, I have something I must tell you, as well. And then, my darling, if you are still interested in pursuing a relationship with *me*, I am yours, dear one."

Mouth open, I watched amazed as she began removing her clothes, one layer at a time. She wore a lot of layers. Finally, though, her breasts were revealed, small, firm mounds that rode high on her chest.

But she didn't stop there.

Her garments were much like Maud herself, plain and utilitarian, able to withstand the wear and tear of life, with a certain sturdy charm all their own.

There was something incredibly endearing about her silent striptease, and I understood that she was bearing not only her body, but her soul at that moment. And when she finally stood naked and hesitant before me, I understood why.

Peeping out shyly at me from the soft brush of her pubic hair was a small, pert penis, head bobbing shyly in its rosy velvet skin. No bullocks dangled below—she was as smooth as a maiden beneath her rousing member. But it was definitely a male appendage that sported there beneath her nether curls.

I looked up at Maud's face, and she blushed, then held her hands out at her sides and slowly turned before me so that I could take in both her feminine curves and her finely muscled frame.

"Maud, I don't . . . what . . . ?"

She faced me once again and gave me a look both shy and earnest. "I am both man and woman, Frank. That is *my* secret. I wish I was as brave as you have been in confessing your secret to me. I wish I was as you are—all one being, even if that being is not widely accepted in our society. Instead, I am neither/nor, both he and she, divided, deceptive, never to be whole. Do you think you could ever even consider accepting me as I am?"

I was speechless. I was delighted. The possibilities were astounding. All was clear now, and I could not have been more enthralled. There was only one answer to give.

"Maud Gage, will you marry me?" I said, and then fell to my knees to engulf her small but exceptionally charming member in my mouth, to run my hands up her firm and muscular buttocks, to cup her small taut breasts in my hands, and get better acquainted with the only woman in my life I would ever love.

Chapter Twenty-Four
Frank: Dinner and a Dance

My parents were inordinately pleased that I was settling down to marry. My father did take me aside at one point to ask if I had noticed that Maud was a mighty plain woman, then let it go at that. The Gages were well-known in New York society; and there was no question of Maud being exactly who—and what—she said she was.

Maud's mother had initially been suspicious of the match. She loved Maud dearly, and was very protective of her, in spite of, or perhaps *because* of, her unique plumbing. Once she realized how very much in love we truly were, however, she declared herself satisfied and did everything within her power to support and promote our union. She even convinced my father to set us up with a business.

My aunt had been doing very well in the theatre, both as an actress and as a teacher of oratory. I myself was enjoying some small success both as an actor and a playwright, and my aunt's enthusiasm finally persuaded my father, ever looking for a new way to make a dollar, to build a theatre in Richburg, and give the running of it over to me.

I loved being the manager of our beautiful new theatre. I began picking and choosing the plays being produced, and with Maud's help and encouragement, many of those plays were mine. Even better than seeing my plays on stage, the audience loved them! I kept my hand in, acting-wise, but with my wife's encouragement, I spent more and more of my time writing.

I had just settled in to doing some last-minute revisions on a play that we had debuted the night before—a drawing room comedy, written by me, called *Matches*. Often, once a play has been put before the audience, small bumps and wrinkles in the dialogue or staging reveal themselves, and a quick adjustment to the script is needed. This was the task I had before me when Maud brought in the day's mail, and I found a most startling note in the post. There was no return address on the plain white envelope, which bore a

Peekskill postmark. But as soon as I looked at the letter, I recognized the flowing script.

Frank

I will be coming to town in the next week or so, and would like to meet with you if possible. Perhaps we could have dinner for old time's sake?

Best wishes

Renny

I could not have been more surprised if I had opened up the letter to find out that the Easter Bunny was asking for complimentary tickets to a show.

Renny? Here in Richburg? And wanting to see me? Last time I had laid eyes on him, he had been standing next to Professor Gulch while I was being humiliated and kicked out of Peekskill Military Academy. Now he wanted to have supper 'for old time's sake'?

I brooded about it for several days, until Maud noticed and teased the news out of me.

When she heard what had me so preoccupied, she frowned.

"This is the same Renny who broke your heart? Now he wants to see you over dinner? For what? To reminisce about his betrayal? To see if he can get you to fall in love with him all over again?"

She looked so fierce I had to smile. "I have no special desire to see him, let alone strike up a new relationship with him, my love. But I do wonder what he wants, and how the years have been to him. He says very little in his note, don't you think?"

Maud looked darkly at the piece of paper in my hand, then back at me. "You are sure it is simple curiosity that motivates you and not a desire to rekindle this old flame?"

I assured her, quite truthfully, of my undying devotion.

She sighed, and her brow cleared. "I suppose it would be the best thing if you went and met with him. You don't think this is some type of blackmail attempt, do you?"

That was a thought that hadn't occurred to me, but to which I found it hard to give much credence. "Highly unlikely, I would think. The pot calling the kettle black? Besides, I have a lovely young bride to give lie to anything he might accuse me of."

I gave her a hug, and she smiled. "Then I say you should talk with him and see what he wants. Otherwise, you'll always be wondering, won't you?"

"Probably. But if it disturbs you in the least, I won't do it. I'd rather suffer some unrequited curiosity than do anything that makes you unhappy, Maud. You mean everything to me."

'We can't change what's already happened,' said Maud, "And I wouldn't change anything that made you the man you are today. You might as well go and give yourself a little peace of mind."

With Maud's blessing, I sent Renny a short note back telling him I'd be delighted to meet him for supper, and suggested a day and time we could meet. I must admit, my curiosity, and my vanity, had been piqued. Was he happy with his defection now that some time had passed? Was he still with Gulch? Had he followed through with his plan to marry some gullible maiden to cover for his true nature?

Sighing, I set aside my questions until such time as I might get some answers, and turned back to doing last-minute line revisions for that night's performance.

Soon enough, the appointed day rolled around, and I found myself unaccountably restless. I must have changed shirts and vests at least three times, and I couldn't stay focused on any task put before me. I caught Maud watching me out of the corner of her eye when I went to the mirror to check my tie yet again, and forced myself to stop, walking over and wrapping my arms around the solid, muscular body of my wife. Laying my head on her shoulder, I sighed. "I don't know what I'm so nervous about, Maud. A little worried he's come here to preach at me, or that I'm going to walk away from tonight feeling like a fool, I guess, although I don't know why. It has nothing to do with having feelings for him—he betrayed me on every level. And I love you, my dearest heart. Only you and always you."

Maud put her hands on my shoulders and held me out at arm's length while she studied my face. Then she gave me a sweet, girlish smile. "You better, Frank or I'll beat you both bloody with the biggest rock I can find." Then she kissed my forehead and gave my tie a final tug to straighten it. "You look fine. Let's go check on our actors, shall we?"

The plan was for Renny to come to the theatre and join me in the owner's box, where we could watch the play together and have a small private supper. I was in the lobby, hobnobbing with those who were waiting to take their seats, when I heard Renny's voice behind me. "Frank?"

I turned and saw Renny. He had aged somewhat, and it did not sit on him well. Without the vital flush of youth, his high good looks had faded. I noticed now the pinched look about his nose, the creases in his face that made him appear as if he had been too long exposed to a noxious smell, or spent too much time badly disappointed in life.

His clothes were plain and neat, but somewhat worn. As our eyes met, I saw him hesitate, waiting to see how I would greet him, and I realized that he was as unsure about the outcome of this meeting as I was. That thought filled me with a confidence, and a kindness, that propelled me forward. "Renny, my old friend! It's good to see you again!"

Folks in the lobby ebbed and flowed around us, as Renny offered me his hand, then stepped back—a fitting public greeting for two old friends, and nothing to suggest we had ever been more than that. I was surprised he had unbent that far, considering our last meeting, but he was the one who had contacted me, so I wasn't sure what to expect.

I gave a few last-minute instructions to my staff, then ushered Renny up to the private box I reserved for myself and family. Maud had set out two snifters and a bottle of good brandy, and I poured us drinks as ushers dimmed the gaslights and the crowd hushed in anticipation of the show.

"To old friends," I toasted, and we clinked glasses. There was a moment of uncomfortable silence, then Renny spoke.

"Frank, you must hate me after what happened. I wanted to

apologize and ask your forgiveness. I was blinded by Gulch. He was everything you ever suspected. Cruel, and cold and selfish and . . . "

" . . . and he left you for someone else," I said, everything coming clear.

Renny tossed down the rest of his brandy, then gave me a desperate look. "He left me for someone else. A student." He shuddered. "A boy. Hardly older than we were when . . . well. You know."

"And so you came here because . . . "

"My eyes have been opened," he said. "Now that I'm no longer bewitched by Gulch—and I swear, I was bewitched, Frank, bewitched! I have decided to come and see if there is any way you could see in your heart--"

At that moment, the orchestra struck up, and there was a burst of applause from the audience. Renny glanced down at the stage, and smiled weakly.

Discarding his previous train of thought, Renny said, "you've done very well since our school days, haven't you, Frank? A theatre of your own, your plays being produced, people talking about you as an excellent writer. I have nothing to show for the last ten years except a worn-out *Bible*." He gave a bitter laugh and glanced down at the stage again. "I heard you have even done what I threatened to, and got yourself a trophy wife to cover your true nature."

Before I could speak, one of the ushers tapped on the door with our dinner, brought over from a nearby restaurant, and by the time were were ready to dine, the play had begun in earnest.

Matches was a drawing-room comedy in three acts, "Brimstone", "Ignition" and "Fire!" As with most of my work, I borrowed liberally from real life experience, although only someone who had lived through it would recognize the inspiration. As I watched Renny watching the play, I realized with a sinking feeling that Renny had, indeed, lived through much of what I drew on as the inspiration for *Matches*. It was the story of a pair of conventional young lovers who are torn apart by the machinations of an older, conniving suitor who just happened to be a school teacher. And while the details differed, the great brush strokes, well-mined for laughs at the expense of the naive main characters, were entirely similar to our own ill-fated love a decade before.

I watched as realization crept across Renny's face, and along with the regret, felt a small spurt of satisfaction. While I hadn't planned it consciously, maybe in the back of my head the idea of seeing himself parodied on stage as the easily seduced nymphet daughter of a clueless military man and his wife had given me a certain amount of pleasure.

It didn't seem to be pleasing Renny. In the reflection of the gaslights that illuminated the stage, I could see his face reddening, the skin of his face drawing tighter and tighter. Oh, no, he hadn't missed the similarities at all.

Finally, he turned to me. He was furious. Another thing that had changed about Renny. I don't ever remember seeing him that angry before. Where had that *rage* come from? His mouth opened, and I flinched in anticipation of the tirade I was sure would emerge, but before he could get a word out, the door to our private box flew open and Maud stepped in.

"Frank? I was just wondering if you and your guest needed anything."

Renny rose to his feet as if pulled by springs, as Maud smoothed her skirts and tried to look as if a jealous thought had never crossed her mind.

"Who is this?" cried Renny, looking her over from head to toe incredulously.

"This is Maud, my wife," I said.

"Wife? *She's* your *wife*? Is this some kind of joke? If that's a woman in those skirts, then I'm a-"

"A hypocrite and a heartbreaking phony?" said Maud passionately, stung by Renny's assessment of her femininity.

Renny roared inarticulately and put up his fists.

If he thought a threatening posture would intimidate my Maud, he severely underestimated her.

Maud didn't bother with fists.

She put down her head and ran straight forward, butting him in

166

the solar plexus and knocking Renny right off his feet and over the short balcony railing of the private box, into the laps of the stunned patrons below us.

As we watched, Renny struggled to his feet and looked up to shake an angry fist at me.

"I'll get you for this, Frank Baum!" He shouted. "You and your dressed-up bulldog, too!"

And on that note, Renny took his leave of the theatre.

As always after one of her little tempers, Maud was the picture of contrition. I comforted her within the circle of my arms.

"Maud, there's naught of blame to stick to you. It was Renny who was rude. You just reacted when provoked. Renny was already of a temper before you came in—some of the scenes in *Matches* apparently rubbed uncomfortably close to our own past experiences together."

Maud frowned. "Well, I didn't care for him, I can tell you that. But I'm sorry he got his feelings hurt. Hell hath no fury like a lover scorned, to paraphrase the bard."

Indeed.

While Renny had professed remorse over his past choices, and indeed, had sounded at one point as if he were considering asking me to resume where we had left off, he had not given up the hypocrisy of living one lifestyle while promoting another. That was one of Gulch's lessons that had stuck with him well. Instead of leaving the ministry after he and Gulch split up, he had become one of those traveling preachers who made his living going back and forth on a loose circuit of small churches in the backwoods of northern New York. For the price of a meal and a warm bed and the contents of the donation basket, Renny would preach the word as he saw it, coached over the years by his former lover Gulch into a true fire-and-brimstone orator.

Maud was right. He was a hypocrite of the worst kind, as Gulch had been, and his perception that he had been mocked by me both in the play and in person fanned the flames of his rage and ego to heights I never would have suspected of the charming boy who had once held my heart.

I got my first taste of what it was like to cross Renny when a vitriolic letter to the editor appeared in the local paper, stating that theatrical productions of any kind were an abomination to God and man. There was no name attached.

A scant week later, another letter appeared. This one went past broad accusations about public entertainment and suggested that a local play currently being put before the public was a cesspool of sin and no good Christian should be caught on the same side of the street as my lovely little theatre.

Ticket sales nearly doubled that week, and I counted myself ahead of the game, except for the fact that a small group of pious crows began to show up outside the theatre before performances, carrying plaques decrying our production.

That raised my temper.

Maud counseled me to caution, which was rather amusing, considering the hot temper she carried under her pretty bonnet. So I bided my time, watching ticket sales go up proportionally to the number of people traipsing around outside the box office.

It occurred to me that I might take to hiring sign carriers for every show I did, it seemed to be having such a positive impact on our profits.

But when a letter appeared questioning the authenticity of my marriage to Maud; questioning the very foundation on which it was based, and suggesting that it was something altogether different than the holy matrimony of a man and woman, my wrath was ignited.

If Maud and her family had not been lifelong, well-known citizens, I shudder to think what might have happened. As it was, most solid citizens just shrugged it off and continued to doff their hats politely when my darling wife and I strolled down the streets, but there were those few who slunk to the other side of the road now, or averted their eyes when we passed, and what I could tolerate for myself, I would not put up with for Maud.

I stomped in a fever to the newspaper to ferret out the information that would confirm my suspicions. When I arrived, I was shown in to the office of the editor, a tired-looking, gray-haired man who squinted at me as if trying to gauge the likelihood that the conversation would come to blows. I did my best to put him at ease.

"I have no quarrel with you, old-timer, although I question the editorial policy that allows you to publish such baseless and scandalous accusations when the writer does not even have the courage or the courtesy to attach his name to the letter."

The editor blinked. "Our policy, unfortunately, is quite clear. We do not censor our editorial letters. If you would like to reply to these accusations, sir, you are welcome to write your own letter. And if this has caused any distress to you and your family . . . "

"If?" I said, rethinking my position about squashing the man's nose.

"I'm new here to the area," said the editor, "and please don't take this the wrong way, but—have you taken a good look at your wife recently? I mean--"

I leaned forward and grabbed his tie, as skinny and tired looking as the man himself. "My wife is the loveliest woman you'll ever have the opportunity to lay eyes on, you cur. And if you value your life, you're going to tell me the name of the person who is slandering her."

At that moment, several bulky pressmen showed up to separate me from the editor's tie, but he stopped them before they tossed me out on the pavement and gave me a look of some sympathy. "My wife was never much to look at either, God rest her soul," he said with a sigh. "I don't know who's writing the letters. They aren't signed, and they come in unmarked envelopes."

"Damn," I replied, as I dangled from several meaty hands.

"But I can tell you what the postmark says. Peekskill, New York. I looked, after we received the second one." He bent to pull open a file cabinet and pulled out a folder containing the original letters. Taking one in hand, he waved it under my nose. Sure enough, it was in Renny's neat, classically flawless penmanship.

I was so elated to have my suspicions confirmed, I hardly felt it when they tossed me out onto the hard cobblestone street on my rump.

I went back to the theatre and penned my own letter to the editor. Now that I was sure who was behind this, I had no qualms about playing tit for tat—and I was a professional writer. I brandished my quill with relish as I formulated a response.

Dear Editor (I wrote)

Several cowardly and anonymous letters have been published recently in your editorial section that defame the fine and ancient art of theatre, myself as a playwright, and the very nature of my beautiful and gracious wife. It has come to my attention that these letters have been written by a jealous former suitor and pulpitless preacher whose jealousy causes him to spread the most evil and reprehensible aspersions not only upon my own meager talents and masculinity, but upon the honor of the loveliest flower of womanhood I have ever had the pleasure of casting my eyes upon. Your letters, sir, are a great mirror, doing nothing but reflecting your own lack of character and nobility back upon you, you charlatan in minister's weeds. Should you ever choose to make your statements to the face of a gentleman who can give as good as he gets, the gentleman will easily be found, as he always is, at his own dear theatre.

Most sincerely, a man not ashamed to sign his name to his letters,

L. Frank Baum

If anything, that merely increased our box office even more, as people came flocking to the theatre to see if the former suitor (whom they assumed must be Maud's) would show up to answer the challenge I had so publicly issued.

It didn't take long.

As I had half hoped, Renny's narcissism led him to read things into my response that no one else would. Feeling revealed and exposed in more ways than one, the ink was barely dry on my editorial response before Henry, a part-time actor and full-time usher, showed up at my office door, looking worried and excited.

"Mr. Baum? You ought to see this. There's some crazy guy down in front of the theatre, preaching that we're all going to burn in hell."

I raised one eyebrow at Maud. "It's Renny," I said, feeling a certain rush of excitement.

"Frank, be careful," she said, as I rose and followed Henry downstairs. Maud stayed right behind me. The box office wasn't open yet, but even so, a small crowd had gathered around to listen to Renny shouting his message of hellfire and damnation. When I stepped out of the theatre door, Renny noticed me right away.

"Sinner!" he boomed, pointing a finger at me. "Knave and corrupter!"

I waited no longer, but flew straight at him and caught him a good one on the jaw, toppling him over. Years with Gulch had left his frame as thin and feverish as his lover's. Renny was not the well-muscled young man he had once been.

"Oh, Frank, I think he hit his head," said Maud, rushing to Renny's side.

I joined her. Sure enough, his eyes were closed, his breathing shallow. A faint cut leaked blood from the corner of his mouth where I had struck him. The gathered crowd stilled. "Knocked himself out on the cobblestones," someone offered.

I stood. "Bring him inside," I ordered several of the ushers. "Let's get him some whiskey and water and see if we can't bring him back around."

Soon, we had him ensconced on a bench, Maud dabbing at his wound with a damp handkerchief, while I swirled watered whiskey in a glass and instructed Henry to lift his head so I could pour some down his gullet.

The whiskey seemed to work. Renny's eyes fluttered open and he coughed and spluttered.

Then he realized where he was and from whom the attentions were coming, and he threw off the supporting arms and sprang to his feet. "You knock me out, drag me into this den of inequity and poor hard liquor into me? What sort of vile debauchery do you think to lure me into, you abomination unto God?"

171

Behind me, Henry sighed. "Well, someone sure is full of himself."

Maud rose and stood next to me. "Watch what you call my husband, you apocalyptic apologist."

Renny gave an incoherent cry of anger and threw a punch which Maud neatly sidestepped. Henry stuck out a foot, and Renny, unable to slow his momentum, headed straight for it, tripping and flailing wildly. In his haste to break his fall, he grabbed a heavy embroidered drapery, which gave a horrible ripping sound and fluttered down from the wall, catching on the gas chandelier as it fluttered down.

Immediately, it burst into flame.

Henry shrieked and doused it with the bottle he held in his hand. Unfortunately, the bottle was full of the particularly fine old whiskey I had used to rouse Renny with.

Flame spread rapidly through the lobby. Henry shrieked and threw himself in Renny's arms. Renny shook him off and pointed at the door. "Go!" He turned to me, a look of distress on his face. "Frank, I had no intention--"

I waved him off. "I know, Renny. Go. Make sure the others are out."

"What about you?"

"My plays are in here. Everything else I can replace, but not those."

"Frank, you don't have time," he shouted at me desperately. "The whole building is going up!"

He was right. In the few seconds since the fire had started, it had already consumed much of the far wall, and the room was filling with thick, black smoke.

I turned to Maud, but she was gone. "Maud? Maud!" I shrieked. I grabbed Renny's arm. "Did you see where she went? Did she go out?"

"I don't know," he shouted back. "But we have to go, now!" He pulled at me, but I tore myself away and turned back. "Maud!" I bellowed at the top of my lungs.

Renny took one last look at me and backed toward the exit.

Then I heard the voice that meant everything to me.

"Frank!" It was Maud, covered in soot and ash, a sheaf of papers clutched in one hand. "I have your plays! Let's get out of here before we get roasted!"

I picked her up in my arms to carry her triumphantly out of the building, but I'd forgotten how much she weighed. Apologetically, I set her back on her feet, and we emerged hand in hand to the cheering crowd that waited for us outside.

The fire brigade came, but there was little they could do to save the lovely theatre in which I had seen my first plays produced. Renny fought valiantly at my side, but finally we were forced to concede defeat. The buildings on either side were saved, however, so I counted my blessings.

When I slumped down on the sidewalk, exhausted and filthy, Maud on one side of me, Renny on the other, Renny hung his head. "Frank, I am so sorry. I had no intention of anything like this happening. You believe that, don't you?"

I looked at him. It actually sounded like the old Renny, the boy I had known and loved. "Renny?"

"Frank. Maud. I don't know what drove me to such extremes. I . . . " he sighed. "Yes, I do. I was jealous. So incredibly jealous, and so ashamed of what I had done. Once Gulch ended our liaison, the enormity of my betrayal of you became so obvious to me. The only way I could live with it was to blame you, point my finger at you, instead of myself. I--"

Maud reached across me to place a finger across Renny's lips. "Hush, now. It's all over. And all forgiven."

"Well, except for one thing," I said. "I owe you an apology, too. You were right about *Matches*. It contained material I had drawn from our old school days that I should never have used. There were private and personal moments between us that I captured and made fun of for public amusement. I'm sorry, Renny."

I took one of the folders—the one labeled *Matches*—which Maud had rescued from the burning theatre and gave her a questioning look. My lovely, sooty wife smiled at me and nodded.

173

I tottered to my feet and staggered over to the smoldering embers of the theatre, and tossed my handwritten script into the coals, where it curled and smoked and flared into ash. Then I returned and held out my hand to Renny. "Friends?"

"Was that what I think it was?" Renny said, eyes on mine.

"The only true copy of *Matches* to survive the fire," I confirmed.

"Friends," he said firmly, placing his hand in mine.

"As long as you remember, I'm the wife," said Maud firmly, placing her hand on both of ours. "If I ever catch even the whiff of a flirtatious breath on the air, I'll rip your arms right off your body."

"Are you talking to me or him?" I asked cautiously.

"Both of you," Maud said with a brilliant smile.

Renny coughed out a smoky breath. "I can live with that," he said.

"Keep your hands to yourself, and you will," said Maud, still smiling.

I wrapped my arms around her tightly. God, I love my wife.

Chapter Twenty-Five
Meanwhile, back on the Farm

We were finally back in the neighborhood of Uncle Henry and Auntie Em's land. As we approached the farm, I was somewhat surprised to notice that it looked even more bedraggled than usual. The sound of the wagon—the creaking of the wheels, the thudding of High Boy's dinner-plate sized hoofs in the dust—must have alerted Uncle Henry to our approach, because he appeared on the front porch as we pulled up the drive, looking nearly as gone to seed as the fields.

I hopped down from the wagon as Frank pulled to a stop, and ran up the porch steps to give Uncle Henry a hug.

"Dorothy? Is that you? Is that really you?" he said in a choked voice, taking me by the shoulders to hold me at arms length and get a good look.

"It really is, Uncle Henry. I can't stay, I'm on my way somewhere else, but goodness, what's happened to the farm? And to you? You look terrible! I mean, if you don't mind my saying so."

Uncle Henry made a harrumphing noise deep in his throat, then looked at Frank. "And who's this?" he asked, without answering my question. "One of those traveling salesman galoots like your mama ran off with?"

Frank stepped forward and held out a hand, which my uncle studied suspiciously.

"No, Uncle Henry. This is Frank Baum, from South Dakota. He gave me a ride back here in his wagon out of the goodness of his heart. He's a newspaper man, and a dry-goods merchant. His wife knows all about it."

"Well, then," said Uncle Henry, finally reaching out to shake Frank's hand. "I guess that's a horse of a different color. Come on into the parlor and sit a spell. Can't offer you much, but got cool water out of the pump that will wash some of that dust out of your throat. Come in, come in!"

175

The inside of the house looked awful. There was a layer of dust nearly an inch thick all over everything, and dozens of opened and empty cans of beans testified as to what Uncle Henry had been living off of. When Uncle Henry sat down in his favorite chair, a puff of dust rose up around him. Frank and I exchanged looks. Auntie Em may have been crazy as a loon, but she'd been a good housekeeper.

"Uncle Henry, what's going on around here? Where's Auntie Em? Did something . . . happen to her?" I asked, afraid she'd gone and done something crazy, like try to fly off the barn roof or jumped down the well.

"She ran off with the hired help," said Uncle Henry after a moment. "Nothing's been right since. She talked crazy, but I sure miss that gal."

"She ran off with the hired help?" I repeated, sure I'd heard wrong. Plain, gray Auntie Em? I tried to think who had been working here last time I'd been around. Who had been there that was crazy enough to take on Auntie Em, at any rate. "Which one?"

"All of em," said Uncle Henry glumly. "Guess they were collectin' more of a bonus than I thought for bringing in the crops, and when it was all said and done, and they decided to mosey on, Em decided to mosey on with them. Damn hussy! Never could keep her satisfied, but didn't think she'd go that far. Man gets tired working all day out in the field. Turns out she was keeping track on a calendar. Do you believe that? 'Day 22—No Sex', 'Day 97—Turned down AGAIN!'. That one was in red letters. By the time we hit day 200, she was ready to go. I wouldn't have thought she knew what day of the week it was, much less how long it had been since I'd hoed her row, but there you have it."

He looked so forlorn that I got up and gave him another hug, trying not to sneeze at the dust it raised.

"It looks like you've let the whole farm go to seed since she left," I said.

"Wasn't much point in it with you and Em both gone, was there?" Uncle Henry replied, patting my shoulder awkwardly. "But now that you're back, things will work out just fine, Dorothy."

"What do you mean?"

"Well, now that you're back, you can take over and do all the things that your Auntie Em used to do—cook and clean and look after the hens and slop the hogs . . . "

"Gee, Uncle Henry," I said. "That sounds great, it really does. But I kind of had other plans."

He stuck out his bottom lip and pouted.

"On the other hand, I guess if something better came along, there's not much holding you to this place anymore, is there?" said Frank, giving me an encouraging look.

I shook my head frantically 'no', but Frank just grinned. "I think a little vacation might be just what Uncle Henry needs, Dorothy."

"A vacation?" said Uncle Henry. "I've never taken a vacation in my life. But where would I go? The whole idea is just crazy."

"Maybe you could go along with Dorothy, Uncle Henry," Frank said.

He actually flinched. "You mean back to that house of ill repute where I found her? I don't think a man who racked up 200 days without putting his plow to the furrow would do very well in a place like that," he said.

"Actually, there's somewhere else I'm headed to," I said. "But if you don't like the idea, by all means, don't let me force you."

"Just a little vacation," chimed in Frank, suppressing a laugh.

"You going, too?" asked Uncle Henry.

"No," said Frank. "Unfortunately not. Promised my wife I'd be back directly. But I'd jump at the chance if I didn't have a family waiting for me at home."

Uncle Henry sighed and looked around at the dirty walls and dusty furniture. "I don't suppose there's much to keep me here anymore. Tell you what. Let me sleep on it, and I'll give you an answer in the morning. How's that?"

"What's the weather supposed to be like tomorrow?" I asked, becoming resigned to the idea. Uncle Henry in Oz. Why not?

"Bad storm supposed to be blowing in, accordin' to the *Almanac*," he replied. "Why?"

"No reason in particular," I said. "But don't take too long making up your mind. Now, how about we get this place straightened up a little so Frank and I can get our stuff in out of that wagon and get settled in for the night?"

I ended up sweeping, and dusting and then sweeping some more, while Frank gathered up all the empty bean cans and disposed of them, then killed a couple of chickens so we could have a decent meal. Out of pity for the chickens, I poured some of Frank's bourbon down their scrawny throats, and waited till they were staggering before I let Frank sneak up from behind and whack 'em.

I have to admit I laced Uncle Henry's after-dinner coffee with some of Frank's bourbon, too, because I wanted to have a nice long talk with Frank and I didn't want any interruptions.

As soon as Uncle Henry was snoring away on his bed, I grabbed a seat at the table with Frank and shook my finger at him. "Are you crazy? Uncle Henry in Oz? What are you thinking?"

He grinned. "Come on Dorothy, have a heart. The poor old guy has worked his fingers to the bone his entire life. He deserves some fun!"

"Yeah, I get that," I said. "But Oz? He's more likely to have a heart attack or something than he is to have a good time."

"Don't be silly," said Frank. "Take him to see Celione and the rest of the KittyCat Dolls, get him hopped up on a good dose of happy dust, I bet you'll be surprised how fast he adjusts."

"Maybe," I said thoughtfully. "It could work, I suppose."

"The girls are still in business, right? Tito and his coppers didn't close it down?"

"Oh, they're going gangbusters, from what I hear. And Tito has a new business now—televangelism."

"What's that?"

"I'm not entirely sure, but involves selling a lot of contraptions called televisions first."

"So he kept his end of the bargain to give Oz back to the Wizard?" said Frank. "But I never did hear how you escaped from Elfa's castle and saved the Emerald City from Tito and his mechanical men. What happened?"

"Let's see. Where did I leave off? Oh, yeah. Leon was in a cage in the dungeon, and Scar was being kept stoned on monkey dust . . . "

Chapter Twenty-Six
Escape from Bitch Mountain

One of the things about being held captive by a bunch of stoned, horny monkeys is that they're a cinch to bribe. Ever try to get a sex-crazed monkey out of his pants long enough to get hold of his key ring?

Exactly. *Easy.*

For that matter, so was Elfa.

Elfa was a major party animal, figuratively speaking—she was a witch, not an animal. It was party in the morning, party in the evening, orgy all night long. Every night. No matter how much we cleaned in the morning, by midnight, the place was a wreck all over again. Which was a big pain in the ass for me, considering I was on the clean-up crew. But it also meant that I had pretty much the run of the castle, and nobody ever asked me what I was doing as long as I had a mop and a bucket with me.

When I judged the time was right, I collected a couple dozen of the phallic-looking mushrooms we had spotted in the forest on the way in. A coat of gold paint, and you couldn't tell the fungi from Elfa's beloved brassies—as long as you didn't try to use them. The imitations were a lot softer than the originals.

When I heard that Elfa's twin sister Nessa was due for a visit, I knew it was time we busted out of there. I wasn't sure how much Nessa might remember by now about the day my shed fell on her, and I didn't want to find out. Plus, the fungi were starting to wilt.

I'd been keeping an eye on Scar, but I couldn't tell if he'd taken my advice or not. If he had, he was putting on a hell of an act at being a drunken, horny fool, but as far as I could tell, his tail hadn't gotten any longer.

I loaded the brassies in a duffel bag and stashed it in the woods near the castle, replacing them in their case with the painted mushrooms, and then slipped down to free Leon. His face brightened

180

up immediately when he saw me.

"Dorothy! Dorothy! I'm so glad to see you! You've got to get me out of here! You wouldn't believe what that disgusting guard wants me to do!"

Actually, I knew exactly what that disgusting guard wanted him to do, because that was how I'd gotten my hands on his keys to begin with. But there didn't seem to be much point in telling Leon that, so I just said, "okay," and pulled out the key to unlock his door.

He blinked at me in surprise. "Dorothy?"

"Come on, Leon, you wanted out, now you're out. Let's move it! I slipped the guard a little something to knock him out, but it won't last forever." I made beckoning motions with my hands, but Leon just stood in his cell and looked at me.

"Leon, dammit! Come on!"

He grabbed his tail. "I don't know, Dorothy, this is kind of sudden—what if we get caught? Have you ever seen Elfa when she's mad? Not good!"

Yes, I had seen her mad, which is why I was in a hell of a hurry. "Leon, if you don't move it right now, you're going to find out what happens when *I'm* mad. Now come on!"

Finally, he stepped timidly out of the cell and began to follow me down the passage. "Where are we going?"

"We're going to find Scar and get the hell out of here!"

"We're what?" He stopped dead in his tracks. "You want me to go up there and take a chance on getting caught? Are you crazy? Let's just go—Scar never did anything for either of us except boss us around. Let him get his own ass out of here, I say!"

"Leon, you are such a fucking coward. Scar is our friend, and we're not leaving here without him."

Leon sighed and pulled on his tail some more. "Well, what about the brass men's brassies?"

I smirked at him over my shoulder. "Already got em, stashed in a bag right outside the castle wall. Which is why we need to get a move on, because Nessa is arriving any minute and there's a big orgy planned. I substituted painted mushrooms for the brass men's privates, and once the orgy starts, there's no way *that's* not going to get noticed. So we need to get Scar and get the hell out of here now, *capish?*"

More sighing, but Leon nodded. "Okay, but you go first. I don't know my way around here very well."

"Follow me," I said, and led the way out of the dungeon and up to the main floor.

Scar had a little room of his own off of the big bed chamber that belonged to Elfa, and we crept quietly down the hallway until we reached Elfa's room. I had left a mop and bucket nearby as a cover, and now I grabbed them before tapping lightly on Elfa's door. When there was no answer, I cautiously pushed it open, and saw to my relief that it was empty. Putting down my props, I crossed over to Scar's room and used the master key I'd gotten from Leon's guard to unlock Scar's door.

He was laying on his bed with his back to me.

"Scar," I hissed, trying to be quiet, but hoping like hell this would be quick. He didn't stir.

"Scar, dammit, wake up," I said, giving him a nudge.

"Oh, he's already quite awake," said a sly, sultry voice behind me.

With a sinking feeling, I turned to see Elfa standing in the doorway, waggling her wand at me, giving me the kind of smile a cat must give a mouse right before it eats the mouse. Behind her, with a collar around his neck and his leash in her hand, stood Scar, looking miserable and furious—and alert.

"Oh, hey, Elfa," I said, as casually as I could. "I was going to mop in here if I could get him out of bed. I didn't want him waking up and tracking all over my nice clean floor."

She laughed and gave a painful jerk to Scar's leash. Her cleavage jiggled invitingly. She might be evil, but it sure looked good on her. "Never try to kid a kidder, kid. I know all about your little escape plan. Leon told me all about it. And did you and Scar really think I wouldn't notice the effect on his . . . performance when he stopped taking the monkey dust?"

182

"I ... I don't know what you're talking about," I said, edging away from her. I bumped into something, and hoped it was Leon. I sneaked a peek and sighed. Just my luck, a Mountie. Hadn't she ever heard of pest control?

"Oh, stop it, Dorothy. I know you've got my penises, and I want them back. I've been bragging to my sister about them for weeks, and I'm not going to have her show up today and think I was lying. Now, tell me where you hid the dicks, or the next one that's going into my trophy case is going to be Scar's, and it's going to be all your fault!"

"You bitch!" I said.

"That's right," she replied, sweetly, giving Scar's leash another jerk. "What's it going to be, Dorothy, a bunch of brass cocks that nobody's going to miss except a handful of mechanical men, or Scar's precious little soldier, which I'm sure he's going to miss quite a bit?"

She jerked the chain again, but this time, Scar reached up and jerked back before Elfa's Mounties could stop him. He pulled so hard he yanked the chain right out of her grasp, and then whirled to slam the heavy links into his guards' faces. When I saw Elfa bringing her wand to bear, I picked up the mop bucket and upended it over Elfa's head.

I grabbed the mop and spun around, jabbing the business end of the mop into the stomach of the nearest Mountie, who doubled over with a satisfying *oof*. I swept the legs out from under the next one, and was getting ready to club a third, when I noticed that none of them were fighting back. Instead, they were all staring over my shoulder at Elfa.

I looked around to see that Scar had been making pretty good headway with his share of the Mounties as well, but like everyone else, he'd come to a halt to look at Elfa.

She'd gotten the upside down bucket off her head. Some of the water had apparently doused her wand, which was sputtering weakly and developing a definite bend. Water was trickling down her face. As I watched, a false eyelash came loose and slid forlornly down her cheek.

And while the trickles of water were green, the skin under them was a rosy, peachy tan.

Elfa wasn't a natural green?

Well.

Elfa was cursing and rubbing mascara and green face paint out of her eyes. The Mounties took a collective step back as her actions only made the damage worse. You know it's pretty bad when your makeup meltdown can scare off a troop of humping monkeys.

"Elfa?" I said, stepping forward.

She squinted up at me, one false eyelash still clinging desperately to a smeary lid, and snarled. She flicked the wand at me and I flinched, but all it did was fizzle weakly and spray me with a few drops of brackish water.

I'd never really noticed how short Elfa was before. As I stood there, looking down at her, I noticed something else: her chest was deflating.

I gestured at her disappearing cleavage. "I take it that was magic that was filling your lingerie, not actual boobs."

She looked down and shrieked.

"What the hell happened to your tits?" said Scar.

"All magic. Now that her wand has flopped, it's . . . melting."

It sure was—from her chest right down to her hips. *Not* attractive. As the water in her hair continued to stream down her cheeks and chin, her pale rosy skin became more and more visible. Something clicked, and I pointed a finger at her.

"You're not a witch! You're a Munchkin!"

There was a shocked gasp from the crowd.

"I am not!" she said hotly, rising to her tiptoes and trying to look taller.

"Then do something magical, right now!"

"I . . . I . . . I don't feel like it," Elfa said weakly.

I looked around at the gathered Mounties. "Have you guys ever actually seen her do anything magical without her wand?"

There was lots of muttering and whispering, and finally, Melvin said, "no."

I gave them a disgusted look. "You let yourselves be dominated by a Munchkin with a magic wand? She probably won it in a card game somewhere, just like she did with the dicks."

"Oh, my God!" exclaimed Leon, pointing at one of Elfa's shapely legs. It was withering and puckering right in front of our eyes. For a second, I thought the rest of her was melting just like her boobs had, then I realized that I was seeing cellulite making itself known up and down the length of her formerly gorgeous thighs. Unfortunately, Munchkins have a tendency to cellulite. There's not much they can do about it. It seems to be a genetic thing.

I snatched the wand from Elfa's grasp, waving it in front of her face. "You had a magic wand and all you used it for was to make your boobs bigger, hide your cellulite and turn your makeup waterproof?" I asked.

She looked at me sourly. "Hey kid, wait till you hit your forties— you'd be surprised what pops up on your wish list."

"Yeah," one of the Mounties stage-whispered. "I could do with a sack tuck, myself."

"Oh, and a chin lift," chimed in another.

"I was thinking about getting one of those hair transplants," said a third. "You know, where they harvest hair off the back of your ass and plug it in to your temples?"

"You'd be a perfect candidate, Stan. You have the hairiest ass in two quadrants," somebody snipped.

I wasn't done with Elfa yet. "Your reign of depravity here is over," I told her. For emphasis, I snapped the wand in two pieces right in front of her nose. "I'm taking my dicks and I'm going back to Oz. And If you try to stop me, I'll . . . I'll dump another bucket of water on your head, and wash the rest of that over-the-top makeup job down the drain!"

With that, I turned on my heel and walked out, Scar and Leon right behind me.

It appeared that Elfa's unmasking as a Munchkin had dampened

185

even the Mounties' ardor—at least temporarily. Or, possibly, it was the deflating of her magically enhanced boobs. But I didn't want to hang around long enough for it to occur to someone that having the brassies in hand gave them a leg up in being the next ruler of Oz.

We left the Mounties still arguing about the best place to harvest hair from, and fled the castle before anyone started thinking about trying to make a grab for the dicks—and the power—for themselves.

We picked up the brassies from where I had hidden them outside the castle and hotfooted it back to Oz.

This time when we entered the Emerald City, however, we played it smarter. First, Scar and I sent Leon ahead to let the brass men know we were coming back with their privates. Then, once we were sure Leon couldn't see us anymore, we hid the brassies in the forest—all accept for one. The smallest, friendliest one of the bunch.

Over several weeks of cleaning and charging up the brassies, I had learned that all metal penises are not created the same. Some are demanding, wanting all the attention; some seem almost angry. Some are full of pride; some are shy and need coaxing. This little guy was happy as hell just to be invited to the party, and he showed it by rubbing up affectionately against my hand as I carried him back into the Emerald City.

This time, we were ushered back into Oz's sanctum without any delay. Tito was sitting behind the big desk, Leon beaming proudly at his side. Anvil and Tongs were busy at another table, but quickly dropped what they were doing and rolled forward when they spotted us.

Tongs' eyes darted over us, then he frowned. "Where are they?"

I stepped forward, hands behind my back. "Where's Oz?"

Anvil turned to Leon and scowled. "I thought you said she had our privates. She doesn't have them."

"Sure she does," said Scar. "Safely hidden away where you'll never find them. Unless you keep your end of the bargain and set the Wizard free."

"How do I know you're not lying?" asked Tito, looking

186

thoughtful.

I pulled the littlest dick out from behind my back and set in on the desk.

Shyly, it tried to climb back into my hand, but I shooed it toward Tongs.

His expression changed. "Little Pecker!" he crooned, reaching to pick up the pint-sized dick and cuddle it affectionately.

When he looked back at us, I swear there were actually tears in his eyes. Well, maybe a little motor oil. But it looked like tears, and the feeling seemed sincere. "You really have all of them? All of our penises? They're all okay?"

"Well," said Scar, "they got a hell of a work out, but they're all fine."

I didn't think it was an opportune time to mention the buffing and the Bondo.

Tito looked at his companions and nodded. "Let me show you to Oz."

He took us on a labyrinthine path through the palace, and down several flights of stairs, until we reached a narrow door in front of which stood a dour looking brass man. Tongs gave him a salute and he stepped out of the way. Anvil gave the door a perfunctory knock and then shoved it open and Tito walked into the room beyond; Scar, Leon and I right behind him.

Inside a small, drab room sat the man we had seen on all those billboards, but he sure looked different out of those long dark robes. He had a long, graying ponytail and in real life his small round, glasses had rose-colored lenses. He wore a short-sleeved, rainbow-colored shirt. His trousers were baggy and made of a faded blue denim, and the shoes on his feet were odd—part fabric and part leather, with neon-colored laces to hold them to his feet. There were beads around his neck, and one of his ears was pierced.

Across the table from him sat a teenage-boy with blonde hair and thickly lashed green eyes. They both looked up when the door opened, the boy warily, the man with a genial smile.

187

"Oh, hey, dude! Glad you're back! Got time for a hand of Texas Hold-em? Hey, Leon, Scar. How's it hanging?"

Scar said, "A little further to the left than it used to, but that's not important right now. Hello, Oz, long time no see."

Leon shuffled his feet and tugged on his tail.

The boy frowned. "Oz, Tito *cheats*. Don't invite him to play cards with us. That's how he got control of the Emerald City in the first place."

Oz shook his head and beamed. "I never really dug the whole 'Great and Terrible Oz, Ruler of the Emerald City' thing, anyways." He shook a playful finger at the boy across from him. "You gotta learn to loosen up a little bit. It's just *stuff*. Easy come, easy go."

Tito took that moment to place a heavy hand on my shoulder and push me toward the table. "Sit," he said. "Let's cut the crap."

I took a chair. So did Leon and Scar. Tongs and Anvil rocked back on their wheels.

"Hey, Tito, you should introduce us to your friend, dude," said Oz.

Tito frowned at Oz, then at me. "Oz, Dorothy. Dorothy, Oz. Now, tell me where the rest of the penises are, or I'm going to lock you in this room with Oz until you're as crazy as he is."

"Dude," said Oz. "Just because I don't share your rigid capitalist value system doesn't mean I'm crazy." He pulled a small pipe, filled it and lit it. A pungent smoke filled the air.

Leon sniffed. "That's not happy dust—what is it?" he asked.

"No, dude. Columbian Gold. Classic. That happy dust is bad for you. You gotta widen your horizons a little."

Tito smiled mirthlessly. "I want those penises, now!"

I was starting to lose my temper. "You promised that if we got them back for you, you'd return the Emerald City to Oz!"

Tito shrugged. "I lied. You want to spend the rest of your life in an eight-by-ten room with a guy that invented tie-dye and wears the footprint of a dove around his neck?"

"You'll never get them, you know, if you don't keep your promise. I hid them some place you'll never find them."

Tito's eyes narrowed as he studied me, then he grinned. "No problem," he said. "I bet Tongs' Pecker knows where they are." He motioned, and Tongs set the little guy on the floor in front of him and opened the door. "Little Pecker," he said. "Go find your brothers. Hurry up, show me where they are."

Little Pecker stretched and turned, as if trying to find the right direction.

"Hey, there, big boy," I said in a silky tone. I gave a low whistle.

When he heard my voice, Tong's pecker gave an excited leap, then hopped stiffly over to my side, where he proceeded to rub himself against my calf. I reached down to pet him, and gave Tito a smirk.

"What the hell did you do to him?" thundered Tongs

"Dude," said Oz. "You may know a lot about passing laws and making rules and stuff, but you don't know dick about ... well ... dicks, if you follow my drift."

I stood up and confronted Tito. "If you and your friends want their dicks back in their pants, you'll let us go and turn the kingdom back over to Oz right now."

Tito rocked back and forth for a long moment, looking at Little Pecker, who was circling my ankles with happy little hops.

"Might as well concede right now, Tito," said Scar. "A dick in the hand is never as happy as a dick that thinks he's gonna make it into the bush."

The brass men advanced on Tito and began giving him not-so-subtle rolling nudges.

Tito nodded and hung his head. "Okay," he said. "You've got a deal."

"Cool," said Oz. "Now can we play some cards?"

The boy, who had been watching all this with suspicious eyes, slapped the table with a hand. "I think we should get the hell out of this room, first, and play cards after."

Scar nodded. "The girl has a point."

"Girl?" I said.

The boy blushed and looked at the table.

"Little of both, actually," said Oz. "He started out as a she, then

189

got turned into a he by Nessa, who raised him, until we found out who he really was, kidnapped him back, and turned him into a girl again. Dorothy, meet Ozma, princess of Oz."

"Wow, that's some story," I said, holding out a hand, which the boy—I mean girl—took and shook shyly.

I gave her a little wink. Us girls gotta stick together, after all.

"I'm still getting used to it," she said, waving a hand at her flannel shirt. Now that Oz had revealed her secret, I could see a certain delicacy to her features that I hadn't noticed before.

"Are you Oz's daughter?" I asked.

"Huh? Oh! Oz—Ozma," Oz said happily. "Nah. The whole Oz thing is more like a title than a real name. I'm actually Tom Brascoe, a street performer from San Francisco, myself."

"San Francisco?" I said. "You're from my world? You don't dress like it. Or talk like it, for that matter."

Oz waved a hand. "This place doesn't sync up with our world, time-wise. It overlaps here and there, but it's a little off. One day I was dropping windowpane and doing a little sleight of hand in Golden Gate Park, and the next minute, I'm sliding down a rainbow and landing right in the middle of an Emerald City high council. They were trying to figure out who was going to take over when the rightful ruler and all his family were kidnapped by a wicked witch. *Bam*! Before I knew what was happening, I was the new ruler. There's a guy over in the Winkie Quadrant that's from the 9th Century—*BC*. It's all good."

"Getting back to what I was saying," interjected Ozma. "I think we should get out of here and get you back on the throne before Hammer comes up with another scheme, Great and Powerful Oz. You and Dorothy can confer, confab and otherwise hobnob later."

"You're right," said Oz, gathering up the deck of cards on the table. "And I know just the thing to keep this from happening again. Let's go upstairs to my office."

A few minutes later, we were gathered around Oz's desk, watching as he wrote out the terms of an agreement between the brass men and ourselves, promising the return and reattachment of their brassies, in exchange for their solemn promise never to try to take over or influence the running of Oz again.

Tito and Ozma both frowned as they studied the document over Oz's shoulder.

"I don't get it," said Ozma finally. "What's going to make them keep their word just because they sign a piece of paper?"

"This isn't just a piece of paper," said Oz, writing the final words with a flourish. "It's a contract. A binding contract. It ... it has a special magic all its own. Because," he said looking at Hammer. "You know what happens if you violate the terms of a contract?"

"What?" said Tito.

"Let me put it this way. What's worse than a drug dealer and two dozen brass men running the government?"

"I don't know," I said. "What?"

"Big brass lawsuit, baby!" crowed Oz.

We all looked at him blankly.

"Trust me. You don't want to go there," he said. "Now, come with me."

He stepped to a back door in his office and opened it onto a balcony opening onto an enormous hall full of the Emerald City's citizens. Oz stepped out onto the balcony and shouted, "Oz has returned!"

People stopped and looked up, craning to see their beloved wizard.

A hush fell over the hall.

"I have thanked the brass men for taking care of you all in my absence," Oz continued. "With Princess Ozma at my side, I will take back up the reins of government as her regent, until such time as she is ready to assume the throne herself."

More cheering. Ozma leaned toward me and whispered, "It's the public appearances. I never know what to wear—flannel or lace, you know?"

At Oz's side, Tito moved restlessly, and I reached into my pocket and pulled out Little Pecker, who bounced happily in my palm.

191

Tongs nudged Tito, who sighed and nodded.

A ragged cheer broke out below us.

"It's time to get rid of the gray and bring back the green!" shouted Oz. He threw his hands dramatically up in the air, and a brilliant green light flew out from them, bathing everything in an emerald glow.

And everywhere the light struck, the dreary, dingy gray fled, to be replaced by sparkling green. Even the citizens below us lost their drab appearance and came vibrantly back to life. A new round of cheers broke out, this time deafening in their loudness and enthusiasm.

Oz beamed. "Now that's some magic!"

"How'd you do that?" I asked. "I thought you were just a plain old mundane person like me."

He shrugged. "I don't know, exactly. Been able to ever since I got here. I think it's just a side effect of too much electric Koolaid at Haight. And it's the only trick I've got. Hence the Emerald City. It used to be a nice shade of magenta. But that and a trunk full of busker's junk got me where I am today. Just gotta be in the right place at the right time. But that's not important right now. Let's get those dicks back their . . . dicks."

"You guys never get tired of penis jokes, do you?"

"Never. But don't worry, the brass men are not going to bother us anymore, right, Hammer? Or Dorothy here will just whistle all your brassies away from you again. You know, once they see her, they're completely under her control."

He paused and looked at me consideringly. "You know, maybe you have a special power, too."

I blinked. "The ability to whistle dick-see?"

"Stranger things have happened."

I considered my whole experience since the tornado struck. "True."

When we recovered the brassies and restored them to their rightful owners, it was party time. Leon was leading the crowd in a medley of show tunes, and Scar was whispering to a giggling waitress with a huge flambe about his experiences at Elfa's castle, when I noticed an iridescent bubble floating through the air and drifting gently toward the dais on which we were seated.

I poked Oz and pointed. "What's that?"

He put down his pipe and squinted through his little round glasses. "Oh, shit. It's Glinda."

"Really?" I asked, not seeing how even the willowy Glinda could fold herself into a bubble that small.

It got bigger as it got closer, though, and by the time it landed next to me, I could see Glinda inside through the translucent walls. She looked softly, whitely beautiful, fluffing her hair with one hand, while peering into the star at the end of her magic wand, held in her other hand as if it were a mirror.

Then the bubble popped.

Bubble juice splattered everywhere. "Eww!" I said.

"Oh, sorry about that," said Glinda, patting her hair one last time. "Fortunately, it only splatters outward, or I'd have to find some other means of travel."

I wiped bubble juice out of my eyes. "Good for you."

"So," she continued, carefully avoiding a little puddle of bubble juice as she stepped forward. "What do I see here? Elfa defeated and unmasked, that stupid second-hand wand destroyed--"

"You knew she was a fake? All along?" I asked. I looked at her wand. "Hey, were you the one she got the wand from to begin with? Why didn't you say so?"

Glinda shrugged. "Look, kid. Oz isn't the only one that played cards with Elfa and lost. She might not have had real magic of her own, but she has a hell of a sleight-of-hand skill. And it might have been my second-best wand, but it still packed a punch. I'm surprised she didn't get Nessa after you, though. She really liked those brassies."

"She tried," I said, "but we bought her off with two leftover penises. When the brass men first discovered their penises were missing, they sent out a reconnaissance party and Elfa blasted them into Neverland. But that's a different story. The point is, there were two extra brassies, and we gave them to Elfa and Nessa. Which reminds me. If Elfa isn't a real witch, then her sister Nessa isn't either. So where did Nessa get *her* wand?

Glinda shrugged again. She didn't have Elfa's enormous cleavage, but it was still a pretty sight. "Okay, I tried for a rematch and lost. Can we move on?" She took another step forward and tried again. "What do I see here? Elfa defeated and unmasked, that stupid second-hand wand destroyed. Tito moving his seat of operations from the poppy field to the big city, Celione in charge of the works factory, Oz restored to power, the brass men, all appendages restored to their proper place, and the Emerald City once again . . . emerald."

"Pretty much," I said, giving Glinda my best smile. "Now that I've fulfilled my contract, what's my reward? Maybe the two of us--"

I never got to finish my sentence. A dusty haze surrounded me, blurring my vision.

"Dorothy!" cried Glinda.

"Dorothy, hold on!" I could hear the panic in Scar's voice. "Oz, do something!"

"I'm trying!" Oz's voice was fading. "She's getting pulled back into her own world!"

Chapter Twenty-Seven
Year of the Not-So-Happy-Dust

"Wow," said Frank. "That explains how you got back here. And you can't control it?"

"Not a bit," I said. "Even worse, when I got back, I landed in a little town called Moose Lick, Minnesota." I shuddered, just remembering. "I've crossed back over twice, but there's some kind of natural magic that keeps kicking me out and snapping me back here, just like I was connected by a giant rubber band. Glinda and Oz have been working on it, but haven't come up with any way to keep me there permanently yet."

"What about Oz? He doesn't go back and forth, does he?"

"No," I replied. "But they're not really sure why. Oz thinks maybe all the acid trips he took shook him a little loose from whatever keeps pulling me back."

"How about that man that lives with the Winkies? Does he go back and forth?"

"No, but he was almost dead when he crossed over. Oz thinks it had the same loosening effect as the acid."

"I'm not sure I really understand the whole 'acid' thing anyway," said Frank. "What is that, exactly?"

I shrugged. I'd never fully gotten it, either. "I think it's like the happy dust, but somehow it involves a lot of moldy bread."

"Doesn't sound like much fun to me."

"Oz seems to like it. He's been working on a way to make more. Something to do with growing a lot of wheat, then letting it all go bad. I was kind of hoping that if he succeeded, I could use some and maybe it would let me stay in Oz, too. The place, I mean, not the man."

"Gotcha."

"So you've come back here to the spot where you crossed over before."

"Exactly. The longest I've ever been able to stay in Oz was when the tornado took me in the shed. I'm hoping that if I can cross over here again, I'll be able to stay a while longer. Glinda and I ... "

"Glinda and you?"

I blushed. "I'm still kind of working on that. No matter what I do, she still thinks of me as the same green kid I was when I first showed up in Oz."

"I had thought maybe you and Ozma."

"Ozma? Why on earth would you think that?"

"I don't know," Frank said. "She's about your age, she's been through a lot, too. Just seems like you'd have a lot in common."

I considered it. "Ozma's still really confused. Some days she's a man, some days she's a woman. The thing I like about Glinda is she really knows who she is. No apologies. Last time I saw Ozma, she was trying to convince Garbanzo to build her a mechanical penis of her own."

"What's so weird about that? Nessa and Elfa seemed to like them quite a bit."

"Not to *use*, to ... uh ... *wear*."

Frank sighed. "Dorothy, I know it's a lot to ask, but I'd really like it if you'd try to do something for me."

"If I can, sure. You're the best friend I've ever had here in this world, Frank. Ask me."

"If this works, and you end up returning to Oz?"

"Yes?"

"Promise me that if it isn't permanent—if you find yourself ever snapped back into this world again? - that you'll try to get word to me? I'd hate to think we'll never see each other again, alright?"

In the short time I'd known him, I'd come to love Frank like a brother. A brother who had excellent taste in women's clothes. "Sure. Cross my heart and hope to die, Frank, if I ever find myself back here again, first thing I'll do is look you up. But how will I find you? What if you move or something?"

He frowned, then brightened. "Tell you what. Whenever anything major happens with us, I'll send you a letter care of Butterfield

196

General Delivery. Just check there, okay?"

"That's probably the closest town to the farm. Good deal. But I'm not going anywhere tonight, and I still haven't heard how you wound up in South Dakota. Feel like telling me the rest of your story?"

"Sure," he said. "After the theatre burned, Maud and I decided it was time to strike out on our own. We thought Chicago would be a good place to get a fresh start, so we packed up and headed out . . .

Chapter Twenty-Eight
Frank: My Kind of Town

We settled on Chicago, a town that we figured was big enough to allow us to start over without anyone knowing or caring about our pasts, while close enough to the frontier to provide plenty of new and novel opportunities for those brave enough to seize them.

Inspired by our change of venue, we decided to make some other changes as well.

I got a job at the local newspaper as a female advice columnist named "Frannie Akers", wearing a wig not unlike this one and a pretty frock Maud gave to me to meet with my editor.

Maud took up the game with enthusiasm, and to my surprise and great pride, developed a new hobby that quickly became a lucrative career—she became something of a sensation on the male wrestling circuit. She shaved her head and took to binding her modest breasts with bandages, and with a codpiece in her tights and a long-sleeved wrestling shirt, no one ever guessed. She also developed an unfortunate habit of going to the local saloon for a few drinks with her fans after each win, which caused more than a few scrapes, but I didn't have the heart to criticize when she was having such a good time exploring this other, underdeveloped, side of her personality.

I must say, our new roles spiced up our love life considerably. As a matter of fact, we were so spiced up that something occurred that I had never even considered possible—Maud got pregnant.

Well, that definitely put the kibosh on her wrestling career.

I was working harder than ever as a columnist, and had branched out by doing novels, with a slight twist on the pen name I used at the paper. It seemed so apropos, considering. We are all fakers in our own way, after all. Floyd Akers was my new pseudonym, and I got busy churning out a series of novels for boys about the escapades of a young adventurer in search of fame and fortune.

It was at this time I began wearing a false mustache, so that I could go both bare and furred, as it were. We moved again, but this time only a few neighborhoods over, so that Maud could resume her feminine persona—while she made a most excellent figure of a man, we doubted anyone would long be fooled once her pregnancy became apparent. I once again became the doting husband, roles we were to maintain for many years. Because once the children started coming, how could one expect a toddler to keep straight the complicated dance of male and female in a relationship such as ours?

Our lives continued uneventfully for a while, with the money I made from the combination of my advice column and my novels keeping our little family financially secure, until a blasted Indian saw through my deception and destroyed our secure little world.

I'd seen Indians before I'd arrived in Chicago, of course. Some of them as inebriated as the stories tell, some not, most of them having that glazed look of lantern-spooked deer—or the survivors of a holocaust, which in fact, they were. They seemed sad and rather romantic figures to me, doomed simply by being in the wrong place at the wrong time. The time, of course, being the colonization of America by the Europeans.

Until I met Rutting Elk. The staff at the newspaper called him Elkie for short, but if ever there was a man less suited to an affectionate and charming nickname, I have yet to meet him.

He was a tall, lean man, with flashing eyes which rarely met those of the person to whom he was speaking, and dark hair that fell nearly to his waist. I had initially made the mistake of assuming he was like the other Indians I had met in the east, and that his avoidance of eye contact was due to his humility and downtrodden state.

Later, I learned he kept his eyes averted to disguise the contempt he held there for all of us.

How he ended up in Chicago, I'm not sure—if ever there was a man born to the open plains, I thought Elkie was it. Gossip was that he had been involved with a white woman, the wife of a colonel in the US Army who had been assigned to keep the peace on Elkie's reservation. When the colonel found out he was being cuckolded, Elkie had no choice but to leave his home forever.

I could believe it. Although he rarely spoke, it wasn't hard to see the traits from which his name derived—he had a lascivious and wandering eye, and had a habit of 'accidentally' bumping into and even rubbing against any attractive woman who showed up in our office. Except for me. For some reason, from the very first, he never displayed any interest in me whatsoever. I didn't know whether to be worried or insulted. However, the more time I spent in his presence, the gladder I was that the bottomless black pits he used for eyes were not directed greedily towards me as they were to the other women he encountered.

Despite the tree-bark color of his swarthy skin and his long black hair, which he kept tied back with a beaded leather cord, Elkie's lustful ways seemed to arouse an astoundingly high degree of reciprocity in the feminine sex. It baffled me. His lips were thin and down-turned in a way that reminded me, oddly enough, of Gulch, with his sense of contemptuous moral superiority; I thought I would sooner sleep with a rattlesnake than Elkie. By the total lack of interest he evinced in my Frannie persona, I guess the feeling was mutual.

His own tale was that he had been abandoned in Chicago by Bill Hikock's Wild West Show for taking his role as an Indian Savage too seriously and coming very near to successfully counting coup with Wild Bill's thinning scalp during one momentous performance. He had somehow ended up at the newspaper offices making the odd dollar here and there by filling in the blanks in our knowledge of western geography and culture with colorful stories that I more than half-suspected were not true. Still, since there was no one with superior credentials available to contradict him, the editor considered him a useful tool and paid him enough so that he could eventually scrape his way on to wherever he was headed.

We collided on the stairs one day, he coming down, me going up, both of us in our own worlds. The collision knocked me on my buttocks, and knocked my wig askew. He looked down on me and his lip curled. Then he went on his way, not offering me a hand or even asking if I was alright. I knew then that he was aware of my true gender.

He didn't share his knowledge, however, and after several weeks passed, I relaxed somewhat. I hoped against hope that either I had been mistaken about the awareness that had bloomed in those loathsome black eyes, or that despite his unpleasant nature, something in his Indian makeup led him to protect my secret.

I could not have been more wrong. He was simply waiting for the best time to use it.

Amongst the newspaper writers in Chicago, there was a sense of camaraderie that transcended the boundaries of which newspaper one worked for. And every year, we all got together for a communal dinner at one of Chicago's great steak houses, where whiskey was drunk and songs were sung and the purplest of prose was read aloud to jeers and cheers, and prizes and toasts were bestowed upon those of us designated the best and worst by our fellows.

The year after our first son was born, Frannie Akers was to be recognized as Sob Sister of the Year, an honor that came with a bottle of excellent chardonnay and a dozen monogrammed hankies. I was thrilled beyond words, and Maud and I had determined that she would accompany me as my cousin, so that she could join me in the festivities and bask with me in the light of my success. At work, my colleagues were full of glad hands and congratulations, and I finally felt as if I were achieving some measure of professional success that was commensurate with what my burgeoning family deserved.

The night before the big dinner, there was a knock on the door of our small but cozy flat. I exchanged looks with Maud. We rarely had visitors to our little nest, except for the occasional neighbor, or—even more infrequently—our super, so an unexpected guest was quite unusual. Maud was wearing a plain dressing gown, while I was in trousers and a shirt, so I grabbed up my phony mustache and slapped it on my face, then went to answer the door.

To my surprise, it was Elkie that was standing there, smirking.

He didn't wait for an invite, simply shoved his way into our home.

"Frank, who is this?" said Maud, eying Elkie suspiciously.

Elkie ignored her completely. Given Maud's generous stature, that's not an easy thing to do.

"What do you want?" I said, not sure if I should acknowledge I knew who he was or not. Although, the odds of him showing up at my home by accident, given Chicago's population of several hundred thousand, were slim, to say the least.

He quickly deflated any hopes I may have had in that direction.

"Money. Give me one hundred dollars and I don't tell your secret, *Frannie*. Or you want to be called *Frank* when you've got your pants on?"

"How dare you!" roared Maud, and she charged at him, fists flying. She landed a spectacular roundhouse, but Elkie took it like he was made of solid oak, and before Maud could blink, he roared back, and hit her with a low tackle. Before I knew what was happening, they were on the floor, rolling around like a couple of barroom brawlers, swearing and sweating and punching for all get out.

I hovered around anxiously, the nearby firepower in my hand, but they wouldn't hold still long enough for me to get a good lick in at Elkie without fear of wounding my beloved Maud. After several minutes, to my infinite horror, Elkie managed to get Maud in a leg lock that looked as if it might snap her gorgeous spine in half. Fear such as I had never felt shot through me—not for myself, but for Maud. She'd never been defeated before. I didn't even think it was possible.

From the floor, Elkie smiled, the first time I had ever seen his lips stretch into such an unnatural shape. The look in his eyes made me shudder. Whatever came next, I was sure it would be loathsome.

"I know what you do," he said, over Maud's labored breathing. "I know who you are. And I like your wife, Frank. Make her part of the deal. I keep your secret."

"What?" I said, shocked to the core.

"You give me money, I take your wife. Simple . . . "

"Never," I cried, outraged. "You can have every dime I possess! Everything I own! But you will never, never, never set hands on my beloved wife!"

As if to show me how little power I had to keep him from taking what he wanted, Elkie reached around Maud and stroked one of her small breasts with his large, uncouth hand. Maud wriggled piteously in his grasp and closed her eyes in what I knew must be shame.

His actions only renewed my determination that either he or I would be dead before he ever left the apartment with my darling Maud. And I told him so in no uncertain terms.

"You foul cur!" I spat. "I'd rather be dead than let the likes of you paw at Maud! I demand you get your hands off her right now!"

Maud opened her eyes and wriggled again in Elkie's steely grip. "Frank, let's not jump the gun on that one."

"What?" I said, sure I had heard wrong.

Elkie smiled some more, and applied himself to more stroking of Maud's breast. Behind the fabric of her dressing gown, her nipples grew hard. I swallowed, both repulsed and mesmerized, watching another man's hands on my wife's flesh.

Maud blushed. "I . . . ah . . . I don't know exactly how to put this, Frank, dear," she said. "But I've never been with anyone but you, and I've certainly never been with anyone larger than me before. Surely you wouldn't begrudge me a little harmless roll in the hay with someone else, would you?"

I dropped to my knees, wounded to the core. "Maud, how could you?"

Besides, my eyes pleaded with her silently, *what happens when he finds out about your . . .*

He must have read the expression on my face.

"I know all about your wife, too," said the spiteful Indian, still grinning that ugly grin, "Miko, the Madman from Manhattan. When I was growing up, there was a person in my village who was half man, half woman. Very popular with both sexes. I was a little young when Squatting Stud was in his/her prime." He sighed with what appeared to be sincere regret."And, unlike you stupid whites, that is okay with me. Now, why don't you take the baby out for a walk, while your wife and I get to know each other better?"

I begged, and pleaded, and even wept, but there was no denying the light of excitement in Maud's eyes, and eventually, I got the baby out of his crib, where he'd managed to sleep through all the ruckus, bundled him up against the night air, and took him out for a walk through the darkened streets, while Maud and Elkie did things that I could all too well imagine.

Well, Maud managed to talk Elkie out of taking all of our savings, and our marriage, while rocky, endured. I started writing adventures—for girls, this time—under the pen name Edith Van Dyke, and am not ashamed to say I used the opportunity to jab at anything Indian whenever I got the chance. It galled Elkie to no end, but between living off my earnings and having his way with my wife, he had little room to complain, so he left me to my minor revenge.

Maud seemed particularly taken with his long, black hair, and while she tried to be discrete in my presence, I came upon them more than once and found her stroking that flowing ebony waterfall with loving hands. The simple gesture made me burn with jealousy. Thus I became convinced to do whatever it took to eject Elkie from our lives.

Unbeknownst to both Elkie and Maud, I was not being completely open about my royalties from the new series. Instead, I was putting away a small but significant sum every week, in the hopes that eventually I would accrue enough to bribe Elkie to leave us be. While Maud's charms were many and hard to duplicate, I was sure that I was correct about one thing, at least—Elkie's lust for money would never be exceeded by his lust for anything else, including Maud.

And in the meantime, I did a little detective work of my own.

Finally, I felt I had enough information—and cash—to confront my nemesis directly. I waited until one evening when he and Maud returned from a night out doing God knows what. They had come up to the flat for a nightcap before Elkie staggered off to whatever cheap quarters he was able to afford with the money he made from the newspaper and the funds he blackmailed from my meager store; instead of being in bed as I usually was at such times, pretending oblivion, I was waiting in a chair by the fire when they entered.

"Frank?" said Maud when she saw me. "Is everything alright? Is the baby ... "

"He's fine, Maud," I said, feeling a tug on my heart at what I was about to do. Despite her perfidiousness in this one area, Maud was a loving wife and a doting mother.

"Why you sitting here like an angry father?" asked Elkie suspiciously.

"I have a deal for you, Elkie," I said.

He grunted, but I could see curiosity in his eyes.

"I have one thousand dollars in gold coin for you if you will pick up and leave us forever."

Maud gasped.

Elkie's face shuttered like a window.

"Show me the money," he said.

"I have a bank draft right here. All you have to do is give me your word to never contact me or my wife again, and I'll fill in your name on the cheque. The bank will honor the draft as soon as their doors open in the morning. I have a statement of my account right here, so that you can verify the funds."

"Frank, no," said Maud, although I wasn't sure if she was trying to dissuade me from bribing her lover or handing him over the funds based on his promise alone.

He looked me over coolly.

"And if I go back on my word?" he asked warily.

"You aren't the only one who can find out things, Elkie," I said. "Or would you prefer to be called Barney Mostaccolli, from Jersey?"

Maud gasped again. "You're not an Indian?"

Elkie sneered. "You New Yorkers are all the same. You'd never dream of sleeping with an Italian guy from the wrong side of the Hudson, but let him grow his hair out and pretend he's some fancy-pants warrior from the west and *Bam!* You can't wait to get caught with your panties around your knees."

"But what about ... about the whole Squatting Stud story?"

He sneered some more. "How naive do you think a kid growing up in Jersey can be? I know a drag queen when I see one. Even a straight guy like me likes a little bit of the old freaky-deaky once in a while."

This time, Elkie—or Barney, as I now knew him to be—didn't see it coming. Maud's roundhouse knocked him halfway across the room.

It took us nearly 30 minutes to bring the rascal around. When we did, he sullenly took his bank draft and slunk off, under the threat of Maud's rock-hard fist. When I was sure he was gone for good, I packed up our things and made arrangements to move to the one place where I suspected Barney Mostacolli would never follow us—South Dakota, home of the Sioux reservation which Elkie had falsely claimed as his home.

My thought was this: Barney's Elkie identity was too much a part of his ego to give up easily, and he would never dare put himself in a position where he could be exposed as the fraud that he was. Along with our reversion to our original names, our move effectively protected us from any further contact with Mr. Barney "Elkie" Mostacolli.

Maud sulked a little at first, but the deception I had uncovered had effectively put an end to her affections for her former lover. Soon, our marriage was as affectionate and close as it ever had been, with the added bonus of Maud giving me free license to pursue the occasional extramarital delight myself without fear of repercussions. She herself had sworn off all such affairs, declaring that after having tasted the forbidden fruits, she was quite happy with the apple pie I put on the table at home.

I myself am quite satisfied with the way things have turned out, although I have never since been able to develop a fondness for either Italians or Indians. Especially the Sioux. As soon as I see that long, black hair, I picture Maud, running her fingers through the silky black strands of that poser, Barney. I know it's not entirely reasonable, but there you go.

Chapter Twenty-Nine
Dorothy: Up the Down Rainbow

This time, when I saw Glinda, I was determined it was going to be different.

I was tired of having her treat me like a kid. And while the fresh-faced, school-girl look had gotten me plenty of mileage with the horny hicks I'd been trying to make traveling money off of, I had a different look in mind for my return to Oz.

With a little advice from Frank, I spent my last night in Kansas putting together a new fashion statement for myself, designed to knock Glinda's socks off. Well, actually, I was hoping it would knock her knickers off, if she wore any—or whatever it was in Oz that stood in for knickers. Frank gingerly cut off my frickin' braids and gave me a spiked 'do that would have been extremely out of place for a young lady in Kansas, but by Ozian standards was barely a blip on the weird-o-meter. I ditched the gingham in favor of something sleek and short and red, and I made use of some cosmetic tricks that I had learned from the girl at Walnut Hall and had never been bold enough to use. I put on a bright-red pair of wedged heels that practically made Frank drool with envy, and threw the silver pumps in my travel bag. I was ready to *rock* that stupid yellow brick road.

By the time Frank and I were done with my makeover, I didn't look like anybody's baby. Actually, I didn't look like anybody from *anywhere* I'd ever been before, but I looked like *me*, and that was just exactly what I wanted, no more and no less.

"Dorothy, you look . . . " Frank stopped and motioned with his finger and I spun around in front of him. "I don't know what you look like. I've never seen anyone who looks like you before. But you look gorgeous. Like a crime waiting to happen, but gorgeous. Glinda's going to blow her top when she sees you."

Which is what I was going for.

Uncle Henry, who used to be so uptight about little things like handymen and hookers, didn't even notice. Poor dear. Auntie Em's desertion had hit him where it hurts. He barely even knew his own name any more.

The next day was everything I had hoped for. Storm clouds hung heavy and yellow in the sweltering skies, and not a breeze to be had anywhere. The few remaining chickens were hiding under the house, and Frank and I worked frantically to reassemble the work shed and then to convince Uncle Henry he should stand around in it with me while Frank sought the shelter of the root cellar.

"Dorothy," Uncle Henry sighed, "we're gonna get kilt out here if a tornado blows up, you realize that? Not that it matters for me anyway, I suppose, but girl, you have your whole life in front of you . . ."

At that moment, the wind picked up, and a thrill ran through me. In a few seconds the shed was rocking on its flimsy foundation.

I threw my arms around Frank and said goodbye, careful not to poke his face or shoulder with my hair spikes.

He kissed me on the cheek. "Don't forget to come and find me if you ever get back this way," he hollered over the sound of the rushing wind, which was now the volume of a small freight train.

He ran out the door, hunching over to keep from getting blown away, and I slammed it shut, then sat down on the floor to wait. I patted the space next to me. "Come on, Uncle Henry, you might as well get comfortable while we wait."

He swallowed. "Dorothy, if it's all the same to you, I think I'm going to run after that young feller that came with you. All of a sudden, life seems a little sweeter than I thought it was a few minutes ago."

I sprang up and gave him a hug. "Oz isn't for everyone, I guess. God bless, Uncle Henry. But hurry, I think I hear the tornado!"

He opened the door, and sure enough, a huge swirling spout had formed on the plain, and was rapidly making its way toward Uncle Henry's farm. He bolted out the door and staggered in the general direction of the root cellar. I hoped he made it. For a moment, as I stood looking out, I had a moment of doubt myself. How crazy was

I, to be standing in the direct path of a Kansas-force tornado, *willing* it to come and get me? Then, behind the tornado, in the distance, I saw the clouds open up and a rainbow appeared.

I looked down at my fire-engine red heels. And I knew it was all going to be okay.

Chapter Thirty
Dorothy: At Last, Oz

My first thought on emerging from the shed Frank and I had built so swiftly was that the land of Oz hadn't changed a bit.

Then I saw Glinda, and realized that while the *place* might remain the same, that didn't necessarily hold true for the people.

Her signature white gown was disheveled, the hem looked like it had been stepped on a few times, her wand was crooked and she was overdue for a root touchup. "Welcome to Ozsh," she slurred as she approached me. "I have schlummoned you here on this very important occasion--" she hiccuped.

"Glinda, are you okay? It's me, Dorothy." I took her arm and shook it gently, and she peered querulously at me as she shoved her tiara back into place. Then she blinked.

"Dorothy? Is that really you?"

"Yes, and—geez, what have you been drinking? You smell like a brewery!"

"Danana Baiquiris," she said.

"Well, ask a stupid question," I said. "Let's get you home and get some coffee into you."

Over coffee, Glinda filled me in on what had been happening in Munchkinland. Glinda had sent Tinker and Bellows to try to find me, because I was the only real supporter she had left. The Munchkins were no longer content to hang out on the farm and gladly accept whatever edicts Glinda the Glamorous handed down.

Over the last year or so, the Munchkins had really changed. It started with a few new societies popping up—along with the Lollypop Guild and the Lullaby League, there was now the Shorties for a Democratic Society, the Malcolm X Order and, inexplicably, Beatlemania.

The new gangs were defiant and disrespectful and even violent. Used to be, all the groups of Munchkins got along together, or at least left each other alone. That was changed. If the SDS came across a bunch of Tiny Tories in the old days, they'd just doff their hats in each others' general direction and keep on going. Now, the SDS would beat the snot out of them just because of the way they were dressed. I'd be the first to admit, those little business suits were really annoying, but still, you can't go around kicking people's butts just because their lapels are too wide.

Somewhere, someone had been filling the Munchkins' angry little heads with a whole boatload of new ideas. The end result was that they had changed from a cheerful, simplistically agreeable farm folk to roving gangs of persnickety, nearly incomprehensible freedom fighters, who refused to be dissuaded from the notion that they were the oppressed and exploited second-class citizens of a tyrannical ruling elite.

Actually, I wasn't entirely sure they were wrong, although based on personal experience I thought Glinda's Munchkins had it all over Elfa's Mounties. But Glinda didn't want to hear it.

One thing nearly all the new Munchkin groups had in common was that they all had a major hate on for Glinda, and they'd been waging a political and image war against her that had quickly gotten on her last nerve.

Glinda had always liked her liquor, and as the situation in Munchkinland deteriorated, she had turned more and more to the bottle. By the time I got back to Oz, Glinda had really changed. Gone was the powerful, self-centered, gorgeous ice queen I had such a crush on, and in her place was a cantankerous, boozy old broad who made Mary Todd Lincoln look ... well, almost normal. Not only had she lost interest in personal grooming, but she'd developed bulgy eyes due to a thyroid condition, and was headed for wicked witch-hood faster than menopause unless she changed her tune pretty quick.

And of course, the new Munchkin gangs were eating it up. At every new outburst, meltdown or drunken brawl, some Munchkarazzi from the *Ozculator* was there to snap a picture and grab a sound bite. Glinda quickly became the most hated person in the North, and there didn't seem to be anything I could do to stop it.

As a matter of fact, I was starting to get a little hate on for her, myself.

Glinda used me as an errand girl, cook, housekeeper, barmaid and nurse for her hangovers. I got tired of that pretty quick, and had started doing my best to make friends and influence people among the local Munchkin population in the only way I knew how—I needed to get some cash together so I could afford to leave and get a place of my own somewhere far, far away from Glinda's troubles.

I finished counting my hidden stash of cash, and cast a discontented glance at Glinda, who was passed out on the couch. The amount of money I'd saved was still a little short of my goal, but Munchkins didn't have a lot of cash, and to earn what I had, I'd performed enough lewd acts to keep the girls of Walnut Hall busy for a year. Suffice it to say, I'd come to know way more about Munchkins than any human girl ever should.

As I studied her, Glinda roused a little, muttering and trying to scrape her hair out of her eyes without moving her hungover head. Since I'd come back, she's swallowed an ocean of banana daiquiris, one blender-full at a time. That and Oz's version of happy dust were all she lived on.

Before she could get it together enough to demand another quart or two of booze, there was a knock at the door. I looked out the peephole and saw a group of dark-skinned Munchkins out there, all dressed in black.

These days, a visit by one of the Munchkin guilds was something to be avoided like the plague, but with Typhoon Glinda looking like she was getting ready to blow again, hangin' with the Munchkins didn't look so bad. I stepped out on the porch and closed the door behind me.

"Hey, girl," said the leader. "We represent the Malcolm X Order."

He paused, and after a minute of awkward silence, I cleared my throat and said, "So, don't you guys have a song or something?"

"Nah, girl, that's old school. We write angry letters and do sit-ins. We hear your . . . *friend* has been dissing our people. We don't like it. That needs to stop." He looked at me meaningfully.

Just then the door burst open and a groggy Glinda half staggered, half fell out onto the porch. She glared at the Munchkins. "Wahdahell yu guys wan? Imm busy!"

Yeah, she was busy, alright - busy pickling her liver.

"Look, you oppressor honky dike, we ain't gonna take anymore shit off of you. Making the Lolly Pop Guild cater your Witchyware party for free, demanding 'udes from the Lullaby League. Those people get good money for their services. From now on, you wanna dance, you gotta pay."

Glinda glared at him, then turned a suspicious eye on me. She was starting to focus. Uh-Oh. She gets really mean when she focuses. "Why'm I the honky dike? What about her? Why isn't she a honky dike?"

The head Malcolm Munchkin looked me over slowly, and then gave me a lascivious smile. Apparently, I hadn't lost my ability to whistle dick-see. "First of all, you're the one who's dangerous; Dorothy don't got a mop, she can't fight her way out of a paper bag. Second of all, I heard she's willing to give it up to a brother in need. Just remember, leave the Munchkins alone, unless you want to find my boot up your ass big time, bitch."

He pointed a finger at Glinda and mimed pulling a trigger. There was some snickering from the Malcolms behind him. Glinda was speechless with fury. All she could do was sputter. Every little droplet of spit morphed into some kind of misshapen bug that slithered away into the azaleas.

That was kinda impressive. It was the first sign of the old Glinda I'd seen in months. I gave her a sultry look. "You want to go inside and . . . do what comes naturally?"

She grimaced. "What I want is a blender full of banana daiquiris. And don't get stingy with the rum."

Unbelievable. I made her banana daiquiris alright. And while I was in there, cranking the blender, I spit in her frickin' rum.

213

Days had turned into weeks, and on the surface everything seemed quiet, but that kind of ominous quiet that portends bad things. While I'd been making my getaway cash, I'd been asking around, but no one was talking about who was filling the Munchkins' heads with all the revolutionary jazz. I was out on the back porch, grabbing a breath of fresh air, when I noticed the Munchkin Mayor's snotty wife watching out the window of their house nest door. She's hates me, although I'm not sure why—my relationship with Glinda, or my relationship with half the male population of Munchkinland? Whatever it was, she looked ready to bust her fat little gut, but she was too afraid of Glinda to do anything.

"Hey, come on over and join the orgy," I yelled at her across our yards.

The window shut with an audible snap, and then I could hear her screaming at her husband when she really wanted to come over and bust me in the chops. What a lame-ass.

The air was getting chilly, so I stepped back in and closed the door. Poor hubby! Maybe I'd pop by sometime when the missus wasn't around and offer him a little neighborly comfort...

... and nearly bumped into Glinda when I turned around. I jumped a foot; she'd been out cold in front of the magic ball—which got great reception, by the way—when I'd gone outside.

"What the hell were you doing?" Her voice, which used to be high and clear as a bell, had first gone smoky, and then deeper still, until she sounded like she'd been gargling with Drano. "Were you flirting with that guy next door?" She took a brutal drag on her cigarette. "Because those Munchkins are *not* that well built. Take it from me." That really pissed me off.

"I was bitching out that stupid little cow next door. And how the hell do you know how Munchkins are built? You said you'd never been with a Munchkin when we got together. So when..."

My voice trailed off as I realized the implications of what I was saying. "You Jezebel! You weren't waiting for me to grow up, were you? You ... you *slut*!" Hypocrite? I don't *think* so. I hadn't pretended to be something I'm not. Glinda had.

Glinda smirked. "I can't help it if you're gullible, kid. Make me a batch of daiquiris. And this time, don't spit in the rum."

I stood blinking at her scrawny form. She looked more like Hymen the Drag Queen than Good Witch Glinda. What was it that made drunken old women invariably choose dingy satin with molting feathers? Before I could answer myself, someone pounded on the front door. Glinda looked back and glared at me. "If it's those fuckin' Munchkins again, tell 'em to get the hell off my property before I turn them all into toads or mushrooms or something. I hate those little pricks."

She went in and sat down on the couch in a huff.

She'd lost a slipper on her way through the house, and looked ridiculous, smoking skinny cigars in an emerald green holder, one foot bare. Her grimy satin robe, set off by a sashed waist and full skirt, along with the requisite feathered neckline and sleeves. She was kicking her slippered foot back and forth like she was wishing someone's ass was in front of it. The slipper, one of those puffy donkey ones, looked like it was going to jump to safety any second. Feathers were floating through the air in tempo with her kicks.

"Really, Glinda, can't you just *try* and pull it together?"

She didn't answer. I sighed and went to the door.

There was nobody there. I had flipped the porch light off and was closing the door when someone hissed at me from the bushes. "Psst! Turn the lights out—I can't afford to be seen here. But I have important news. Can I come in?"

I looked back at Glinda, that two-timing bitch, and then shrugged. "Sure, whatever." Never rains but it pours. I saw the hausfrau looking out her window again, so I flipped her the bird and then hit the light switch on the wall. Instantly, the living-room was plunged into darkness.

I heard a thump and a muffled, "fuck!" and winced. Glinda must have been in the middle of crossing the room when I turned out the lights. A small figure slipped by me, and I shut the door and turned the lights back on.

The little man looked more like a mole than a Munchkin. He blinked and shuffled in the light. "I -- "

There was second thump, followed by another muffled curse. We both turned to see Glinda rubbing a shin, while balancing a lit cigarette and a pitcher full of daiquiris. The end table was now a banana bush. Damn! I liked that table. Too bad she couldn't magic up a rum bush—free rum would save us a hell of a lot more money than free bananas. When Glinda got to the couch, she dropped down on it hard, and glared.

"I represent the Society of Snitches and Sell Outs," he said.

"Never heard of 'em. What the hell do you want?" Glinda had decided to be her usual charming self. "It's three o'clock in the morning, dammit."

Actually, it was about nine-thirty, but I didn't bother to tell her that.

"We have a jingle, and everything." He cleared his throat, but before he could sing a single note, Glinda cut him off.

"If you just came here to exercise your pipes, you can get right the hell out of my house, half-pint. I've got better things to do."

"No, no," he said hastily. "I've come here with an important message, oh Glinda, Good Witch of the North."

"What's that, tiny?"

He coughed into his hand, one of those polite, not-really-a-cough kinda coughs. Glinda rolled her bulgy eyes and reached for her bag. She pulled out five bucks and handed it to the Snitch. He looked at it, looked back at Glinda, whose face could curdle milk, and decided five was enough.

"The Guerrilla Guild has put together a plot to overthrow you, Glinda the Good. The Malcolm Order, the Lolly Pop Guild, the Pawnshop Party, the Lullaby League and the Castro Commissars are committed, and we think the Stalin Society and possibly the Fascist Funsters are about ready to sign on."

"They think they can overthrow *me*?" To our amazement, she burst into laughter.

It took her nearly a minute to get herself back under control. Her laughter sounded like a rusty chainsaw, and she didn't stop until it triggered a coughing fit. It sounded like she was ready to hawk up a lung. Then her face changed and she looked at the snitch and hollered, "get the hell out of my house, you lying sack of shit!"

He blinked and stepped back, then looked fearfully at the door. "But... but..."

"Brag about your butt on your own time, shorty." She pointed an imperious finger his way and magic sparked off the tip. Snitchy made his decision. Glinda in his face was scarier than whatever might be waiting for him outside. He flung the door open and rushed out onto the porch, then stopped, trying to figure out which way to go. In that second he paused, a shot rang out from the dark, and Snitchy's head exploded all over the front steps.

Glinda stood and walked over to survey the mess sourly. "Go out there and clean that shit up. And get my five bucks back while you're at it."

What I actually did was drag Snitchy into the neighbors' rose bushes, and then hose off the porch. For my trouble, I stuck the five bucks in my stash. The next morning, I was hanging out in the kitchen, waiting eagerly to hear the hausfrau's screams of terror, when Glinda came stumping in.

"Geezus, Glinda. It's nine a.m. You can't really be looking for booze this early, can you? And good morning, by the way."

"Pack a bag. We're off to see the Wizard."

"The Wizard? What the hell for? I mean, it would be nice to get together, just for old time's sake, but don't you think we ought to get to the bottom of this Munchkin stuff first? We can't just take off on a whim."

Glinda scowled. "You idiot. I want to get him to help us. And I'm not leaving you here on your own to screw half the neighborhood while I'm gone. You're either with me or against me. Make up your mind." A jitterbug fluttered by Glinda's head and she absently zapped it with her wand, blowing a three-foot hole in the wall behind it in the process.

217

I packed even quicker than I had gotten rid of Snitchy.

We didn't bother with any of that 'follow the yellow brick road' bullshit. We traveled in style, in a big bubble that smelt faintly of rum and bananas, and arrived in Emerald City before lunch. It was great to see Oz again. He was no longer the ruler of Oz, Ozma having come of age and taken her rightful place on the throne, but he still lived in the palace, in a suite of rooms decorated with posters of his idols from the mundane world, eerie purple tube lights that he said were black, even though they obviously were not, and furniture that consisted mainly of giant floor pillows and various smoking apparatus.

Oz's pony tail had gone nearly white, but he still wore his rosy colored glasses, and he seemed delighted to see us, until he found out why Glinda was there.

"Glinda, you can't be seriously asking me to bail you out of this mess. In the first place, I have work to do here," he said, gesturing to a far table where Bunsen burners and mysterious beakers boiled and bubbled. "And in the second place, those Munchkins are totally right on. I don't know how you lasted as long as you did, zapping people all over the place, making the seamstress sect sew all those little sequins all over everything you wear . . . "

Glinda narrowed her eyes. "Look, *Tom*, I don't want things to get ugly here, but us wizards and witches need to stick together. And if you won't help me voluntarily . . . "

Glinda made a threatening motion with her wand, and Tom's eyes widened.

"You can't seriously be threatening to harm me if I don't help bail your ass out?" Tom asked, seeming more amused than afraid. "I may not be as magical as you are, Glinda, but I've made good use of my time here. And I've learned a lot from Garbanzo Tinker--"

She snorted. "Tinker? He's a fool. Ever since I let him hide in Munchkinland from King Evoldo, all he's been doing is parading those stupid Munchkins up and down his ladder to the moon at two bits a pop."

"Not true," said Tom. "You've had your head too far up your ass to notice that Tinker and I have been spending some serious time together. My busker trunk has been heavily augmented--"

"Tinker is in Munchkinland?" I interrupted.

Glinda glared at me. "Yeah. I gave him a little place in the country to prop up his ladder, in exchange for the use of some of his mechanical men for riot control. That's why he was around when I needed to send someone after you. Why?"

I slapped my forehead with my palm. "That's it!" I said. "All those Munchkins are going up to the moon and looking through his telescope. But there's something wrong with it—he told me when he came to give me your message. All you can see when you look through the telescope is the mundane world—70 years in the future!"

Glinda looked blank, but I could see that Tom got it immediately. "And seventy years in the mundane world's future . . . " He started laughing uncontrollably. "It's the sixties, dude!"

"The sixties?" asked Glinda.

"The biggest period of unrest and social revolution the world has ever seen," Tom replied. "Glinda, you are *so* screwed."

She waved her wand again. "Then you better be ready to help unscrew me, Tom. Or I'm going to make a hole in your head that all the happy dust in the world won't fill."

Tom stopped laughing and sighed. "Glinda, you really don't want me involved in this."

"I'll take my chances, rainbow man. Now help me figure out what to do."

They were still arguing when I left to go shopping. The gist of it centered around whether or not Oz would go back to Munchkinland with us.

I decided to go get my color refreshed and a couple of tubes of bright red lipstick to match my heels. We agreed to meet up when I was done. It was the first time I'd been to the Emerald City since I'd gotten back. I had a list of things as long as my arm that I wanted to do there while I had the chance.

When I got back to Oz's place, Oz and Glinda were still yacking. As I walked in, I heard him saying earnestly, "Glinda, for the last time, I don't want to be on the side of *The Man* against the Munchkins."

Glinda replied sourly, "You better take a good look around you, you sorry excuse for a wizard. You're a member of the oppressive ruling class now, and if one of us goes down, all of us go down. There's a tornado coming, Tom, and this time we could all end up with a house on our heads . . . "

Us? Our? What the hell did she mean, *us*? The Munchkins were pissed at her, not me. "Uh, you guys? You look like you're still pretty busy. I think I'll just go and see if Manic Manicures is still open. Nobody gives a French tip like the Molls of Manicure."

Glinda waved me absently away.

Last I heard was Oz saying, "Hold that thought for a second. I've got to go take a wiz."

My first—well, actually, my only—thought was to call and beg Ozma to help me. I was getting a little worried about getting caught in between a schnockered Glinda and the Munchkins bent on taking her down. Last time I had seen Ozma she had been pretty distracted with the whole mechanical penis thing, but she'd been a good friend. Maybe she'd let me crash with her in the palace until the whole thing blew over.

I had to get past her snotty secretary first, which turned out to be none other than Fucking Leon. It took me a good half-hour of badgering to find out she wasn't even in the office—she'd gone shopping at the local men's big and tall shop. Finally, he sighed and told me I could use the talkaphone on his desk to leave her a message.

She apparently had been working on all those pesky gender identify issues since our last get-together. She sounded happy and feminine, if the soprano warble of her voice was anything to go by. "Hello," she trilled. "You've reached the desk of Ozma, Ruler of Oz, and also the hotline for Transgender Anonymous. We've missed your call, because we're either out shopping for shoes or bowling, so please leave a message, and a guy or gal—or both—will get back to you soon. Ciao!"

I left a message, then went out in search of raspberry mocha and a little more retail therapy. Not necessarily in that order.

I was standing in front of a shop run by the Jiminy Choo Society, looking at a hot pair of smokin' Choo-Choo wedgies—the thick soles were fashioned into train engines, and made soft "I think I can" noises with every step, when I turned around and nearly bumped into Ozma.

"Ozma, is that you?" She was in man mode today, and if I hadn't known her as a boy, I wouldn't have recognized her.

"Dorothy? Wow, have you changed! Hubba, hubba," she said, wiggling eyebrows that were thick and dark under a short brush of honey-blond hair.

I'd have been flattered, but I had other matters on my mind. "You won't believe what's going on in Munchkinland!"

"I've been hearing rumors, and it's Ozman, today, if you don't mind."

I should have known.

"Ozman, got it. You've heard about it all the way over here in Emerald City?"

"Word travels. I also got that Glinda has totally flipped her lid, turned into a complete dictator. Are *you* okay?"

Briefly, I described what was happening.

"And she came to see that hippy-dippy Oz, to try to mount a counter attack, instead of coming to see me, and looking for a peaceful solution, huh? That tells you something right there, sweet cheeks. Not good. Not at all."

I can't tell you the relief I felt in putting the burden on Ozman's broad shoulders. "So, you'll do something before anybody else gets killed? I think she's going into holocaust mode—I swear to God."

"I hadn't realized things were in such a crisis state. Let me get a few things together. And have a little tête à tête with Tom myself."

"Ozman, you're my hero."

"Chin up, Dorothy. I'll be in Munchkinland before you."

Feeling better than I had in weeks, I went back to the hotel to wait for Glinda.

We waited until dark to bubble back, Oz traveling above us in a rainbow-colored hot-air balloon, lugging a carpet bag full of God knows what. I didn't know if Ozman had been able to get that tête à tête or not—nothing about Oz's reluctant demeanor gave it away, so I just crossed my fingers and hoped for the best.

Even though it was dark, when Glinda's magic bubble landed in our backyard, I saw the snap of blinds on the house next door. The little Munchkin hausfrau had been waiting for us. She must have gotten a talkaphone of her own, because less than ten minutes later, a rock was thrown through our living room window, scattering shards of glass everywhere.

"*Come on out, White Mamma,*" it read. Oh, boy, it was the Malcolms again. I could tell by the lingo. "*Get out here and apologize for what you been doin', before we jam that wand up your ass.*"

Glinda turned red and swelled up like a toad when she read it. Oz started looking nervously toward the back door, but he couldn't move half as fast as Glinda when she was pissed off. She grabbed him with one hand and me with the other, and dragged us outside with her to confront the angry mob. Oz barely had a chance to snag his bag as he passed it.

On the porch, Glinda squinted and glared in the light from the torches. There must have been a hundred Munchkins out there, all armed with something or other—from pitchforks to machetes.

"Get the hell off my property," she screamed, veins popping out on her neck. Her hair magically freed itself from the neat waves I had persuaded her to have it done in while in the Emerald City, and now snapped wildly around her head, strands whipping back and forth like snakes. Her face flickered with strange light, throwing the angles of her cheekbones into a sharp relief that made her look like one of the undead. And she grew in size until she nearly bumped her head on the overhang above the porch.

Oz, apparently emboldened by the sight she made, stepped up to her side and opened his carpet bag.

"What you got in there, hippy? Another set of love beads?" It was a scornful voice from the mob, and people began snickering.

"More like a plastic Ozzie semi-automatic," he shouted back, and held it aloft. There was some worried muttering and our audience took a collective step back. Everybody knew how dangerous an Ozzie was—if the bullets didn't get you, the incessant bitching would. And the top-of-the-line Sharon Silencer cost a bundle. "I don't want to hurt anyone, but I'll use this if I have to. Everybody needs to calm down, *now*."

The Malcolms were manning up for battle, when there was a shrill neigh from the edge of the crowd. I shielded my eyes against the flaming torches, and then waved and called out excitedly. "Ozman! You made it!"

Glinda looked at me in disbelief. "You knew that freak was coming and you didn't tell me?"

I shrugged. "I want to survive this in one piece."

Ozman had dismounted from her rocking horse, which was currently a strong, manly navy. She had completely lost her sense of fashion, and was wearing a ten-gallon hat, plaid shirt, jeans and cowboy boots. I understand the whole transgender thing, I really do. But why does switching off cause her to wear such really horrible outfits? Emboldened by Ozman's arrival, someone in the mob threw a rock at the porch, narrowly missing Glinda's head. All of a sudden, a sense of style—or lack thereof—didn't seem to matter so much. I jumped to the lawn and scrambled to get to Ozman's side.

"Hey, Ozman," I gasped gratefully. "Thanks for coming. If you want, when this is all over, we could have a spa day. And go shopping. My treat!"

Ozman nodded absently. She might not appreciate my offer now, but once the Ozma side kicked back in, I knew she'd be delighted.

To my surprise, Oz took that moment to join us.

Stung by the betrayal, Glinda drew back the hand with the wand in it, and Oz raised his gun. I winced and tried to make myself smaller. Showdown in wizardville. Not *good*! Unfortunately, when the rest of the crowd is under three feet, I really stand out.

Glinda's wand sizzled, and someone right next to me turned into a sloth. A flaming arrow, a product of the Gay Archer's Guild, landed on the porch by her feet. She raised her arm for another shot, and Oz pulled the Ozzie to his face and took aim.

"Stop!" thundered Ozman at my side. "As your Queen and your . . . *queen*, I order you all to stop this right now!"

"What the hell are you gonna do with that bitch, if we stop? We can't live like this anymore. We want some guarantees." That had to be one of the Malcolms.

Ozman stepped forward until she reached the porch, and then turned to face the crowd, a grin on her face. "I have a solution that's way better than some stupid guarantee."

"What's that?" said one of the Lolly Pop Guild members suspiciously.

"What is it?" said Glinda, distrust in her voice.

"Tom, show them the magic weapon!"

Obligingly, Tom reached into his bag and pulled out a strange looking contraption covered with buttons and glowing lights.

"What the hell is that?" someone shouted.

"Glinda, I'm really sorry," he said, even as he held it up.

"It's a device our wonderful Wizard picked up at the Technology Exhibit of the Chicago World's Fair of 1893. A Shrink Ray Gun."

The audience got quiet as they tried to figure out what exactly that meant.

Ozman turned and looked at Glinda and smiled nastily. "Now, I'm going to provide you with a little off-the-cuff sensitivity training."

Before Glinda could say anything else, Tom squeezed the trigger of the shrink ray gun. An eerie blue light shot out, enveloping Glinda in its strange glow. There was a blinding flash, and then the blue light disappeared. We all looked at Glinda.

It was still Glinda, but different—the top of her head just barely came up to Ozman's belt buckle.

"Oh, my God," screamed Glinda. Her voice was about two

octaves higher and about 20 decibels quieter, which was a total improvement. "What have you done, you bitch?"

There was scattered giggling from the yard, and then some outright guffaws. Pretty soon, the whole place was rocking with hysterically laughing Munchkins.

"What am I supposed to do?" Glinda was whining. "I don't know how to live like a Munchkin."

Ozman was laughing too, but managed to get it under control enough to call out to the crowd. "Now, who's going to volunteer to help Glinda get a better understanding of what it means to be a Munchkin?"

Hands flew up into the air.

I smiled. "Why don't you start your own Munchkin gang—how about the League of Duplicitous Dictators?"

Ozman turned and gave me a look so intense I blushed. "And I think it's time you and I got to know each other a little better, Dorothy. Hell, a lot better."

Before I could react, she swept me up in a kiss that had my toes curling. A cheer went up from the Munchkins.

Yeah, there's no place like home.

Chapter Thirty-One
Dorothy: Old Friends

After that, things settled down quite a bit. I moved into the palace with Ozma, and she showed me some of the magic tricks she'd learned with the penis Tinker built her, and I had to admit, a woman with a penis of her own was pretty remarkable. For one thing, they share. Something a man just can't do. Sorry, fellas, but there's no comparison on this one.

Once the hubbub about Glinda died down, we discovered that all of the Munchkins' radical ideas had been coming from the trips they'd been taking up Garbanzo Tinker's magic ladder to the moon. When they'd looked through his telescope, they'd seen seventy years into the earth's future, and really gotten an eyeful. From what I heard, it didn't sound pretty—I was happy to be in the when and where I was, as long as it included Ozma.

Eventually Ozma persuaded Oz to take another look at the problem of me snapping back to the mundane world, and he determined that it was the clothing I wore—the stuff that had come from my old world, that is—that caused me to keep getting pulled back. "But when I got to the Emerald City the first time, the Brass Men's servants made me change into completely gray clothes," I protested. "And then in Elfa's castle, I had to wear maid stuff. I didn't have on anything from my old world."

"Not knowingly," he responded.

I couldn't figure it out. The only thing I hadn't changed out of in Emerald City or Elfa's castle had been ... "Nessa's shoes!" I exclaimed.

"You got it, Dorothy," he said.

"She got them in my world?"

"Bingo. Ever hear of online shopping? No, of course not. I forget you're from a different *when*. But the short version is: it was the shoes, and as long as you were wearing them, they kept pulling you back. Once you finally ditched them for the red stilettos, your problem was solved, and you didn't even know it."

I hugged him, which caused him to break into a fine sweat, which I pretended not to notice. I was a one-woman girl now.

Just then, I saw a familiar face. Ozma's social secretary, Leon. Who had wasted half-an-hour of my life, making me beg for Ozma's phone number when I was desperate.

"Listen, Oz, would it have the same effect on anyone else who put them on?"

He frowned thoughtfully. "I suppose so, eventually. You wouldn't be able to predict exactly when or where, but . . . sure. One minute, you're skipping down the yellow brick road, and the next minute, *Bam!* Cleveland."

Over his shoulder, I watched Fucking Leon saunter across the room in a skin-tight lame number. "Oh, Leon! Hey, I have a pair of shoes I think you'd just love!"

Oz was all gangbusters to get back to his spoiled wheat, but I managed to wring one more favor out of him before he got away—a small magic mirror that would allow me to say the name of a person in my old world and talk to them, as long as they were looking in a mirror, too. It was a little bit like the talkaphone, but you had to sync things up right for it to work.

It took several weeks to catch Frank looking in the mirror. You'd think a man in a wig would check more often, but that was Frank. Or Frannie. When I did finally catch him, he was so surprised he nearly dropped the one he was holding.

"Frank! It's okay, it's just me, Dorothy! Whatever you do, don't drop that mirror!"

Once he got over the initial shock, he was delighted. "Dorothy! After all this time! I can't believe it! How are you? How is everything? How did things go with Glinda? Are you happy?"

I caught him up on all the news, including my new, domestically settled life with Ozma, and he smiled. "I thought when you told me about her she sounded like a better match for you than Glinda, but I knew that was something you'd have to figure out for yourself," he said.

"How about you? How's Maud? The kids? And whatever happened to Uncle Henry? Did he make it to the root cellar in time?"

Frank grinned. "He not only made it to the root cellar in time, his brush with near death shook him out of his doldrums and gave him a whole new lease on life. He had nothing to stay here for, so I took him back to Dakota with me, and he and my mother-in-law hit it off right away. They're in Japan for their honeymoon, right now!"

I tried to picture Uncle Henry and Matilda the suffragette together, touring Japan and inciting rebellion in all the prim little geishas. I returned Frank's grin.

"Oh, and Dorothy, that's not the best part. After you left, I . . . I wrote down all your adventures, and made a book of them."

"A book? About me? You're kidding. My story would burn the ink right off the pages," I said, perplexed. In my old world, people would be lined up to lynch the publisher that would print a story like mine.

"Well," said Frank. "About that. I did change it around a little bit. Cleaned it up. It's a children's book now, actually."

I sat down. "And you did well with it?"

"Well? I've made a fortune. It's become so popular that Maud and I have decided to move to a little village in the middle of nowhere in California just to get away from all the excitement and publicity."

I pursed my lips. "How are you going to keep your *lifestyle* a secret in a little village like that, Frank? Won't it be tough?"

He laughed. "I have a young friend who lives there. There's this most amazing new industry starting up—*film making*, and I want to be in on it at the beginning. My friend has been telling me about it. He thinks there could actually be a commercial market for films, of all things—and he's invited me to come out and stay a while, to see if I like the place. I haven't described our . . . *lifestyle* in so many words, but I believe he understands what I'm looking for. He says the people are the epitome of discretion and good manners."

"Well, good luck with that. Who is this guy, by the way?"

"Barrymore. Errol Barrymore. Delightful young man. Worships the ground Maud walks on. I do believe he has a great future in this 'film' business. I have great hopes for our new home there. Errol says it's a paradise on earth. Green, unspoiled, and with only a few hundred people scattered over a broad expanse of wooded land and gently rolling hills. A veritable garden of pastoral delights."

"Sounds great, Frank. I hope you and Maud are very happy there. What's it called?"

"Hollywood. Hollywood, California. We'll be moving this spring, after Matilda and Henry get back from their honeymoon. I think Matilda is planning on running for governor."

I hoped Uncle Henry had remembered to pack his good pants.

Chapter Thirty-Two
Dorothy: Home for Good

Home. Now that I reflect back on it, my whole tale has been about home—finding it, then earning the right to call it my own, finding someone I loved to share it with.

Just as my good friend Frank found his home and his happiness with his beloved wife Maud. Through Frank, I discovered that the true magic of Oz was not the . . . well, the *magic*, but the fact that I had found a place where I *belonged*. It wasn't the place I was born, or the people I was born to. It was the place I fit in, and the people who loved me, and whom I loved in return.

And wherever your home may be, gentle reader—and rest assured, it's out there somewhere, just waiting for you to find it— once you find it, hold onto it with gentle hands. You can't force a house to be a home, and you can't make your lover love you. But once you're there, no matter what it looks like, or where it's located, or who it's with, you'll know it in your heart for the peace it gives you, and you'll never have to look any farther for happiness, ever again, than your own backyard.

ND - #0481 - 270225 - C0 - 229/152/19 - PB - 9781907133220 - Gloss Lamination